30 DAYS
OF
NIGH
D1273949

A Novelization by Tim Lebbon

Based on the Screenplay by
Steve Niles and Stuart Beattie and Brian Nelson

Based on the IDW Publishing Comic by
Steve Niles and Ben Templesmith

Pocket Star Books
New York London Toronto Sydney

The sale of this book without its cover is unauthorized. If you purchased this book without a cover, you should be aware that it was reported to the publisher as "unsold and destroyed." Neither the author nor the publisher has received payment for the sale of this "stripped book."

Pocket Star Books
A Division of Simon & Schuster, Inc.
1230 Avenue of the Americas
New York, NY 10020

This book is a work of fiction. Names, characters, places, and incidents either are products of the author's imagination or are used fictitiously. Any resemblance to actual events or locales or persons, living or dead, is entirely coincidental.

Copyright © 2007 by Columbia Pictures Industries, Inc.
All rights reserved.
Motion picture artwork and photography © 2007 by Columbia Pictures Industries, Inc. All rights reserved.

All rights reserved, including the right to reproduce this book or portions thereof in any form whatsoever. For information address Pocket Books Subsidiary Rights Department, 1230 Avenue of the Americas, New York, NY 10020

First Pocket Star Books paperback edition October 2007

POCKET STAR BOOKS and colophon are registered trademarks of Simon & Schuster, Inc.

For information about special discounts for bulk purchases, please contact Simon & Schuster Special Sales at 1-800-456-6798 or business@simonandschuster.com.

Manufactured in the United States of America

10 9 8 7 6 5 4

ISBN-13: 978-1-4165-4497-5
ISBN-10: 1-4165-4497-6

30 DAYS OF NIGHT

TWO DAYS AGO

OUT OF THE HAZE of snow, as if from nowhere, came the Stranger. His eyes were red rimmed, yet they sparkled with determination and excitement. His stubbled chin and cheeks were spotted with ice. He looked weary, wretched, and in pain, yet his expression suggested that he could walk on forever.

Pausing and glancing over his shoulder, he could just make out the shadow of the ship. Closer, his rowboat had already been caught by the currents and dragged away from shore. He smiled. He would not be needing it again.

The Stranger marched across the plains of snow and ice, tightening the fur coat across his chest, zipping it up beneath his chin so that the hood gathered around his face. But there was little that could protect him from a storm such as this. Snow melted on his exposed face and froze again as ice, coating his eyelashes and stubble and pinching his skin. He felt hot from exertion, but his breath froze in the air before him. Once or twice he stumbled and fell, coating his clothing with wet snow, an unintentional camouflage. But there was no need to hide. This was the first bad storm of the season, and no one in their right mind would be outside.

He drew a clear map case from his pocket, checked the compass hanging around his neck, and grunted. Right way. Not long now. He looked up at the sky, but all he could see were a million snowflakes dancing groundward. They said that every flake was different and unique, but he didn't really care. For the Stranger, there was merely us and them.

An hour later he started up an incline. He was struggling by now, legs shaking and breath rasping in his throat. He needed warmth, shelter, and food, but more than anything he needed to succeed. Anything else was unthinkable.

Dreaming of what would come, he mounted the ridge and stopped. Ahead of him, way across the snow desert, lights winked in the blizzard. He dug out a pair of compact binoculars from his pocket.

Several dozen low buildings hugged the landscape, all but buried in snow. Oil drilling derricks ringed the outpost, tall masts topped with red flashing lights stood away from the settlement to the north and south, and dozens of poles suspended a web of power cables at eaves level.

Lights burned in many of the buildings. There were even a few illuminated signs on show. In this place of Arctic storms and fields of snow, the town looked almost warm.

"Barrow," the Stranger remarked.

And then he grinned.

TONIGHT

THE SUN WAS GOING DOWN, and the last thing Sheriff Eben Oleson needed was a problem. Not now, not today, and not right here. This was a special place for him, and he had no wish to see it tainted. He sat on the hood of his 4x4, eyes closed, remembering the good times.

"Eben? You there, Eben? Come on." Billy was calling him on the radio, but for a few more seconds Eben remained in his own world. Here, all those years ago, up on the ridge with her. Watching the sunrise. Already thinking that maybe she was the one.

"Eben? Come in, Eben, you there?"

Eben sighed. "I'm here, Billy." He slid from the hood and thrust his hands in his pockets. He was a tall man, wiry and strong, with a grim face that would have looked better wearing a smile.

Billy Kitka stood halfway up the slope, fidgeting from side to side. The fortyish deputy was obviously excited at his find, but perturbed as well. "Eben, really need to show you this." He waited until Eben reached him, then they walked up the slope together to the hole in the snow.

Eben stood with his back to the sun, protecting his eyes from the glare of its dying light. He looked down into the hole and grew still. "Strange," he said.

"Ain't it? Who'd do a thing like this?" Billy shined a flashlight into the hole. It contained a mess of burnt cell phones, their plastic casings melted and warped into weird shapes. A rush of wind blew a sprinkle of snowflakes into the hole and they melted.

"Still warm," Eben said. He knelt down, picked up the remains of a phone and shrugged.

"Someone got a little upset about roaming charges?" Billy said.

Eben ignored the crack, stood and shook his head. "*Stealing* satellite phones'd make sense, you could hock them, maybe run up charges on someone's account. But burning them?"

"Kids? Pulling some prank?"

"Nah. There'd be a message. 'Fuck you' to their parents or the world or whoever. Not a bad thought—" Eben broke off, distracted by the sight of the sun bleeding across the horizon. There was still light snow in the air from the storm, drifting with the wind and giving the sun a blank canvas on which to paint its demise. He walked along the ridge to watch.

The sun had touched the horizon, and it looked as though it was burning its way into the frozen Alaskan landscape, ready to hibernate for a month. It would leave them dark, cold, and abandoned. Alone.

"I remember I brought Peggy here on our first date," Billy said.

"We all did," Eben said. "Hey, not Peggy, I mean, just . . ."

Billy chuckled. "I gotcha. Last sunset for months always works, don't it?"

"For me it was the sunrise," Eben said. "Best damn date I ever had."

"Yeah," Billy said, uncomfortable now. He fidgeted again until he had a sudden thought. "Hey, Eben, c'mon, let's do the sign."

Eben stared across the icy desert, trying to cast himself back in time but unable to do so. His insides were as cold as this Arctic landscape, and as barren. He sighed, craving to feel that warmth again.

"You okay, Eben?" Billy asked quietly.

"Yeah." Eben turned and started back down the slope. He passed the ruined cell phones with a glance, and by the time he made it back to the 4x4 he could hear Billy following him. Dependable Billy. Caring Billy, who could never find the right thing to say.

At the outskirts of Barrow, Eben stopped the 4x4 next to the town sign. It had obviously been written by a tourism bureau with a sense of humor: WELCOME TO BARROW, ALASKA—TOP OF THE WORLD!—POPULATION 563—WARNING! DANGER! POLAR BEARS!

In the passenger seat, Billy chuckled with the anticipation of what he was about to do. He'd chuckled last year, and the year before that, and he would laugh next year as well. Eben so wished he could find humor in such things.

The deputy jumped from the vehicle and approached the sign, pulling out some metal tags from his coat pocket.

Eben leaned from the window. "Nobody's gonna see that sign for the next thirty days, Billy."

"You tell me that every year," Billy called. "But it's a tradition!" He hung new tags over the "population" number, reducing the 563 to 152 for the coming thirty days.

So many people couldn't handle that much darkness. Even for those who stayed behind, it sometimes caused problems. It was a busy month for Eben, but one he strangely looked forward to every year. He'd always enjoyed Barrow's isolation, and the thirty days of night—what Barrowites had named the Dark—made it even more intense.

Billy climbed back in, and Eben gunned the motor and drove them past the drilling derricks and into town.

"Home sweet home," Billy said. At last, Eben found a smile.

Barrow was a town like no other. It was the northernmost settlement in North America, isolated from the rest of the world by hundreds of miles of snow desert, and almost exclusively accessed by aircraft. Its people were hardy—the bulk of them employed by the oil companies, and they and their families suffered the harshness of Barrow for the rewards it offered. Though in truth, for many of them, the suffering was slight; they enjoyed such an existence and found that it offered rewards other than money. There was isolation, a sense of truly living with nature, and a simpler way of life.

Much of the town had its own unique architecture. Homes and stores were built on thick timber piles to protect their structures from the stresses of shifting ice. Beneath the buildings were crawl spaces of various depths and sizes, some of them boarded in with timber sheeting to prevent animals from sheltering there, others open to the elements. Here and there, snowdrifts from the recent storm reached window level. Some residents had tried to dig through, forming tunneled pathways past their homes, but most had not bothered. The weather was unforgiving here, and it would always win.

The roads were cleared periodically by the town's snowplow, forming banks of snow six feet high on either side of the roads. There were walk-throughs dug about, mostly in front of the handful of stores, bars, and restaurants that served the town. Business was business, and even in Barrow it helped to keep your customers happy.

Crawl spaces, walkways, tunnels through drifted snowbanks . . . here, the Stranger was very much at home. Plenty of places to hide. Lots of cover for when he wanted to move around. He'd found them to be trusting people, leaving doors unlocked and possessions open to view. That had helped, but the approaching darkness seemed to make the inhabitants more cautious, and now his tasks were becoming more difficult and dangerous. Not that he was at all afraid of being caught, just not yet. He had no wish to spoil the surprise.

And now the huskies were barking, and they would give him away.

He finished rooting around in the trash can for food scraps. The sled dogs still barked, and he thought much of it was from fear. They had growled to begin with, baring their yellowed teeth at him, hackles rising, hunkering down as if to leap. But he had merely growled back, and their fear had set them off.

The Stranger chewed on the remains of the hamburger he'd found. *Nuked. Damn, don't these people like a bit of blood with their food?*

The dogs' barking became louder and more frenzied.

The Stranger turned on them and put his hand inside his coat pocket. The huskies fell silent. And as he advanced on them, the growling began anew.

When he reached for the first hound, it snapped at him. He kicked it to the ground, grabbed its chain, dragged it to him, knelt on its neck, and plunged the knife into its chest.

The husky howled, and the other dogs started whining in terror.

He withdrew the knife and sniffed at the blood. Foul. They deserved to die.

A minute past the town sign they came across the snowplow, swerved off the road and half-buried in a drift. The hood was up, and Beau Brower was working beneath it.

Eben stopped the 4x4 a dozen paces away and sighed. Beau paid no attention to their arrival. Even from here Eben could see the stain of spilled oil beneath the truck.

"Let's see what's going on," Eben said.

"You know he's goin' to be pissy," Billy said, making to climb from the cab.

Eben shook his head. "Stay here, Billy—no need two of us getting cold again." He climbed from the 4x4 and approached the truck. The back was covered with a tarpaulin, one corner loose and flapping in the breeze. He paused and watched Beau working; he was an ox of a man, with sometimes the temper to match.

"Little problem?" Eben asked.

"Nothin' I can't handle my own fuckin' self." Beau didn't even look up.

Eben sighed again. *Not now,* he thought. Beau had never caused him trouble—not physically, at least—but he could be an argumentative son of a bitch if the mood took him. Which was often. He lifted the flapping corner of tarpaulin and peeked underneath. In the weak streetlights, he could see several oil canisters, rolled together in a jumble.

"This for generators?"

"Mostly."

"I can't have it leaking all over the roads, Beau. You know I'll have to cite you for that." He took out his citation book and started writing, just as Beau's expected outburst began.

"Fuck's sake, Sheriff. You don't *have* to cite me. You don't *have* to do anything. That's why we live up here, ain't it? So we've got a little freedom?"

Eben glanced up, but Beau was looking over his shoulder.

"Why don't you run Billy on home so he can cuddle with that cute wifey of his? Only fair that one of us oughta get laid tonight, at least." The big man grinned.

Eben stepped forward, ripped the ticket, and stuffed it casually in Beau's coat pocket. "Happy motoring," he said, turning his back on Beau.

"Yeah. Fuck you very much. I'll add this to my collection."

Eben smiled as he climbed back into the 4x4. *Didn't go so bad,* he thought. *Least I'm not laid out in the snow.* He felt a sudden tightness in his chest, but he didn't like using his inhaler in front of other people. Even Billy. He started the motor and pulled gently away, feeling Beau's gaze burning into him.

"Beau's not that bad," Billy said. "Why do you bother writing him up?"

Eben shivered and turned up the heat. "He lives all by himself in that cabin on the south ridge, y'know? A little citation now and then reminds Beau he's part of this town. Good for him, and when it snows, good for us."

Billy nodded. "I guess. But he's right though, Eben."

"Right about what?"

"You really should drop me at home. The wife always likes the first night of the Dark." Billy chuckled, and Eben could not help being infected by the man's humor.

Lucky for you, Eben thought. *Some people sleep alone.* But there was not an ounce of malice in this thought. Eben knew well enough that some who slept alone had no one to blame but themselves.

"Another hour on duty, by my watch," Eben said. "Maybe she'll keep warm for you."

The radio crackled, startling them both. *"Eben, come in, Eben."* It was Helen, their dispatcher, and Eben could already hear trouble in her voice.

Eben picked up the handset. "Roger, Helen."

"Eben . . . something bad's happened to John Riis's dogs."

Eben and Billy glanced at each other, and Eben sighed. *Long night ahead,* he thought. *And it's barely begun.*

As night fell, Barrow became a town of good-byes. Some people could handle the long period of darkness without going mad; indeed, some welcomed it. Others found it oppressive and disturbing, and resorted to the bottle or fist to appease their stress. It was these who left, whether voluntarily or, in several cases, by the suggestion of other townsfolk. In Barrow, it was hard enough dealing with what nature had to throw against them, let alone handling someone driven to the edge by such harsh conditions.

Mainly these were cheerful farewells, given in the

sure knowledge that people would be reunited again in a month. The main street had something of a carnival atmosphere as the stragglers prepared to head for the airport. Horns honked, the lights strung between buildings shone bright, people wandered here and there laughing, hugging, and shaking hands. Those who were staying promised that they would take care, and those leaving were told not to have too much of a good time. There was excitement in the air, but an underlying sense of melancholy as well. Beneath all the enthusiasm lay the knowledge that Barrow was a town very much ruled by its environment. That was always a challenge, but sometimes . . .

Sometimes it was dangerous.

Tom Melanson knew that Dianne's parents disliked him. They smiled, but they couldn't hide the ice in their eyes. Maybe that's what came of spending their life living in the snow. And that was exactly why he was taking his time saying good-bye.

"See you in the light, baby." He pulled back from whispering in her ear and kissed Dianne again, closing his eyes and darting his tongue into her mouth. He knew she liked that. He knew that beneath her heavy clothing her nipples would be growing hard, her legs quivering. He reached down and squeezed her butt, and she slapped his hand away.

"Tom! My parents!"

"Yeah," he said. He could see them over her shoulder. They were trying to look everywhere but at their daughter, and their attention was completely on her.

"Be good," she said. She wriggled from his grasp and grabbed his heavy coat's collar. *"Be good!"*

"Who would I have to mess around with? Half the town's leaving today."

Dianne frowned, pouted. "Don't people get kind of wild sometimes in the Dark?"

"But I'll be good while you're gone—I promise." He grinned at her, remembering the previous night. She blushed. Damn, he thought that was so cute! Shy and innocent today, but last night . . .

"Anyway," Tom continued, "it's you I should worry about, living it up in Seattle. You're the one everyone hits on."

"Tom!" She acted all coy, but when they kissed again, it was her tongue in his mouth this time.

Tom pulled away. "Your parents."

"Yeah." Dianne grinned.

Doug Hertz was middle-aged, rotund, and determined not to reveal his sadness at being left alone. He didn't want his wife leaving him behind like that.

"I'm sorry, it's okay, sweetie," Lizzie said. "I know I say I'll try every year, but I just can't take a month with no sun. Just seems wrong. I'm so sorry."

"Stop apologizing! Every year you say sorry, and every year I tell you it's fine."

"But do you mean it?"

Doug nodded, and he *did* mean it. "It's fine. We chose this life and what goes with it." He kissed her and hugged her tight. "Just give my love to your folks. And I promise I won't live on Oreos and Snapple."

"Yeah, right." Lizzie laughed and rested her head on his shoulder.

"Really," Doug protested. "Honest!"

Kirsten Toomey loved her dad, but she also relished the thought of time on her own. She was twenty, but sometimes he still treated her as though she was twelve. A month of night, four weeks of the Dark, and she was planning to play much harder than work.

"Wish you'd come with me, Kirsten," he said. "I hate this place in December. Nothing here but twenty-eight miles of roads, and all of them dead ends."

"I'm gonna get all caught up, Dad," Kirsten said. "The taxes, invoicing, January's orders. Don't worry! Have fun in Seattle!"

He smiled sadly, nodded. "Okay, fair enough. Anything you want me to bring back?"

"Got everything I need here."

He hugged her. "You take care."

"I will. It's a break from life, Dad. I like the thought of things slowing down for a while."

Charlie Kelso hammered the last boards across the windows of his house. It wasn't that he didn't trust the people he was leaving behind—he'd known many of them all his life—but a month was a long time to be away from home. And his house was *nice*. He'd worked long and hard on *making* it nice, and he was damned if he was going to leave it unprotected. Peace of mind, that's what he called it. Paranoia, his wife said. Whatever.

"Charlie," his wife called from behind him. She was waiting impatiently beside their Land Rover, their two teenaged daughters already sitting inside, expressions surly enough to melt ice. "Do you want to make it to Maui or not?"

Maybe, maybe not, Charlie thought. *Sometimes I wonder.* He'd often thought of suggesting that he remain here through the Dark, watching the house and catching up on business. *Yeah, and catching up on some other stuff, too . . .*

But he'd never actually had the guts to go through and say it out loud.

Charlie sighed. "Almost done." He hammered the last few nails home, taking his time and resisting the urge to smash the hammer straight through the timber.

Stella Oleson had been back in Barrow for eight hours, and already she wanted to leave.

Since she'd left the first time, she'd been working for the Alaska State Fire Marshal's office, and now it seemed that they were doing their very best to help her return. Twelve hours before Barrow closed down for the longest month of its year, they'd sent her here, requesting that she inspect and test the foam fire-fighting tanks housed inside Barrow's own small fire station. It could have been done at any time—a month ago, or two months down the line—and would still have complied with guidelines. But no, now was when she had to do it. And here she was.

She hadn't even told Eben she was back. She was confused enough with life right now . . . why confuse it more?

Stella was in her late twenties, good-looking, trim, and athletic, and she commanded respect from everyone who knew her. She was good at her job, and knew that she'd be good at *any* job. Life was too short for average. She was aware that some people called her hard, but to her knowledge no one had ever called her cold. Other than Eben, of course.

One of the volunteer firemen, Adam Colletta, walked by. "Kinda put this off till the last minute, didja, Stella?"

"Tell me about it. A lot of small towns in this state, and my boss wants all their gear inspected and certified by the thirty-first."

"And I notice you saved Barrow for last."

"I was sent here, Adam," she said sternly. "Didn't come of my own accord."

Adam's face fell a little. "Oh. Sure you don't wanna stay? Jeannie and I were kinda hoping you and Eben—"

"No," Stella said, shaking her head. She moved on, examining another piece of equipment, tapping a dial, and she sensed Adam moving away behind her.

My *business,* she thought. *Wish people would leave it the hell alone.*

She closed her clipboard and sighed. "Adam," she said. She turned around, and Adam was standing expectantly a few paces from her. "Thanks a ton. I've gotta make the plane. It was nice seeing you again. You take it easy."

"You too, Stella."

She smiled, zipped up her parka and headed out to where her rented 4x4 was parked. She glanced at her watch; plenty of time. The notion of being stuck here for the month . . . *No thanks,* she thought.

She fired up the 4x4 and skidded out of the fire station driveway.

Stella passed a few people still on the streets, but she waved to no one. She hoped that none of them saw who was driving. This was meant to be a quick in-and-out—she'd never intended hanging around to rediscover old friendships. Most of them were gone now anyway, either waiting at the airport for the last flight, or back in their homes to get used to thirty days without their husbands, wives, or families. Perhaps it said a lot about Stella's current state of mind when she thought that many of them would be looking forward to the break.

She hated it when those blessed enough to have families complained about being around them all the time.

She pushed down angrily on the gas, corrected the steering when the 4x4 slipped out from under her, and then a shadow emerged from the night, bearing down.

Stella jumped, then relaxed back in her seat. It was only the trencher—a huge truck mounted on tracks instead of wheels and bearing a massive chain saw on its nose. A mean-looking vehicle driven by Malekai

Hamm, she had seen it around many times when she'd lived in Barrow. It looked pretty damn intimidating right now, illuminated by her headlights reflected up from the snow, windshield like a dark mouth above its own lights, chain saw inactive but still pointing threateningly ahead.

"My right of way," Stella muttered. Still, she eased up on the gas. Years of driving in the snow sharpened her instincts.

The trencher started flashing at her, honking its horn, and for a crazy second she thought Malekai had recognized her and wanted to stop and chat. Then it struck, throwing her against her window with the impact and sending the 4x4 fishtailing across the road.

Stella held her breath and tensed up, everything she knew she shouldn't do in a crash. The 4x4 came to a shuddering halt in a snowbank, and she found herself still gripping the wheel. She gasped, shaking her head. *Something bad there. Grinding metal.* For a moment she dreaded what she'd find when she got out, but then the fact that she was still alive hit home. It could have been a whole lot worse.

She had to shove her door hard to get it open. The impact must have buckled metal somewhere, bent the frame. She walked a couple of steps, turned and surveyed the damage. Her front tire was shredded, the wheel itself gouged by the vicious links of the chain saw. The wheel arch was rumpled as well, a subtle texture in the metal that could hide a lot more damage underneath.

"Goddamn it, Malekai!" she shouted. "Don't you know what 'right of way' means?"

Malekai jumped down from his cab. "I'm sorry, Stella, the brakes jammed."

Stella looked at the trencher. It had suffered hardly a scratch. "Well *you're* all right!"

"Eben wanted this back from the airport before the storm hits, I was just trying to—"

Stella shook her head and went around to the back of her truck. *Just my luck! Oh, I can't be stuck here, I can't, I can't.* She opened the door and pulled out her carry-on bag. She sensed Malekai standing behind her, shifting his weight nervously from foot to foot.

"Didn't even know you were in town," the trencher driver said.

"Nobody knew," Stella said. She spun around. "So now who's gonna run me to the airport?"

"Wouldn't Eben—"

Stella sighed. "Of course he would. But I just popped into town for work, and he doesn't know I'm here. I didn't want things to get messy, today of all days." A few snowflakes were dancing in the air now, so light that she couldn't be sure whether they were fresh, or fallen snow gusted up from the ground. A couple landed on Malekai's eyelashes and he seemed not to notice. *Go easy on him,* she thought.

"My mom could bring the tow truck," he said. "But, uh, you know she doesn't move so fast."

"Thanks, Malekai," Stella said, and the anger was still there, her short temper showing through again. The driver averted his eyes, abashed, and it was too late now to try and apologize for snapping at him. Later, maybe. The brakes jammed, he'd said. She shook her head. She *had* to arrange a ride to the airport, and she was only delaying the inevitable.

She pulled out her cell phone and speed-dialed Eben's number.

He answered after three rings, obviously having seen her name on his caller display. His voice was cautious, defensive. *"It's me."*

"Surprise," Stella said flatly. She closed her eyes. This was more difficult than she'd thought. "Eben, I need a ride to the airport."

He did not respond for a few seconds, obviously processing the words and what they implied. *"Wait . . . what? You're in town? And you didn't want to talk?"*

"What about?" Stella said. They were both silent for a moment, displaying the honesty of her statement. A million things to say, but neither of them wanted to say a thing. "Look, Eben, I had Fire Marshal work here at the station, now I'm stuck at Ransom and 355. I've had a fender bender with Malekai, the airport'll close soon, and then I'll never get back to Anchorage. I'll be stuck here for a month. I need to get back, Eben. You want to talk, we can do it on the drive to the airport." She fell quiet, seeing Malekai's discomfort through her hazed breath. The telephone ticked and crackled. Then she heard Eben moving about and the sound of a car door opening.

"Billy!" he shouted. *"Hey, Billy! Stella's stuck at Ran-*

som and 355; can you get her to the airport before the plane leaves?"

He's sending Billy? Stella thought, but she would not say anything. Let him play his games.

After a pause, Eben came back on the phone. *"Listen, John Riis needs my help with something, so Billy's on his way. You let me know if a day comes when you* do *want to talk."*

"Eben—" But he was gone. Stella cursed at letting the conversation end like that; Eben at an advantage. This wasn't a fucking game, she knew that, but . . . well, it really was, wasn't it? Hadn't it always been a game between the two of them? She shook her head and thrust the phone back into her pocket.

Malekai was kneeling down beside her rental, pointlessly touching the crunched bodywork and tapping the tattered wheel with his knuckles. She stood beside him and checked out the damage. Not good. It'd need a tow truck. She moved over to the trencher, for something to do more than anything else, and sighed with frustration when she saw how unscathed it was.

Malekai beeped a number into his cell phone behind her. *Anything to avoid actually talking to me,* she thought.

She knelt in the compacted snow beside the trencher, took a small flashlight from her pocket, and looked underneath.

Malekai started talking to his mother, asking her for a tow and speaking like a berated child when she obviously launched one at him down the line ("Yeah, Mom, Stella asked the same thing. Could you just give me a tow?"). Stella smiled, then felt sorry for the poor kid.

She shined the flashlight around beneath the trencher until she saw something hanging down, a pipe almost touching the ground. A few drips of fluid seeped from the end, darkening the snow. *That's not right,* she thought. She lay down on her side and stretched her arm underneath.

The brake cable was hanging down. And she was no expert, but from what she could see it looked as though it had been cut.

Frowning, she stood up and brushed snow from her parka. She checked her watch and hoped Billy would hurry the hell up.

The dogs had been slaughtered.

Someone had gone at them with a knife, that was clear, and their still-steaming blood and insides were now splashed across the Riises' backyard. Eben tried not to breathe in the steam, because he knew where it came from.

"What sick jerk would *do* something like this?" Ally Riis wailed. She was in her late thirties, small and athletic, and Eben knew that she often went out with the dogs.

"Every kennel," John Riis said, his tone flat. "Every dog we had."

"You have a fight with anyone lately, John?" Eben asked. Riis was known for saying what he thought, and sometimes his thoughts weren't that pretty.

John shook his head. "Y'know, somebody always freaks out a little once the sun's gone, but it usually takes two or three weeks." He was lost in grief and shock, and Eben suddenly felt very sad. Angry, a little bit afraid . . . but sad as well. For the Riises, this was an awful beginning to the long night.

"I'll kill them," Ally said. "When we find out who did it, I'll kill them."

"Hang on now, Ally—" John began, but his wife shrugged his hand off and stared at the bloody mess of their backyard. Then her face crumpled, and she leaned into John as the tears came.

"It can't be somebody we *know*," John said, his own eyes watering.

Eben shrugged. "But the bodies are still warm. This wasn't done long enough ago that you could get to the airport afterward. Whoever did this . . . is still in town."

"These dogs were *strong,*" John Riis said. Then he and his wife went inside, leaving Eben to the steam and blood.

Malekai was smoking a cigarette, and Stella was sitting on her bag beside the wrecked rental when she heard a motor. *Let it be Eben,* she thought. And at the same time, she fervently wished it was not.

Billy's voice gave her answer. "Your limo's here, Mrs. Oleson!"

Stella stood and heaved her bag at Billy when he jumped down from his cab. "Service is going downhill," she said.

Billy was about to say something, but Stella turned to Malekai. "You'll be okay, Malekai?"

"My mom will be here soon to tow me in."

Stella nodded, glanced at the trencher. *Brakes cut. Who the hell would want to hurt Malekai?* But maybe she'd been mistaken. It was dark after all, and perhaps the pipe she'd seen hadn't been the brake cable at all.

Stella then turned and threw up her hands at Billy. "Where've you been?!"

"Sorry I'm late, Stella," Billy said. "The car keys weren't where I thought, and then I was like, wait, Rogers and 355, or Ransom? And then when I—"

"Never mind. Let's go—we've got to hustle if I'm going to make that plane." She scrambled in the cab and waved back. "Take it easy, Malekai."

The trencher driver waved, offering a tentative smile. "See you again?"

Stella closed her door without answering.

"Hey, Stella," Billy said. He sat there waiting for a response, and she shook her head.

"Billy, I just need to get to the airport! No bullshit, no psychoanalysis, just a drive from here to there. Is that okay?"

"Sure thing," Billy said, but in his voice she heard that it was not okay at all.

Billy drove fast. But still Stella checked her watch every thirty seconds, willing the time to slow down, staring at the minute hand in the hope that it would retreat five minutes and give her some sort of safety zone. She fidgeted in her seat and tapped her fingers on her knee. She stared into the sky ahead of them, terrified that she would see the blinking taillights of the last plane out of Barrow as it hauled itself skyward. She willed Billy to drive faster.

It took three minutes for him to break his silence.

"You want to know how Eben's been doin'?"

Stella sighed. "You're going to tell me whether I ask you or not, right?" She looked across at Billy and he returned her a lopsided smile. "Billy, just drive, okay?"

Billy's smile dropped, he stared ahead at the road, and Stella was sure she sensed him driving faster still.

As they approached the small airport building—little more than three large rooms, baggage sorting, toilets, and a two-man control tower—the lights started going out.

"No!" Stella shouted. She banged her hand on the dashboard, urging Billy to drive faster.

"Stella, this doesn't look good," he said.

"I didn't see it take off!"

"Runway heads east, we're coming in from the west. It'd be a mile away, at least. And the clouds—"

"But they must have *known* I wasn't on board. My ticket! They should have waited for me."

"Stella . . ." Billy began, but he drifted off and let her vent her rage.

More lights flicked off, and by the time Billy skidded to a stop in front of the main building, the security guard was locking and chaining the front door. The only illumination left inside was the one emergency light, and this would blink out within the hour.

Stella leapt from the 4x4 even as it was rocking to a

standstill and ran at the doors. "I can't have missed it!" she hollered.

The security guard looked up, shrugged, and walked away without saying a word.

"Hey!" Stella shouted. She *hated* being ignored.

The guard turned around, shoulders hunched against the cold and scarf hiding everything but his eyes. "Sorry, ma'am," he said, voice muffled.

Stella walked to the doors and stared inside. The jolly sign on the door really pissed her off: CLOSED—SEE YOU NEXT YEAR!

"No," she said. "No, no, I am *not* trapped here for a month. This is a bad dream." She closed her eyes, opened them again, and everything was real.

The car door slammed behind her and Billy approached. "Ohh, there'll be someone you can bunk with, Stella."

"Don't start, okay?" She turned, ready to give him hell.

Billy held out his hands and uttered a nervous laugh. "Hey, no, I meant Lucy, or Denise. Or hey, Peggy and me could even move the girls into one room and you could—"

The reality of the situation really hit home then, and the practicalities of what was happening, and Stella felt a creeping sense of panic. "But I *can't* stay here! I've got bills to put in the mail, a dentist's appointment next week. And my plants will die!"

"Well, you can call somebody from our place to handle some of that, can't you? You gotta know someone in Anchorage who can help?"

"Damn it, Billy." From anger, to panic, to hopelessness in the space of thirty seconds. *Shit, Eben really did a job on me didn't he? Or did he . . . ? Maybe it was the other way around.* She wanted to scream. Hell, she wanted to shoot something. "*Damn* it!"

Billy stepped closer and gave her a friendly tap on the shoulder. "Come on, it'll work out." He paused, and Stella could see him debating whether or not to say something. *No, Billy,* she thought. *Not right now—*

" 'Course, the price of rent at my place might be explaining to me and Peggy what the heck's wrong with you and Eben."

And there it was. "Not enough time in this century to cover that, Billy." She sighed, took one final look back at the darkened airport and nodded at the 4x4. "Let's go before we freeze to death."

Helen Munson sat at her desk, staring at the radio and waiting for Eben to arrive. She had some more news for him, but she knew he was on his way back to the station, and she'd rather tell him this face-to-face. Give him time for a break and a coffee, at least. Helen had lived through many month-long nights in Barrow, and the first day or two always had the potential to be troublesome. But this was something more. As dispatcher, she heard of everything that happened, and here—the cell phones, the Riises' dogs, and now the vandalism—she was beginning to see a pattern. It just wasn't a pattern that she liked very much.

She had also heard from Billy that Stella was in town. Awkward.

Her fifteen-year-old grandson, Jake, was playing Risk at a desk behind her. Normally she'd have joined in, but she was too troubled to concentrate.

"It'd be easier if you played, Grandma." He glanced up at her with his piercing blue eyes, and he just about broke her heart, he was so gorgeous. How his parents could leave him here for so long . . . but she supposed it was a break for them. And Jake had always loved the Dark, ever since he was a little kid.

"Not right now, Jake. I don't really care for games like that, if you want to know the truth. Besides, don't you learn a lot when you play against yourself?"

"Yeah, yeah, yeah," he said. "Playing against yourself builds character and yadda yadda . . ."

Helen grimaced as a wave of nausea passed over her. She turned away, closing her eyes and tensing her jaw.

There were only a handful of people who knew about her cancer.

She was trying to maintain a positive attitude to fight it, and listening to the sympathies of a multitude of family and friends would not help her one bit.

Jake knew, of course. She'd have never been able to hide it from him.

"Grandma?"

She raised her hand and waved his concern away, and then Eben arrived. He seemed not to notice. Or if he did, he gave her the privacy he knew she desired.

"Try your brother. See if he wants to play," she said to Jake.

"'The Classic Game of Global Domination,'" Eben read, mock jolly. He took a blast from his albuterol inhaler, something he only did amongst family. "I'm a little jammed today, Jake. Can't even keep this little town from going to hell."

Helen stood, pleased that she'd sent the sickness down yet again. Sometimes she won, sometimes she didn't. "Sorry, Eben," she said. "Grab a coffee, but keep your coat on. While you were busy with John Riis? Carter and Wilson called about a vandalism problem at the Utilidor."

"Jesus," Eben said. "Can it wait?"

Helen shook her head.

Eben sighed, poured a coffee and clicked the lid on his cup. "Okay. Helen, do me a favor and call Point Hope and Wainwright, see if they're having any troubles. This just feels odd." He took the dispatch sheet from Helen. "You okay, Grandma?" he asked quietly.

"Don't call me that," she scolded. Then she nodded. "I'm fine." She glanced across at Jake, who was making a great show of examining a game he wasn't even really playing. "I'm having a good day."

Eben smiled, pecked her on the cheek and left.

Helen closed her eyes as another wave of nausea came roaring in.

• • •

Eben stood by his 4x4 and stared at the Utilidor Sewage Plant. For a town as remote as Barrow, it really was a marvel of engineering, built with oil money that seemed as bottomless as the wells from which the black gold sprang. There was a pump house, a large square building containing the huge shredder, and two connected storage tanks which towered more than a hundred feet into the sky. They were the tallest structures in Barrow, and if it had not been for the flashing aircraft lights that topped them, their heads would have been lost to the darkness. But expensive though the technology was, and cold though the wind may have been, the air here always carried a hint of what the plant was here to treat.

"Phew," Eben muttered. He zipped his hood up around his face and started for the plant. *Weird shit going on here,* he thought, smiling at his unintentional pun. *The cell phones—how the hell were they stolen from so many people without one of them seeing who'd taken them? Then the Riises' dogs. Strong, hardy, vicious if provoked. Now . . . this. Whatever "this" turns out to be.*

The door to the pump house swung open and Carter Henry emerged. He was a huge barrel of a man who Eben rarely saw wearing anything other than jeans and a T-shirt. How he had never frozen to death was a mystery. Tonight he was wearing an Alaskan Tourist Board T-shirt reading ALASKA B4UDIE, glaring white against his dark skin. He shouted over to the Jayko twins, Paul and Xavier, who were working on a huge sewage pipe one hundred feet to the north. "Guys, you can't get that pipe fixed tonight. Seal it off from the town and come back tomorrow. Have a beer. Dream of retirement."

"Good enough!" Paul called. He waved to Eben, and Eben waved back.

"Lord, Carter, it's gotta be ten below out here. Can't your wife send you a sweater or two?"

"Damn things give me a rash. Besides, I'm such a fine figure of a man, why cover myself up?" He smiled, then turned around as Wilson Bulosan appeared in the doorway behind him.

"Hey, Wilson," Eben said.

But there were no niceties. "You need to see this, Eben," he said, jerking his thumb back over his shoulder.

"Yes, you do," Carter said, and the smile dropped from his face. "Let's go inside."

The pump house was where Carter controlled and monitored Barrow's sewage system. Shit Central, Carter called it. His control panel was scattered with knick-knacks and family photographs, shots of his four kids in school, his wife riding a horse, and a couple of casual snaps from their wedding. A big gruff guy he might be, but Carter obviously missed his family.

"So when are you bringing the whole tribe back here, Carter?" Eben asked.

Carter shrugged. "They'll come when they're ready, I guess."

"A family oughta be together, Carter."

Carter nodded, turned away, and followed Wilson

through another door into a smaller, noisier room. There was an open trapdoor in one corner; racks of tools, protective clothing, and coiled rope fixed to one wall; and beyond another door Eben could make out a couple of shower stalls.

Another wall was taken by a bank of shelving, and here there was a variety of strange, unlikely objects. Books, kids' toys, clothing, a picture frame without a picture, a pile of CD cases, a scattering of eating utensils, a smashed food blender . . . most of them impact damaged or stained by dirty water, all of them worthless.

Carter waved a hand at the shelving. "Welcome to my Museum of Shit. So . . . I've found all kinds of garbage here over the years. Amazin' the sort of stuff people try to flush away, y'know? Blue jeans. Bikes. Sometimes I can yank 'em out before the Muffin Monster chews 'em to shit."

"The Muffin Monster?" Wilson asked.

"Mmmhmm. Something falls in, it gets shredded." He pointed at the open trapdoor in the corner.

"Is that where that delightful smell is coming from?" Eben asked.

Carter sniffed, shrugged again. "Can't say I notice it. Come on. I've already told Wilson what I found, now I can show you both."

The three men stood before the Muffin Monster, a high-torque, four-shaft shredder. It was not as noisy as Eben had been expecting, and the smell wasn't quite as rank either. Perhaps, as Carter had hinted, you got used to it after a while.

"Welcome to Barrow's stinking underside," Carter said.

"Like somethin' out of *Blade Runner*," Eben muttered.

"Not quite so high-tech," Carter said. "Every pipe ends here, and the Muffin Monster chops it all up. Main sewer from town has a couple of baffles, stops bigger stuff coming through, and earlier I found this." He lifted a trash can and showed them the contents. "Saw Wilson's logo on it, pulled this stuff out before it got totally trashed, so I called him and he said not to touch it till I called you."

Wilson took the trash can from Carter and emptied the contents onto the floor; a tattered seat belt, pipes and leads, a chunky metal device that looked as though it belonged inside an engine, dashboard controls with a Polar Tours logo on it, and a bloated wet book with the words *Top of the World Tours* fading on the cover.

"You keep your copter under lock and key, don't you, Wilson?" Eben asked.

"Yeah, of course. I put it in dry dock when the tourists headed south. Haven't looked at it for days. Then Carter called me, told me about this, and I swung by on the way over here. It's a mess. Totally fucked up."

"Could you fix it up if you needed to?"

"Not without parts from Anchorage. This is my living, Eben. Why would someone rip the hell out of my bird?" Wilson stood and threw some of the pieces angrily into the Muffin Monster, which chewed them up with startling speed.

Why indeed? Eben thought. *The phones, the dogs, now Wilson's helicopter. Almost like someone doesn't want us to leave. Shit.*

Back in his 4x4, Eben reached for the radio to call Billy. As he grabbed the mouthpiece it crackled and squawked, startling him.

"Eben, you there?"

"Here, Helen." He could hear the concern in her voice. "What's up now?"

"Some stranger's causing trouble up at Lucy's diner. Lucy thinks he's a vagrant."

"A vagrant in Barrow?"

Helen uttered a brief laugh. *"Yeah, I know. But that's how she described him."*

"Hell, a stranger in Barrow is weird enough," Eben said.

"I'll tell her you're on your way."

"I'll be there yesterday."

Lucy Ikos was a tough, willful woman in her sixties, and in many ways she reminded Eben of his grandmother. She'd run the Ikos Diner for two decades, and while serving oil workers all that time, she'd had her fair share of disturbances. Usually a harsh word from her was enough to calm things down. For her to call something in, it must be pretty serious.

"How are things at the Utilidor?" Helen asked.

"Just a bit of graffiti," he said. "Nothing to worry about."

"Oh. Okay. Out."

Eben wasn't sure why he'd lied. Perhaps lying to himself? Several hours in, and already the Dark was starting to feel like it had settled down for a long, long time.

Beyond the northernmost limits of Barrow lay the satellite dish tower, bristling with antennae and topped with the dish itself. Not far past the tower ran the Trans-Alaskan oil pipeline, a visible indicator of the riches to be found in the area. The tower boosted all cell phone signals, and was also the relay station for all the radios in Barrow—police, medical, and the several radio hams who liked to keep the outside world apprised of events in this unusual town.

Gus Lambert had retired to Barrow and taken the job of maintaining the tower. As he liked to tell people in the town, he'd come as far north as he could, then gone a little farther. He liked to think of himself as the northernmost working man in North America, yet most of the time he had to admit there was little real work to be done here. He was certainly no communications or electronics genius, and any real problems that arose were usually fixed by men flown in by the oil companies. He was the caretaker here, really—cleaning up the control room, making sure the doors and windows were kept free of ice, keeping the heating cranked up—and he was just fine with that.

He flicked on the external lights, glanced outside, and saw that it had started to snow. Little flurries for now, but he knew this was just the beginning. "Here it comes," he said, turning the lights off again.

Gus sat at his table and poured some tea. There was a portable DVD player before him and a book upended fifty pages from the end, but Gus sat back in his chair and sang himself an old swing-band tune as he waited for the tea to steam cool. He'd already guessed how the book would finish, and he'd seen his DVD collection three times over.

Sometimes he thought about what he'd do when this all became too much for him. He was still fit and healthy, but his joints played him up now, and every time it snowed his left eye ached. He didn't have a clue what that meant. *Gettin' old,* he thought. A time would come when he'd have to move again. Into Barrow, perhaps, or maybe back down south. He shook his head. No point thinking about that right now. He was in his twilight years, and now more than ever he was trying to live for the moment.

He finished his song. The tea smelled good. Ah, screw it—maybe he'd give that book one more try.

There was a noise outside. Gus opened his eyes, holding his breath. "Wind?" he said aloud. He guessed so. The air sang all sorts of songs around the antennae. "Damn storm's coming in faster than I thought." Gus talked to himself a lot. He had always liked his own company, and he rarely answered back.

He reached for the cup, and that was when he heard

the distant howl, starting low but rising in tone, until Gus could no longer hear it.

"What the fuck . . . ?" He stood and on instinct dug his old revolver from the table's drawer, and tucked it in his belt. Another howl, this one farther away. Wolves? They'd been seen around Barrow before, but none since last year. Maybe now the Dark was here and the storms were descending, they were coming closer to the town in search of food.

Another howl. This one seemed to come from right outside.

Half the illuminated dials on the control desk flicked out.

Gus gasped and stepped back, nudging against the table and spilling his tea. "Shit." He thought of calling in to Eben, but the damn long night had only just begun, the storm was coming in, and he didn't want to seem like a panicked old man.

"Probably a power surge," he muttered. There were arrangements to deal with this, fail-safes, backup computer programs that would automatically reboot and reset the whole system—

But what the hell had made that noise?

He shrugged on his parka, zipped up, transferred the revolver into his coat pocket, and went for the door. If there were nasty critters out there, they may be damaging the tower. One shot would probably see them off. "Whatever they are," he murmured.

Gus opened the door and snow wafted inside. He stepped out and closed the door quickly, eager to keep the warmth in the tower. He'd be back inside in a minute, brewing a fresh cup of tea, maybe settling down to watch *The Thing* for probably the tenth time, and then planning on what to have for dinner.

He crunched through the snow a dozen steps from the tower, turned, and looked up at the array. "Seems okay," he said, but yet again he admitted to himself that he was no expert.

Gus heard the secretive crunch of a footstep behind him. He gasped again, breath stalling in his throat, and spun around. He tugged the revolver from his pocket and brandished it at the shadows. "Nothing there," he whispered.

Another series of crunches, more distant, as something walked with steady determination.

He turned and staggered for the tower, and spotted the set of footprints crossing his own. The outside lights weren't that powerful, but he was sure he saw the shapes of toes in those prints.

Human toes.

He hurried on, reached the safety of the door, sighed in relief, and the shadows came at him from around the side of the tower, growling and drooling and reaching for him with inhuman hands.

The Ikos Diner was much more than a place to eat. It was the main bar in Barrow, as close to being the center of the community as anywhere. When the sun was up, workers and their families came here to eat, drink, and catch up. During the thirty days of night, when

Barrow hunkered down and let nature take the lead, it was an important meeting place for those made lonely by the Dark. Its owner, Lucy Ikos, was well loved in Barrow because she never took advantage of anyone. Those whose families went south for the Dark often ate in her diner every day, eager for the company of others, and Lucy never raised her prices. Sometimes she even lowered them, if times were hard. Her diner was as much a part of Barrow as the oil derricks, the pipeline, and everyone who worked them. In many ways, it was the heart of the town.

Now, the heart had a murmur.

They were used to strangers in Barrow—transient oil workers often drifted in and out of the town depending on labor demand. But *never* at this time of year. The man who'd walked in half an hour earlier was recognized by no one. He'd taken a seat at the counter, and Lucy had been around the block enough times to spot trouble when it reared its head.

This time, she smelled it as well. The man stank. Within five minutes of his arrival—and his silent contemplation of everyone in the diner, that smile, those eyes that seemed to bore right into your own—Lucy had slipped out back and put in a call to Eben. She was used to handling the rough stuff on her own, but that was with people she knew. This stranger could be packing, and no one needed that.

"No *whiskey*? No *rum*?" His voice was a sibilant, slimy whisper, yet audible to everyone in the diner.

"I told you, alcohol's illegal this month. You're not

from 'round here, so there's plenty you don't know. Folks have a hard enough time in the Dark without booze making it worse."

"Booze always makes things better," the Stranger responded.

"Ask me if I'm surprised you think that."

The man stared at her, and Lucy averted her eyes. *Damn him for staring me down,* she thought, but there was something distinctly unpleasant about him. As though he'd seen everything and she, spending much of her life up here, had seen nothing. He looked to be half her age, but his eyes held twice her experience.

"Forget the liquor, Lucy. Bring me a bowl of raw hamburger."

"You can only get meat two ways around here, mister; frozen and burnt."

The Stranger sighed and shook his head, looking down at the counter again so that his long hair obscured his face. Lucy glanced around at the uneasy patrons—the ones who hadn't already quietly left—then at the door. *Come on, Eben,* she thought. *This is going to turn into a shit storm, I can just—*

"You won't give me what I want to eat," he said, the gritty whisper seeming to reverberate off the counter. "What I want to drink." He looked up, reached out, and ran a grimy nail through the air inches before Lucy's face. "What kind of hospitality *is* this stinking shit-pit of a town able to offer?"

Something in the air changed. Lucy gasped, and for a split second she was terrified. Then she saw a big shadow shift behind the Stranger and she realized that help had arrived.

"That's enough, pal," Eben barked. "Leave the woman alone."

The Stranger slipped from his barstool and stood. Eben was six feet tall, but this guy had a good four inches on him. The Sheriff sized him up with one glance; scruffy, unkempt, a confident look in his eyes, a sly smile, and stains on his coat that could have been blood.

"Time to hit the road."

"What's wrong with a man wanting a little fresh meat? A drink or two?"

"I'm sure Lucy has told you that no one drinks around here in the Dark. Not townsfolk, not strangers."

"That so?"

Eben nodded. The Stranger chuckled. It was not a nice sound, and Eben tried to shrug off the tingle it sent down his spine. The door opened behind him, but he did not turn to see who else had left. Besides, the Stranger was glaring right at him. Eben was damned if he was going to let this punk stare him down.

"If you refuse to leave," he said quietly, "I'll escort you out of here myself."

The Stranger stepped forward, halving the distance between them, and Eben's hand slipped three inches closer to his gun. "I'd like to see that," the man said.

"I would, too," another voice said.

The Stranger glanced up, his eyes registering an instant of surprise as a gun was placed against the base of his skull. Even then Stella had to point it upward.

Billy stood behind her, his own weapon not yet drawn. He looked terrified.

"But then," Stella continued, "Lucy'd have to clean up after Eben kicked your ass. It's more trouble than you're worth."

The Stranger's lips compressed, his bearing changed as he tensed his muscles, and Eben threw Stella a glance. *What the hell are you doing?!*

She nodded, held his gaze for a second longer than she needed to, then looked back at the Stranger. "Not a fucking breath," she said.

Eben pulled the man's arms roughly forward and snapped on the cuffs.

"Nice and tight," the Stranger said, and this close Eben could smell his breath. Stale. Rotten. No booze, so that ruled out a drunk-and-disorderly. Who knew then what this guy's story was? This environment had a way of playing with someone's sanity. Eben squeezed the cuffs until he heard the man's sharp intake of breath, then stepped back.

He nodded to Stella. She took three steps back, now pointing the gun at the Stranger's back.

"Fire Marshal's office lets you carry that?" Eben couldn't help asking.

Stella shrugged and gave him a small smile. "Funny thing, I never asked them."

Eben looked at Billy. "My able deputy could have helped me, I'm sure."

Billy shifted from foot to foot, still fingering his sidearm. "Yeah, but . . . well, Eben, it's Stella."

"Go home to Peggy, Billy. Been a long day."

"Longer night to come," the Stranger said. He uttered what may have been a giggle.

Eben glared at him. "Shut the fuck up. You're already in enough trouble." The Stranger looked up at the ceiling, closing his eyes.

Eben offered Stella a smiled *thank you* for her help, which she returned as a shrug. "Missed your plane?" he asked. "That sucks. Where are you gonna stay?"

"Billy said he and Peggy would put me up."

Eben nodded, not trusting himself to say anything more. *This will make everything even more confusing,* he thought, *but right now I'm glad she's here.* He glanced at the Stranger, then back to Stella.

"Need to get him to the station. Well. Talk to you sometime, I guess."

"Maybe the lady don't wanna talk," the Stranger rasped. Then he chuckled again.

"Eben, Stella, can you two dance around each other outside?" Lucy said. "Right now I want this guy somewhere I can't see or smell him."

Eben smiled apologetically at Lucy and glanced around at the other patrons. "Carry on, folks," he said.

"Carry on, folks," the Stranger mocked.

Eben shook his head. "Pal, I've had a bad day and you're really grabbing my shit."

The man tittered and nodded at the door. "After you?"

Eben held out his hand, a silent *after you* gesture. The Stranger smiled and walked for the door.

"Maybe I'll tag along," Stella said. She'd holstered her pistol and zipped up her coat. "Say hi to Jake and Helen?"

Eben nodded, but he had mixed feelings. He had work to do—lots of it, after the day's troubling events. And while he was already attributing much of them to this stranger, there was still paperwork to get done and an interview to carry out. Having Stella in the station . . .

Well, she and Jake got on well. It would keep him out of mischief, at least.

The three of them left the Ikos Diner, each swaddled in their own thoughts.

"Jesus," Lucy Ikos said when the door swung shut behind them. "Talk about cutting the atmosphere with a knife." The Dark always brought a bit of trouble. She hoped that this year, she'd had hers early.

The journey from the Ikos Diner to the police station was less than a mile, but Eben still used a second set of cuffs to lock the Stranger to the roll bar in the back of the 4x4. He was taking no chances. Too much weird shit had already happened today to do that.

With the Stranger inside, Eben jumped out and slammed the door, turning to face Stella. But she had already circled around the back of the truck to get in the passenger side. "Guess Stella rides shotgun," Eben muttered. He remained there for a few seconds, looking around the silent streets and watching the snow start to fall. He loved the beginnings of a storm, that moment between good weather and bad, and he could actually see the snow front advancing up the street. At least the bad weather would hopefully keep everyone inside. And now that he had this guy in cuffs and soon to be behind bars . . .

Well, hopefully things would calm down into the Dark.

They drove in silence for a minute or two, neither Eben nor Stella eager to speak first. Stubborn: she'd called him that many times. Well, fair enough.

While he'd been locking the prisoner into the 4x4, he'd noticed marks on his wrists and hands that could be dog bites. The guy had looked down at his knees, offering nothing. Now was not the time. He'd have plenty of opportunity to question him back at the station. Thirty days, in fact. There was nowhere else for the Stranger to go, and Eben didn't like the thought of releasing him back into Barrow. As long as he could pin something on him quickly he'd have the authority to keep him locked up for the duration of the Dark.

Eben glanced at the man in the rearview mirror. The silence was becoming uncomfortable. "Haven't seen vandalism like this in a long time," he said. The Stranger said nothing.

"Don't you know how to take care of this town without me?" Stella asked.

He was sure she hadn't meant it as a slight, but Eben took it that way. And if he'd been in a self-pitying mood perhaps he could tell her how being apart had shattered him, blown his confidence out of the water, and left him high and dry, emotionally parched in a landscape of ice and snow. He *could* tell her that . . . but there was so much more besides. And with him and Stella, things had been complex. Once they eventually started talking—and he hoped they would, maybe one day soon—he had a feeling the discussion would either be brutally short or very, very long.

"I think somebody screwed with the brakes on the trencher," she said.

Eben nodded, glanced again in the mirror. The Stranger's head was still dipped, lank hair shielding his face. He knew the guy was not asleep.

"Hell of a day," Eben said.

"Just wait." The voice was as slimy and rough as before.

"Keep it shut," Eben said.

Just wait. What the hell did that mean?

He glanced at Stella and shook his head slightly. *Let's talk later,* the look said. Stella nodded. Damn, they could almost read each other without saying anything.

No wonder the good thing between them had broken apart.

None of them spoke again until Eben had slammed the cell door in the Stranger's face. It was only a holding cell in a corner of the station's main office, and yet again he wished they could stretch to building a proper cell block. This was little more than an area partitioned off by bars. If they had to keep the Stranger locked up here for the next thirty days, it would make for an uncomfortable time for all of them.

The tall man sat slowly on the cot, hands still handcuffed before him, hair hiding his face. Eben couldn't help thinking that the son of a bitch was smiling, and the idea was unsettling. *Just wait,* he'd said back in the 4x4. A comment that left so many things unsaid.

And there was other stuff unsaid as well. Helen and Jake hadn't spoken since he and Stella had entered with their prisoner, and Eben could feel the loaded silence behind him. They'd want to know why Stella was back, what she was doing helping him with a prisoner, what about her and Eben? He could feel the questions building up, loading the air fit to burst.

"You don't work at the refinery," Eben said. He was certain that questioning would be useless right now, but he had to break the silence. "You'd have been seen flying in. So when did you get here?"

The prisoner said nothing. Eben glanced back at Helen, who raised an eyebrow and looked at Stella. *Not right now,* he thought. *Please, Helen. Not right now, in front of this scumbag.* For some reason Eben didn't want this man to know anything personal about him, or any of his family.

"We've got a long time to figure this out," Eben said in response to the Stranger's silence. "They won't be coming to take you away for a month. Plenty of time locked in there. People watching you eat, sleep, and shit. Must say, doesn't appeal to me very much, but I'm prepared to do it."

The Stranger looked up and raised a skeptical eyebrow. The smirk was still there, too, and Eben had a brief, violent image of wiping it from the man's face with his fist. And at the same time there was something intensely threatening about the Stranger, a potential of violence that was almost palpable.

The room remained silent but for the humming of the computer and the soft breathing of all those present. The prisoner lowered his head again and looked at the floor, and his shoulders began to shake as he laughed.

Eben went to his desk and tossed the cell keys into the top drawer. He went to close it but it jammed, and after a couple more efforts he reached in and pulled out a clear plastic bag. It was filled with pot.

The Stranger giggled. *Something else private.*

"What the hell is this?" Eben asked, looking at no one in particular.

"Pot," Jake said. "It helps with her cancer."

"It eases the pain," Helen said. "I didn't want to tell you, I've got a little greenhouse at home, Eben. Didn't want you arresting me." She smiled, but Eben saw a mixture of embarrassment and fear in her expression.

"Pain," the Stranger whispered. Eben ignored him. It was either that, or mace the fucker.

Eben looked at Jake. "Now I get why you wanted to move in with Grandma."

"Noooo, I just thought you and Stella oughta have privacy."

Eben smiled without humor and glanced at Stella. "Yeah, that worked out real well."

For a second, the lights flickered and Eben looked straight at the holding cell. *This is when he'll try something,* he thought. Barrow often experienced intermittent power cuts, and though they only lasted a few seconds, they were unpredictable. The lights returned and the Stranger had not moved. *But what could he do, cuffed and in a locked cell? Nothing. Bastard's got me spooked, that's all.*

"Oh, criminy! Computer's down." Helen was busy rattling keys and trying to restart her machine, actions as useless as tapping the screen.

"Power surge?" Eben asked.

"No, don't think so."

"I'll call Gus. He's fallen asleep again, I expect." Eben lifted the phone and dialed Gus's number out at the array, finishing it before realizing that the phone was dead, too. For a second, he considered not letting on. Too much strangeness for one day, and a pattern to the troubles that was slowly turning him from worried to outright scared. *Someone's getting us ready for something,* he thought, not for the first time. He dialed Gus's number again, and again nothing. He held the receiver to his ear for a few seconds.

"Phone's dead, too," he remarked to Stella.

"Mr. and Mrs. Sheriff. So sweet," the Stranger drawled, his voice like rubber on glass. "So *concerned.* I can taste it in the air, the fear. I can smell it on your breath. So helpless, all of you, *helpless* against what's coming."

Jake slipped across to Helen, trying not to look at the prisoner but unable to tear his gaze away. *Only a kid,* Eben thought, looking at his terrified brother.

"He's just trying to freak us out," Stella said.

Jake nodded. "It's working."

"*What's* coming?" Eben asked. The prisoner just laughed again, shoulders flexing slightly as the humor rumbled through him.

"Thirty days of shitting in a bucket, that's what's coming for him," Stella said.

Eben silenced her with a glance. "Well, we've got better things to worry about right now. I'll check on Gus, find out why comms are down."

"Check on Gus," the Stranger said. He stood, but did not approach the cell bars. "Board the windows. Try to hide. They're coming and this time they're gonna take me with them, honor me for all I've done."

"Shut up," Jake whispered.

" 'They'?" Eben asked.

"Well you might ask. They been here long before us, lawman. God made 'em to . . . thin the herds." He moved to the bars, clasped his hands beneath his chin, and pressed his face forward with a quiet, twisted pride. "Now they're here."

Eben looked at the Stranger, rested his hand on his pistol, and shook his head. "You need to shut up now," he said quietly, injecting as much threat into his voice as he could.

The prisoner smiled, shrugged, and said no more. *Just playing along with the game,* Eben thought, as the lights went out again. This time they didn't come back on.

"Flashlight," Eben said, but Jake had already grabbed one and switched it on.

The man in the cell was sitting down again, head lowered as though he'd never moved. "Board the windows," he said again. "Try to hide."

The windows went dark as the streetlights blinked out.

"I'll hit the generator," Jake said.

Eben nodded and grabbed more flashlights from a cabinet. "I'm heading for the cell tower," he said. "Gus may need help."

"Help doing what?" Stella asked.

Eben glanced at the prisoner. "Fixing things," he said. But when he looked back at Stella he saw the understanding there. Of course. She was sharpest out of them all. *Things are going wrong.*

"We have to stay here with him?" Jake asked.

"Sure. We can sit here and mock him," Stella said. "Like, who's he trying to look like in that coat? Some ugly extra from *The Matrix?*"

Jake smiled at Stella, then glanced at Eben. *Glad she's back,* that look said, but Eben didn't bite. "Helen," he said, "as soon as the lines are up, get Billy over here. Stay on the walkie-talkie with me till the power's back."

Helen nodded as Eben exited.

Damn it all, he hated leaving the people he loved in there with that stranger, but it had to be done.

Besides, Stella was there as well. She could certainly look after herself.

Eben drove through the darkened streets, seeing lights flickering at many windows where the residents had got their individual generators up and running. Shadows flitted here and there, and a couple of them waved at Eben. He waved back, half-blinded by the glare of headlamps against the snow.

Leaving Barrow felt like going out into the wilds. It was a feeling he experienced every now and then, but never quite this strong. He knew the dangers of living up here, knew that going beyond the town, past the drilling sites, and into the desert of snow was a risk unless you were very well prepared. But tonight it felt as though there were dangers out there that no one could be prepared for.

The snow had started properly now, reducing visibility and laying a thickening blanket across the road that slowed his progress. It was over a mile to the array, and Eben had to concentrate every inch of the way.

The first thing he saw was Gus's truck. *Good,* he thought, *he's still here.* What was not good was that the array building was in darkness. The generator had not been started, and that meant that Gus was either happy sitting there in the dark, or something was terribly wrong.

Eben parked the 4x4, grabbed the flashlight, and drew his pistol. He checked that the safety was on and held the gun by his side as he exited the vehicle. He didn't want to look too threatening to whoever might be here . . . although with what was happening in town, he didn't for a minute think they were here for anything friendly.

Just in case, he thought, comforted by the weight of the weapon.

He pointed the flashlight ahead of him, lighting the way between where he stood and the square building. The entrance door was around the corner, and between Eben and the building was a smooth blanket of snow. If Gus had been out to his vehicle for any reason, it had not been recently.

He checked out Gus's truck. Door locked, no one inside.

"Gus!" he called. The snow dampened his voice and swallowed any echoes. No response.

Eben started walking, and when he rounded the corner of the building, he froze. The fence that separated the array from the northern wastes had been torn down. *The wind,* he thought, then he shook his head. Aiming the light along its length, he could see that holes had been ripped through the metal mesh here and there as well. It wasn't the wind, and no polar bear had ever done damage like this.

"Gus!" he called again, a loud whisper this time. He looked over his shoulder at the trucks, and already his footprints were being made hazy by the snow.

A breeze breathed across from the north and something creaked above him. He stepped back and looked up, raising the flashlight and pistol as one, and gasped. The dish was broken and bent, aerials snapped, and wires sparked feebly here and there. A wisp of smoke rose from one wrecked connection, whipped quickly away into the snowstorm.

"Holy shit, what happened here, Gus?"

And the danger came down and struck him then, full force. An unknown variable for sure, but Eben knew that Barrow was in big, big trouble. Someone had systematically destroyed their means of communicating with, or traveling to, the outside world. That guy back in the holding cell was part of it, but there must be others to have done this much damage. Thieves perhaps, terrorists, some sort of dispute gone bad between oil companies—

And where the *fuck* was Gus?

Eben reached for his walkie-talkie to speak to Helen, and his flashlight swung across something dark in the snow. He hurried over to it, bent down, and saw the rich, dark red of splashed blood.

Lots of blood.

"Oh Jesus." He grasped the pistol tighter, flipped off the safety, and spun around on the spot. There was no movement other than the shadows thrown by his flashlight. He started walking, following the spatters of blood that still showed through despite the new snowfall. *Still warm. Melting the snow where it hits, still warm and—*

And he found Gus, tangled with a mess of wires and torn metal. His clothing was ripped, spewing the pink of raw, ripped flesh. His head was missing.

For a few seconds, Eben could not move; could not even process what his eyes were seeing. This was Gus, and yet the part of Gus he had spoken to many times, listened to, laughed with, was missing. The part that made him Gus was gone, and this ruined body was meat steaming into the night.

He stepped back and tripped over something in the snow, going down onto his rump, flashlight falling and resting against his foot. Six feet to his left lay a tangle of metal that had once been fixed to the tower. Atop this tangle, pinned there, was Gus's head.

Eben shouted.

Gus's tongue lolled out, one eye closed.

He stood and backed away, desperate to swing his flashlight away but unable to take his eyes from Gus. *So wrong. So wrong!*

The caretaker's mouth was open in a scream, his face all twisted up.

Eben spun around again, shining the flashlight everywhere, aiming his gun, sure that he'd see who- or whatever had done this creeping toward him through the fresh snow. He seemed to be alone.

Then he looked north.

Something moving out there.

He pulled out his pocket binoculars and put them to his eyes. Shapes . . . shadows . . . obscured somewhat by the snow, but shifting from side to side as they walked.

God made 'em to . . . thin the herds. Now they're here.

"Here they come," Eben whispered. Then he turned and ran like hell for the 4x4.

They didn't have much time.

"Helen, Gus is dead," he said into the walkie-talkie as he drove like a madman. Her astonishment was evident in her silence. "Is Billy there?"

"No, but, Eben—"

"Tell Stella to break out the shotguns. Get ammo. And watch that bastard in the cell!"

"Eben, what the hell—"

"I'll be there soon," Eben said, then he signed off. *The ones I love,* he thought, picturing Helen, Jake, and Stella panicking and confused over what he had just told them. But he also had a duty to others.

As he approached the town limits he switched on the external loudspeakers and grabbed the handset.

"This is Sheriff Eben Oleson. This is not a drill. Stay in your homes. Lock your doors. Load your firearms. Barrow is under curfew."

He drove farther, repeating the message several times as he raced on, then a block away from the police station, he saw a group of shadows emerge from beneath a roof overhang. He skidded the 4x4 to a halt and reached for his pistol, then he recognized them as residents of Barrow—the Jayko twins from the Utilidor, and the Robbins family, the little girl Gail giving him a sweet wave as he wound down his window. *Jesus, I could have shot them.*

"Eben?" Frank Robbins asked, his voice uneven with worry.

"Frank, Michelle, you got your generator running?"

Frank and the Jayko twins nodded.

"Good. Get home and lock the doors. Tell anyone without a jenny to meet up at the diner—Lucy'll have heat and power."

"What is it, Eben?" Frank asked.

Eben glanced at Gail, then back to Frank. "Keep your weapons with you," he said.

"Against what?" Paul Jayko asked. Eben knew that he and his brother had quite an array of weaponry in their basement. He thought of those shadows, coming in from the north toward the already shattered antenna array, the already dead Gus . . .

"Not really sure," he said. "But Gus is dead."

"Damn." Frank stared at Eben for a second or two, then turned and quietly ushered his family along the street.

Eben pulled away and headed toward the station.

Just as John Riis slammed his back door, he heard Sheriff Oleson's voice in the distance. He wiped diesel from his hands—damn generator was leaking—and opened the door again, just a crack. Ally was upset enough over the dogs. If Eben had something bad to say, John would just as soon keep it to himself.

"Lock your doors!" the Sheriff said, voice tinny and crackly through the loudspeaker. *"Load your firearms . . ."* The voice soon faded along the streets, but John had

heard enough. Ever since they found the dogs, he'd known that something bad was going down. He was a hard man, true, but he'd never fallen out with anyone bad enough for them to come and kill his dogs. There was a reason behind that slaughter. Ally couldn't see it just now, she was still too tied up in the blood and guts and grief of the thing. But John could see it. He'd been dwelling on it as they sat together on the sofa, drinking coffee laced with forbidden whiskey, listening to the silence usually broken by growls and yelps. Ally was still crying, and he'd wiped a few tears away from his own face. But mostly all he felt was anger.

Someone doesn't want us going anywhere, he thought.

And now the lights were out, communications were down, and Eben was riding around town telling people to lock their doors and load their weapons.

John shook, and to begin with he thought it was fear. But as he unlocked his gun cupboard and pulled out his shotgun, he recognized it as something else. The urge for revenge. And the certain knowledge that vengeance would be in his sights very soon.

He walked back into the living room to find Ally on her feet, laying the table for dinner and lighting candles around the place. "Let's have dinner, John—please? It'll take our minds off . . ." She sat in a chair below the window, closing her eyes.

"Eben just drove by," he said.

Ally opened her eyes, looked at the shotgun in his hand, and frowned.

The window exploded inward, glass shards and gusting snow immediately extinguishing half of the candles on the table.

A shadow reached in, blurred and confused by the flickering light and the waving, torn curtains.

Ally screamed.

John raised the shotgun and aimed, but then Ally was lifted from the chair and held for an instant across the window before being dragged through into the dark. On her way out, her scream changed from shock to pain as smashed glass ripped into her clothing and skin.

"Ally?" John took a tentative step toward the window, gun still aimed, and then his wife screamed again from their backyard.

"John!"

He darted back through to the hallway. *They'll expect me to jump out the window . . . I'll go this way, circle around . . . surprise them. . . .*

Ally's scream came again as he kicked the front door open, echoing from neighboring buildings, and surely someone must have heard that? Surely someone must be coming to help?

At the corner of his house he paused, took a deep breath, blinked snow from his eyelashes, and then stepped into the backyard. *Where the hell is she?*

Ally shouted, muffled and yet close by, and then John knew where she had been taken. He dropped to his stomach and pointed the shotgun into the crawl space beneath the house. Trying to regulate his panicked breathing he squinted his eyes, trying to see into—

Something flashed out and lashed at his face. If he hadn't moved back in surprise it would have taken his eyes, but he still felt a burst of blood from his nose and right cheek, and his finger involuntarily tightened on the trigger. The gun fired into that enclosed space, the brief flash revealing an image that his terrified mind could make no sense of, its disparate parts orbiting each other and refusing to coalesce. . . .

The shotgun was ripped from his hands and shadows lashed out again, spinning him in the snow and grasping his leg, letting go only when he kicked and kicked again, and now he howled in pain as he felt the hot rush of agony envelop his shattered calf. He blinked against the snow and saw the smeared pink of splintered bone protruding from his leg.

But he could just make out Ally now, fighting and thrashing beneath their house as something fought to drag her in deeper. He could see its human form and was surprised and shocked, because somewhere deep down he'd been thinking *bear, it has to be a bear,* because no man was this strong and he'd *emptied both barrels of his shotgun into it at point-blank range.* That was the image he did not understand, but which now presented itself in its whole bloody glory: that face, briefly illuminated by the shotgun blast into its chest and throat, grinning at him like the face of a dead man.

"John," Ally whispered, gurgled, and John lunged for her. Their hands clasped, slippery with blood and snow, and then Ally was dragged beneath the house.

For a second, their grip held and John went with her. But then their hands parted, and Ally croaked another wounded scream, and John watched her disappear into the shadows.

Aaron and Gabe had been making plays for Denise all night, and she was happy to string them both along. They'd been working together for more than a year, and neither of them had made secret their desires. They were both good guys—fit, dependable, though sometimes not as much fun as she'd like—and she knew she could do a lot worse. Thing is, this was her first Dark. It made her feel . . . sexy. And the dilemma of which one to go for was rapidly ceasing to matter.

While Denise was realistic about her looks, she knew that, out here in the wilds of Alaska, she was Catherine Zeta-Jones. She could pick and choose.

Right now, though, Aaron was hogging the JD. That would never do.

"Going to keep all that to yourself?" Denise asked. He grinned and offered her the bottle. She took a small sip and passed it on to Gabe, smiling sweetly at Aaron's brief look of anger. "Share and share alike," she said, trying to inject deeper meaning into her remark. Aaron must have been too drunk to see it.

"So where are we going?" he said. "I'm freezing my balls off out here."

"Look, I told you, my landlady doesn't want pipeline workers keeping her up. She won't let us all into my place. So it's yours or his." She nodded at Gabe, who had already developed a thousand-yard stare from the whiskey.

"Denise is right," Gabe said. "Let's head over to my place."

"Let's go to mine," Aaron said. "I've got better music."

"*Neither* of you is getting me alone," Denise teased. And damn, a year or not, she still couldn't work out which one of them was cuter.

"Then we'll share!" Gabe said. "Right, Aaron? None of us have to be greedy."

Aaron nodded. "Sure, none of us is like that."

"C'mon, we'll be good," Gabe said.

Denise smiled sweetly. "You will? And where's the fun in that?"

"Okay," Aaron said. "All right, fuck this. Rock paper scissors—whoever wins, we go to his place. Right?"

"Right," Gabe said. He frowned and cocked his head for an instant, then faced off against Aaron. They banged fists, counted to three, and revealed their weapons of choice.

Aaron's fist was a rock, while Gabe opened his fist and wriggled his fingers.

"What the fuck is that?" Aaron asked.

"Nuclear explosion. It burns up rock, paper, *and* scissors." He winked at Denise. "I win."

"Talk about desperate," she muttered.

Gabe shook his head. "Okay, we'll do it the boring way. Let's go again, one, two—"

Gabe screamed as he was ripped away into the darkness.

Snow swirled in confused patterns where he had been standing, and Aaron and Denise froze, staring after their suddenly missing companion.

"Uh . . . Gabe?" Denise said.

"What the fuck is he doing?" Aaron asked. "He was holding the JD!"

Something growled in the shadows. And then there came a crunching, wet chewing, a brief cry, and Gabe appeared again, spraying blood and twitching as he flew through the air.

Gabe's body landed at their feet, still shuddering. Throat ripped out. Face lacerated and bleeding. Coat tattered, flesh torn, blood pulsing from his terrible wounds to form a steaming pool in the snow.

Denise ran. She turned around briefly, afraid to look but terrified of what she *couldn't* see.

Aaron was standing like an ice sculpture, unable to take his eyes from the thing emerging from the snow. It had a terrible, ashen face, blood on its chin, and a grin displaying large teeth.

And on those teeth, fresh meat.

Stella guessed it was shock. Helen still sat at the radio even though it was no longer working. Her fingers tapped the table in a regular rhythm. She glanced at the radio every few seconds, as though expecting it to crackle back into life. Or maybe she was trying to re-imagine what Eben had told them all.

Gus is dead.

Stella and Jake sat playing Risk, not talking. None of them had spoken, not even the prisoner. But when Eben's call had come in over the walkie-talkie, Stella heard the Stranger giggle to himself, and whisper *"Gus."*

Five minutes had gone by. They avoided each other's eyes. And Stella didn't know why it should be like this. They should be comforting each other, trying to lessen the fears that Eben's words had planted in all of them.

Perhaps it was because of *him.* And as if thinking of him brought him around, the Stranger began to talk.

"No way out of town, not now. Nobody to come help."

"Shut up," Jake said.

"Ignore him, Jake." Stella touched the pistol she'd put on the table, shifting it slightly so that they all heard the metal scraping wood.

"Who'll go first, I wonder. The woman who thinks a gun'll help? The scared wimpy kid? Or the dying old gal?"

"Shut up!" Jake shouted. He stood and nudged the table with his thigh. It tipped, Stella caught the gun as it slid off, and Jake lobbed a handful of tokens at the prisoner. Some rattled against the bars, most went through, and the Stranger reached out quickly and plucked one from the air.

"Thanks for the plastic," he said. With a snick he snapped the token in two, held one half up to the weak light. "Perfect." He looked straight at Jake, and his stare was so intense that Stella felt immediately excluded. "I can use this to pick the lock and get out," he said. "Then the sharp edge will be perfect for cutting." He slipped his hands between the bars and fiddled with the lock, glaring at Jake as he did so.

"No you won't," Jake said.

"Jake, he's just—" Stella began.

But Jake was not listening. He darted to the cell and lunged, but the Stranger was much faster. He grabbed the boy's arm, spun him on the spot, pulled him clanging back against the bars and pressed the snapped plastic token to his throat.

"Flick of my wrist, lady, and you'll be bathing in his arterial blood." The prisoner's eyes half closed, as though luxuriating in some sick image.

Stella had already lifted the gun and pointed it at the man's forehead.

"Jake," Helen said, but Stella waved her back with her free hand.

"That's right, dying lady, stay back."

"You need to stop talking now," Stella said.

"No, *you* need to shut the fuck up, bitch!" He jerked his hand and Jake winced, the plastic pressing into the side of his neck. "Lower the gun and pass me the keys. *Now!*"

Stella hesitated, glancing across at Eben's desk where the keys lay in the top drawer.

"Now!"

"I'm not lowering this gun."

The Stranger rolled his eyes. "Fine, but just *get me the fucking keys!"*

Stella edged sideways, still keeping her gun trained on the prisoner, and reached into the drawer.

"Good girl. Hurry, now. Gun on the floor first, then keys over here and in the lock."

"I *can't* put this gun down, you know that—"

"You don't and . . ." The Stranger's arm tensed and pulled tighter around Jake's throat, and Stella saw the first dribble of blood running down the boy's neck.

She squatted, put the gun down and then felt for the drawer. The keys were where Eben had dropped them. Stella walked forward slowly and slid the key into the cell door. *Damn it, damn it.* She kept focused, remembering exactly where she'd put the gun, ready to fall backward and snatch it up as soon as the opportunity presented itself.

"Now turn the key, lady."

"You let Jake go first."

The Stranger glared at her, and Stella shivered beneath his gaze. *His eyes . . .*

"Turn. The. Key."

Stella unlocked the cell.

"Good, now back away—" the Stranger said as a bullet struck his left bicep. He fell sideways against the bars, eyes wide with shock, and Jake darted away into Helen's embrace.

Stella fell back and snatched up her gun, but she didn't need it. Eben kicked the office door open—shattered glass falling from the viewing window he'd shot through—and stepped forward, gun held in both hands.

"Back of your cell, or the next one goes into your temple."

The man looked up, lips wrinkled in anger, eyes blazing.

"I mean it," Eben said quietly. And everyone in that room knew that he did.

The Stranger slid backward on his rump, pushing himself to the rear of the cell and leaving a thin trail of blood behind. He was grunting and moaning, and Stella liked that sound. *So the bastard* can *bleed,* she thought, and the gun felt heavy in her hand.

"You okay?" she said to Jake. The boy nodded, protected behind his grandmother's embrace. There was a spot of blood on his throat, that was all. *Could have been worse,* she thought.

Eben walked past her, gun still trained on the prisoner. He went into the cell, and for a second she thought he was going to kick the Stranger. *Good for you,* she thought. But Eben motioned with the gun for him to stand.

"Raise your arms," the Sheriff said.

"You shot one of them."

"Then it'll hurt. Step forward to the bars, raise your arms, or I'll shoot the other one and do it myself."

The Stranger did as he was told, groaning with each movement. Blood was flowing freely down his arm now, spattering to the floor in uneven rosettes. Eben took a spare set of handcuffs from his belt and locked the prisoner's original cuffs to the bars of his cell. Then he backed out, shut the door and locked it.

"Helen, get the first-aid pack," Eben said. "Not that this son of a bitch deserves it."

The Stranger smiled. Even through the pain, he managed a feral grin. *Should have shot him in the head,* Stella thought, and she was unsettled by that. Dangerous he may be, but she had never been one for bullying or excessive violence. *Shot him in the head when he first came to Barrow.*

"How long have you been here?" she asked.

"Time to talk. Answer the lady." Eben stood before the prisoner, gun still in his hand.

"Fuck the both of you." The man lowered his head and stared at the growing puddle of blood.

Eben tapped the man's cuffed hands with the pistol until he looked up. Then he leaned in close, only the cell bars preventing the two men from touching foreheads. "See, it's like this," Eben said quietly. "I think something bad is about to happen here. I think there'll be bodies. And as far as I'm concerned, I've no problem at all with you being one of them." He reached out quickly, grabbed the man's hair and clanged his head against the bars. "Who're you here with? Who wanted the copter screwed up? And the cell phones burned? The sled dogs killed? And why would anyone do that to Gus?"

Face pressed against the bars, the Stranger still managed a malicious grin. "You'll see for yourself. Won't be long at all. You're dead already, all of you. No point talkin' to dead men."

"If we're dead," Eben replied, "nobody ever lets you loose from here."

"I'll just take that chance."

Eben raised the gun and pressed the barrel against the Stranger's left eye, breathing heavily, lips pursed.

"Eben . . ." Stella said.

"Don't," Jake said. And it was probably the fear in the boy's voice more than anything that made Eben lower the gun.

The Stranger said nothing. *Even he knows when it's time to shut up,* Stella thought. Eben turned to her and glanced down at her gun. Nodded. *You'll be needing that.* Stella nodded back and checked her magazine.

Helen went to the prisoner and took a look at his wound. She reached in and wound a tourniquet around his arm, none too gently. "I can take care of this for now," she said, "but Doc Miller should really stitch it up."

Eben shrugged. "Call Doc when the power's back—this fucker can wait till then."

"So what now?" Stella asked.

"There aren't many places his friends can hide. Billy and I can work our way from South Street toward the pipeline."

"I'll join you, too."

"I can handle it."

Stella shook her head. *Is he really being macho?* "Eben, right now you, me, and Billy are the authorities. Be stupid not to take more help. And whatever your faults, you're not stupid."

Eben glared at her. *Oh, that hit home.*

"We've got the walkie-talkies," Helen said. "We'll be

fine in here." She pulled tight on the Stranger's bandage and he let out a grunt. "Won't we, Jake?"

"Fine and dandy," Jake said.

Eben looked around the room, considering. Back at Stella. She nodded. "Keep the doors bolted," he said. "Keep the walkie-talkie on and the lights off. Helen, Jake, if he gives you any trouble—and that means farting, coughing, or giving you lip—there's a Taser in the back." He pointed to the prisoner. "Keep it shut or you'll find thirty thousand volts up your ass."

He turned back to Stella.

"So?" she said.

"You drive. I'm riding shotgun."

Stella drove them through the deserted streets. There wasn't a soul around. The streetlights were still out, and heavy swirls of snow turned the few illuminated windows into vague ghost lights in the darkness. Chains clanked on the 4x4's tires, biting through fresh snow to the hardened ice beneath.

She glanced at Eben now and then, careful not to let him see. He looked strong, determined, troubled. She liked his profile, always had. She'd told him that he could never hide what he was thinking when viewed from the side. She supposed it was something to do with believing he was unseen.

"Stop!" Eben said, lifting his gun.

"What?"

"Stop the fucking truck, Stella!" She knew his tone,

knew there was something badly wrong, and she slid them to a halt. He reached over and pushed the windshield wipers onto rapid, killed the lights, leaned forward so that his forehead rested against the glass.

"What is it?" she asked.

"I know I saw something out there. Along the street."

"Night goggles still in the back?" Eben nodded, and Stella reached over between the seats and found them straightaway. As she slipped off her hat and fitted the goggles over her eyes, Eben opened the door and jumped down from the cab. She glanced across at him—glaring skin, shining eyes—then looked forward along the street.

The landscape was washed green by the goggles, the surface of snow thrown into sharp contrast against the blocky buildings, and then what Stella had thought to be a bank of shadows started to move.

"Get in the truck, Eben."

"What?"

"Get in the fucking truck!" She ripped the goggles off, threw them in the back, hit the lights and was already moving by the time Eben jumped in. As he slammed his door she did a rapid three-point turn, burying nose and tail into snowbanks, before accelerating back the way they had come.

"How many?" Eben asked, staring back into the darkness they had just left.

Stella shrugged. "Maybe—"

Something hit the roof. *Snow falling from a building?*

She glanced across at Eben. He looked at her, then pointed his pistol upwards.

Stella flipped the wheel lightly to the left and right, trying to dislodge whatever had landed on them . . . and then something started *pounding* on the roof, rapid impacts that put huge dents in the metal above their heads. She glanced up. The metal had already torn in a few places, and she could see something moving out there.

The gunshots were shockingly loud in the confines of the cab. Eben fired five or six times, then they both heard something slipping from the roof and bouncing from the rear of the vehicle. Stella put her foot down, glancing in the rearview mirror to see a shape flapping and rolling along the road behind them.

"What. The hell. Was that." Her heart was pummeling, foot aching where she pressed it to the metal, and Eben touched her arm.

"Ease up a little," he said. She could hear the fear in his voice. That did nothing at all to set her mind at rest.

Eben ejected his magazine and inserted a new one. The pistol's barrel was hot. *Second person I've shot today,* he thought, but then he wasn't so sure. Person? He glanced up at the damage to the cab's metal roof—dents, rips, tears as though put there by sharpened metal tools—and then across at Stella. *She's hanging in there.*

"You okay?" she asked.

"Fucking dandy."

"Eben, just what the hell—?"

"Look." He pointed ahead, where a dancing glow was splashing orange and yellow across a snowdrift. As they cleared the building to their left they both saw the blazing car. Stella began to slow but Eben shook his head. "Can you get by?"

"They might need—"

"If anyone was inside, they're dead."

Stella edged them around the burning vehicle, and Eben could feel the heat even through the windows. *What the fuck is happening to my town?* he thought.

"Eben?"

Ahead and to their right the whole façade of a shop had been shattered. Glass and broken timber lay against the snow banked up beside the road, and inside they could make out the flicker of flames. Stella slowed again, then sped up, gasping.

"What is it?" Eben asked.

"Bad feeling." Her hands gripped the wheel, her knuckles white.

"We should get to the diner," he said. "I told everyone without a jenny to go there. And I shouldn't have, that was *stupid.* It's *way* too exposed."

"Gunshots?" Stella tipped her head to one side, still concentrating on the road ahead.

"Keep driving." Eben holstered his pistol and lifted the shotgun, pumping a round into the chamber.

"What're you doing?"

"Just keep driving," he said.

"Eben, what the hell is this? I'm scared."

"Don't know. And yeah, me too." He smiled at his estranged wife, and he knew that the two of them took strength from that. A brief image flashed across his mind, unexpected and shocking: Stella lying in the snow, blood splashed all around her and her throat ripped out. He gasped and shook his head, dislodging the image. Then he reached for the door handle.

Stella kept moving as Eben stood in the open door. He glanced at the truck's roof first, just to make sure, then tilted his head to the wind. He nursed the shotgun in one hand, ready to bring it up at a moment's notice.

The wheels crunched through the snow, erratic gunfire sounded from ahead, a howl or scream came from behind them. More gunfire, this time closer and from their right. Eben aimed the shotgun that way, then he heard breaking glass and a dull explosion, and the horizon to the east briefly lit up.

They passed by Barrow's small church. Its door was open, insides glowing with weak light, and on the steps lay the minister. He was decapitated and sprawled in his own blood. Hanging on the church door by its hair, the minister's head.

More gunshots, this time the sustained echo of several weapons firing at once.

"Eben?" Stella said from inside the cab.

"Where's it coming from?" Eben said. *"Where's it coming from?!"*

"Everywhere," Stella said. "Eben . . . Helen and Jake?"

Eben cursed silently. What was he thinking? He

dropped back inside the cab and plucked the walkie-talkie from his pocket.

"Helen? Jake? Come in. Listen to me, take the keys and lock all the doors. Get the Taser and lay the prisoner out straightaway—I don't want him awake in there with you. Then get the spare shotgun and hide. You hear me?"

When he lifted his finger from the transmitter, Helen's scream was his only response. *"Eben!"* There were other noises in the background, noises Eben could not identify and didn't really want to think about. Helen screamed again, and this time there were no real words in there. Only pain.

"No." He dropped the walkie-talkie as though it was alive and ready to bite.

He didn't need to say a word to Stella. She floored the accelerator, fishtailing the 4x4 for a few seconds before getting it under control. Left at the next junction, past a burning house, past a body lying spread-eagle in the street, past a car on its side with a shape crushed underneath.

Eben wanted to close his eyes, but Barrow was his town. So he bore witness.

They waited for a minute, sitting with the engine idling in case something came at them.

Eben wanted nothing more than to leap from the truck and storm inside the station, but he'd do no one any good by getting himself killed.

Jake. Helen. He could think only of them. There

were people dying in his town, but he could think only of his brother and grandmother. The other person he really loved in the world was sitting next to him, but even through the fear there still stood their colossal differences, like a monument to all that had gone bad between them. He felt immensely comforted that Stella was with him right now, and he hoped she felt the same. Though all things considered, he guessed she really wished she'd made that plane.

"Looks quiet," Stella whispered. The station was still lit weakly within by the generator. The front door stood open, top hinge broken and barely holding the door to the frame. The snow before the door was churned up as though there'd been a struggle there.

No blood, Eben thought. *At least I can't seen any blood . . .* But then he remembered Helen's final scream, and he knew that there must be blood somewhere.

"Whatever happened here—" Stella began, but he cut her off.

"Don't." He reached for the door handle and snicked it open. Jumping into the snow, he heard Stella turn off the engine and open her own door.

Eben went first, low, crouching in the doorway and shining his flashlight inside. Stella stood above and behind him, watching their backs.

"Go," she whispered. Eben went. Through the lobby, the waiting room, scanning left and right for shadows that moved when they should not, and even before he kicked open the door through to his office, he could smell the blood.

It was a mess. Furniture lay broken and scattered across the room, windows were smashed and letting in snow between the grilles. The Stranger was slumped in his cell sobbing quietly, still handcuffed to the bars.

Eben sensed Stella right behind him. He nodded at the cell then went left, checking behind his desk where it was turned on its side, his senses heightened by the threat that whatever had done this might still be there.

He froze. "No. Oh no." Behind the desk there was a large patch of blood and gore on the floor. Shreds of Helen's clothing lay in it, and other pieces were scattered about, torn and seemingly chewed. He closed his eyes but imagined worse, so he opened them again and looked across at Stella. "Helen," he said. He gasped, vision becoming hazy, and as he reached for his inhaler he saw Stella's eyes go from sad to furious as she closed in on the Stranger's cell.

"Jake?" she said.

Eben shook his head. "Not here. *Jake, are you here?!"*

Stella glanced as he shouted, then joined in herself. They both swung around slowly, guns trained ahead of them, calling for the boy. "Jake!"

"Jake, are you here? Jake, are you here?" a voice said, and for a second, Eben didn't recognize it as the Stranger. Gone was the slimy whisper, the threat in every word, and now the man wallowed in some sick self-pity. "They just laughed."

He walked to the cell and kicked the Stranger's hands where they clasped the bars. The man howled in pain, and Eben pointed his gun. "Where's Jake?"

"Eben, if we shoot we may attract attention."

"I *want* attention," he said. "I want to ask where my brother has gone."

"They didn't take me . . . they just laughed . . . after all I did, they just laughed . . ."

"Where's Jake, you fuck?" The Stranger was crying and laughing or maybe both in response, and Eben pursed his lips, ready to put a bullet in the bastard's leg. *"Who are they?! Who the hell did this?!"*

"Eben . . ." Stella said.

"Finish me," the prisoner said, shaking hair from his face and looking up. He'd been beaten, one eye swollen shut, lips split, teeth missing. "Kill me, please."

"Tell me who they are," Eben said. The Stranger only lowered his head and started jabbering again, blood and tears foaming across his lips.

"We can't just leave him here," Stella said.

"We can. We have to find Jake, Stella, and get help."

She glanced dubiously at the prisoner then back at Eben.

"Finish me off," the man said again, and Eben and Stella locked eyes. She shook her head, ever so slightly. *He saw my grandmother die,* Eben thought. *He saw whatever happened to Jake.* He turned around slowly, raised his gun and placed it against the man's forehead.

If the Stranger hadn't sighed, Eben would have pulled the trigger. But in that sound he heard relief at the escape from what was to come. So he lowered the gun and watched the man start pleading again.

"You stay there," he said, "and get whatever's coming to you." He turned the pistol and cracked the prisoner behind the ear. It took three more hits before he slumped down against the bars, drooling blood and mucus. "Now you can shut the fuck up," Eben said.

"Eben—"

He stood, turned around, and walked past Stella toward the door. "Not a word, Stella. I could have killed him. Easily. And if you weren't standing there behind me . . ."

"Where now?"

He paused in the doorway. He could still smell the blood. "We need to check at the diner, make sure people are holding up. Ask if any of them have seen Jake. We'll deal with *him* when we're ready." But before leaving the station, he looked around again at the chaos, and he could feel Stella staring at him as he walked outside.

The Stranger cried piteously after them. *"Finish me . . . !"*

They were the hungry ones, doomed forever to walk the night and loving every minute. They were gathering at an intersection, watching the 4x4 pull away from the police station, certain in the knowledge that the people in the vehicle would be theirs very soon.

The whole town would be theirs.

They had made a good start, after all, and it felt as though this night could go on forever.

All of them had pale faces painted red with their victims' blood. Some had ragged teeth protruding from receding gums, a few had true fangs. All of them had black, black eyes, adapted to the darkness with no use for seeing in sunlight. They hissed. Spat. It was their language, ancient and unrecognizable to anyone else alive . . . or dead.

Their leader, known only as Marlow, walked in their midst, a tall figure with feral looks, hooded eyes, and the easy gait of someone used to being in control. Others bowed down to him, some crawled at his feet, and he spared none of them a glance.

He growled a few words in their unknown language. "Smell the blood. Taste the flesh. The heads must be separated from the bodies. Do not turn them. Is it understood?" He waved his hand at the sky, and most of the group of invaders split up and disappeared into shadows.

The one called Zurial stood there admiring the town. "There's enough feasting here to keep us strong for a year, Marlow . . . all without the sun."

Marlow gazed upon the small community, eager to sample the delights that waited within. "We should have come here ages ago." Marlow looked down at the vampire at his feet. Iris. Young, inexperienced . . . his protégée.

"Iris," he said, "come. Learn."

The weather was changing. A long, cold storm was about to begin.

Denise had not stopped running. She'd seen Gabe snatched away by something, heard the noises which she'd come to realize were the sounds of him being killed, and she'd taken off. Instinct took her. *Nothing I could have done,* she kept thinking as she ran, *I couldn't have done* anything *to help him.*

Or Aaron.

She'd only glanced back once, and Aaron had been surrounded by shadows . . . with something coming out of them.

Maybe I imagined that, she thought. *That thing, that face. Heavy snow, and I was shocked, and drunk.* But she was sober now. The terror had seen to that.

Nothing I could have done . . .

She tried for home first, but there was a burning car and spilled fuel on Barrow Way, so she turned back. She heard screams and gunshots, and once or twice the roar of motors. She'd hidden from the cars—she had no idea who was driving—and even when she saw the police cruiser speed by, she'd fallen behind a snowbank. She reasoned that whoever had killed Gabe and Aaron could have taken the Sheriff as well. She wanted help, she wanted contact, but more than anything she wanted somewhere safe to hide.

The streetlights were out and the snowstorm made navigating difficult. Once she saw the glow of a window in the distance and she approached, edging along the side of a building. She paused every few steps, holding her breath and listening for signs of life. Nothing. And when she reached the window she saw why. There was no life in this place, only death. Smashed window, a wrecked room, a splash of blood across one wall, and something wet in a chair, all illuminated by the weak light that flickered as the generator ran out of diesel.

So she ran again, and when she passed the Ikos Diner, she saw a face peering out at her.

She dropped to her stomach, panting, crying, feeling the cold burning into her fingers and toes. When she looked up a minute later, the face was still there, and she almost cried in relief when she recognized Doug Hertz.

Denise looked both ways before dashing across the street. Fear drove her on. As she hit the diner door she realized that but for Doug, it would have driven her on forever, beyond the edge of town and out into the wastelands.

The door burst open and someone fell in, snow gusting, wind howling behind them as though it had been seeking access for an age.

Jake pushed himself back against the wall, trying to crawl even farther beneath the table. *Could be one of them, maybe, their eyes their teeth their claws . . .*

"It's Denise," Doug said. Still he stood back, gun clasped at his side, and Jake nodded his silent agreement.

Could just look *like Denise,* he thought. The girl looked up, all panic and fear and breathlessness from whatever she had been through. She and Jake locked gazes for a second, but then he looked away. *Could just* look *like her.*

"What the hell's happening?" Denise said. She tried to stand but slipped, and Doug reached out to help her.

He guided her to a table and Lucy Ikos appeared as if from nowhere, a mug in one hand and a jug of freshly brewed coffee in the other.

"Drink this," she said, and then she moved on.

Jake watched Denise staring at the steam rising from the coffee. Her eyes were far away. "What's happening?" she said again, voice rising. "Who are they?"

"We don't know." That was Wilson Bulosan, sitting in the far corner with his crazy old man. Grandma had told Jake that Isaac wasn't nuts, he had Alzheimer's, but sometimes he mumbled, and sometimes he scared Jake. Jake lifted his head slightly until he could see across the top of the table. Isaac wasn't scaring him now. The old dude sat there and let his son stroke his hair, and every now and then he told no one in particular that he wanted to go home.

Jake felt guilty at thinking he was crazy. *Same age as Grandma,* he thought, but even thinking her name brought those images back to him and he closed his eyes, tight.

"Shoot 'em and they keep coming!" Doug said. He stood close to Denise staring down at his gun. Shaking his head. Turning the gun this way and that as if looking for something wrong with it, but Jake knew that Doug never let his guns get dirty. "I put four into one of them and she . . . she . . ."

"How's that possible?" Carter asked. He was on his third slice of Lucy's pie, sitting there in a T-shirt while the rest of them shivered in the meager heat produced by the generator.

"Don't know," Doug said. He was pacing again—had been for ten minutes—and Jake kept his eyes on the pistol. *He'll blow his own foot off,* he kept thinking, and the more he thought it the more the idea made him want to laugh. "Maybe they're coked up, or whacked on some other drug," Doug continued. "Something so they don't feel pain. I only got away in the end because they found Kay Lopez, and . . . I couldn't help. Couldn't save her. They just fell on her and . . ." He shook his head, stopped pacing, stared down at his gun yet again.

Denise spoke through the steam from her coffee. "They took Aaron and Gabe. Must be strong."

"They took my grandma," Jake said. He and Denise locked eyes again, and though she did not smile, he took some comfort from the contact. As if she understood.

And the names came again, Denise's entrance giving everyone the excuse they needed to run through the list of dead once more.

"Reverend Pfeiffer," Carter said, "Malekai Hamm, the Dale family—"

"John and Ally Riis," Wilson said. "Their house is all smashed up. Doc Miller's, too."

"Is there *anybody* left?" Denise asked. She was looking directly at Jake, but he knew now that she was not really talking to anyone. He saw panic in her eyes, and disbelief. He wished he could go where she seemed to be going. Slip away, go insane, be like old Isaac just wanting to go home.

And then Jake heard the doors smash open again,

and a voice he recognized accompanied the angry roar of the weather.

"Kill the lights. And get the hell away from those windows!"

Jake stood, ran for Eben and barreled into him, crying and hugging and welcoming his brother's embrace.

"Jake! Oh Jake, I thought . . ."

"They got Grandma," Jake said, pressing his face into Eben's chest. The lights went out and his tears blurred his vision even more.

"I know." Eben hugged him tight, and when Jake turned his head he saw Stella looking at the two of them with tears in her eyes. He smiled and she smiled back. She was carrying her pistol in one hand.

"Has anyone seen Billy?" Eben asked. Nobody answered. "Carter? Doug?"

"Nope," Carter said.

"Not me." Doug was pacing again, looking at his gun.

"What is it?" Eben said.

"I shot one. It kept on coming."

Eben eased Jake away from his chest, looked down and tried to smile. But Jake wasn't fooled. "Doesn't surprise me," Eben said. "Now listen, all of you: we can't stay here. Too many windows, too much open space, and it's the first place they'll come looking."

"Who the hell *are* they, Eben?"

"What do they want?" Doug shouted.

"He's not good," Jake whispered, and his brother moved away from him.

"Take it easy, Doug," Eben said. "Remember you've got a loaded weapon in your hands."

"Lot of fucking good it did me."

Eben took control then, and not only because he was Sheriff. Jake had seen this before; his brother was a born leader. Shy sometimes, maybe not quite as sure of his abilities as everyone else, but he was always the calm one in a tough situation, always the one to offer comfort. There was little comfort to offer right then, but Eben stayed calm.

"I don't know who they are, but right now that doesn't matter. What *does* matter is that they're here. I don't know why they're here or what they want, but we're in danger, and we need to hide until we can answer some of those questions."

"We should call for help," Wilson said.

"Anyone here still got their cell phones?" Eben asked. A couple of people raised their hands. "The antenna array is fucked. They'll do no good."

"How about the high school?" Carter suggested. "The clinic?"

"They already hit the church," Stella said. "They'll scope out any other public place. Including here."

"Right," Carter said. "Hey, there's a generator at the Utilidor."

"It's way out on the edge of town," Eben said. "We need someplace close to hide. Now."

There was silence for a while, broken only by the sound of the wind playing around the eaves, whistling through the chains that held the sign up outside. Jake stared at the window, convinced that if he looked long enough he'd see those frantic snowflakes merge into a pale, vicious face.

"There's Charlie Kelso's attic," Denise said quietly. "It's boarded out and has a couple of vents. There's a pull-down ladder; you can't tell it's there. Few bits of furniture. It'd be tight but we could all fit."

"He would've boarded up his home before he left," Stella said.

"Which is why it's a good idea," Eben said. "We pull down a board to get in, then tack it back."

"Could work," Carter said. "And an attic should be easy to defend."

"Defend?" Doug scoffed, but Eben ignored him.

"Carter," the Sheriff said, "when I say go, lead people close to the buildings, roll under crawl spaces if you hear anything. Go straight to Charlie's house and get up into that attic." He looked down at Jake. "Go with Carter, Jake. I'll be with you again soon."

Jake bit his lip and tried not to cry, to shout *I don't want you to go again.*

"Where'll *you* be?" Doug asked.

"Loading up with all the ammo, flares, and bear traps a 4x4 can carry. Like Carter said, we can defend an attic. And *something's* gotta slow them down."

"What about . . . ?" Denise began, but the room had fallen silent and she seemed unwilling to finish.

"What about everyone else?" Jake said.

Denise nodded and looked back down at her coffee.

"They'll be surviving," Eben said. "Hiding away. Arming. We can't all hide in the same place."

"But—" Wilson began, and Stella cut him off.

"Let's take things one step at a time," she said. "Let's do what Eben says and get away from here."

"Right," Eben said. "Besides, maybe it's best we *don't* all hide in the same place." He hugged Jake hard and went for the door.

Stella followed him. Jake knew she would and wished she wouldn't. "I'll cover your back," she said.

Eben nodded grimly. "One minute, Carter." He smiled at Jake and then he and Stella left the diner.

"You okay?" Jake asked Denise. As a teenaged boy he was more than aware of her looks—big eyes, nice hair, curves in all the right places—but now she seemed like a little girl. She seemed to be drifting away again, her gaze set way beyond Barrow.

Denise looked up after a few seconds, as if suddenly remembering where she was. She stared at Jake. "No."

Eben and Stella waited outside the door for a few seconds, huddled in shadows. The darkness was heavy, the snow blinding, but there were still lights here and there along the street. Perhaps they had been left on when people fled their homes. Eben hoped so, at least. If they indicated where people were huddled around lights and a heater, then they would soon draw whatever had come into his town.

"See anything?" he whispered.

"No. Too damn dark." Stella had brought the night vision goggles with her from the truck, but she'd broken one lens when she dropped them earlier. Eben was now more inclined to trust his own eyesight.

"Let's go. Longer we stay here, more chance we'll attract attention." He darted to the passenger door of the truck and sensed Stella shadowing him, swerving away to climb in the driver's side. As soon as he was in, Eben reached up and killed the interior light. He closed the door gently, rested the shotgun across his lap, and sat back.

"Let's wait until they've all gone. We're a target now," he said.

"At least it'll draw attention away from the others." Eben looked across and saw Stella leaning back in her seat, staring in the wing mirror.

After a minute, she stirred and reached for the steering wheel. "They all away?" Eben asked.

"Yep. Straight into the crawl space beneath the diner. I could hardly see them from here, just shadows. They'll be okay."

"Yeah."

She looked across at him, reached out, and touched his shoulder. "Jake'll be okay."

"Yeah," Eben said again, dropping and checking the magazine from his pistol, even though he'd yet to fire a round from this one.

Stella reached for the keys, then paused. "Dead quiet out there," she said. "This'll be loud."

"The snow throws sound around," Eben said, but he grinned at the absurdity of his comment. As if the people doing this would be fooled by false echoes.

"Here goes." Stella turned the keys and the engine sounded painfully raucous, coughing as if to purposely attract attention.

"Move it," Eben said, hands clasping the shotgun. The pistol was heavy in its holster. *I shot one. It kept on coming,* Doug had said. He smelled burning for an instant, before it was stolen away on the breeze.

Carter went first, leading them all beneath a house, nervous but empowered by Eben's trust in him.

Jake followed close behind. He was terrified.

"Not too fast!" Carter hissed. "No sudden moves."

"I'm cold," Jake muttered.

"You'll be colder dead."

There was a sudden crack and an icicle fell from above Jake's head. It shattered beside his hand, dark instead of light. Even without touching it, he knew it was made of blood.

They turned a corner into Ransom Street and Stella pressed on the gas. A house was on fire two blocks away, a smudge of light and heat in the snow-filled darkness. Eben sat up straight, thinking *moths to a flame,* and then they were both thrown forward as the vehicle jerked to a sudden stop. Stella groaned, winded against the steering wheel, and Eben slammed both hands against the dashboard, barely avoiding a bloodied nose.

"What did you hit?" he said, but Stella was shaking her head.

"Nothing. We're not moving." She gave it more gas, the engine screamed, but they both felt the front wheels spinning on the road, chains slapping at the ice and churning up clouds of shattered ice and snow behind them.

"I'll see," Eben said, and already he had a very bad feeling about this. He opened his door and leaned out, shotgun aimed before him in one hand.

He could see the shadows behind them, holding on to the back of the car, teeth glinting in the poor light and hair waving in the wind, and they hissed at him as he swung the shotgun around to face them. He pulled off one shot before dropping back into the cab and slamming the door shut behind him.

"Floor it!" he shouted.

"I am!"

"I *mean* it!"

"What's happening?"

"They're behind us, holding the truck—"

"Holding it? How can they be holding it?" And then the rear of the truck began to lift.

"Eben—" Stella said, but by then they were both slipping into the dashboard, the rear of the truck lifting higher and higher. Stella's foot came off the gas and the 4x4 stalled, but it made no difference.

"Grab your gun!" Eben shouted. He positioned himself so that he was facing his side door, shotgun aimed at the dark glass.

The 4x4 was balanced impossibly on its front grille now, metal creaking and tearing in protest.

Stella's door was ripped open. Eben glanced back over his shoulder, wincing as she fired at the thing that stood there before her. The sound was shocking, but what he saw was worse: the bullet gouged a finger-sized wound out of the creature's skull. It didn't even cringe. Its tongue lolled, sharp teeth glinting as it opened its mouth wide, swiping the gun from Stella's grasp.

"Eben!"

He struggled to turn. The shotgun became wedged against the seat, and then the 4x4 fell forward onto its roof. The windshield shattered and metal shrieked as it struck the road, lights crushed beneath it, and he and Stella tumbled to the ceiling. Disoriented, Eben tried to pry the shotgun loose from where it had become jammed.

More glass broke, though he was not sure where.

Creatures, he thought. *They're not people. They may look like people, but they're not.*

Shadows flailed and he felt something scraping across his cheeks, a shape thrashing in front of his face before grasping onto his jacket collar, pulling, fingernails ripping through his clothes and pricking into his shoulder. He dropped the shotgun at last and reached for his pistol, but a scream brought him up short.

"Eben!" It was Stella, and she was being dragged through her broken door by two of the creatures. They were grabbing at her hair, her clothes, her waving arms, and when they both got a good grip, they tugged.

Eben aimed his gun at the thing grabbing him and fired. He had no idea whether the bullet found its mark, but it gave him a second to shift. He rolled, kicked out through his own broken window and brought the gun around to bear on Stella's aggressors. He fired twice, saw a splash of blood on one of the feral faces, and then hands grabbed his knees and thighs and hauled him backward through his window. He fumbled the gun, dropped it, and watched it disappear in shadow.

"Eben!" Stella shouted again, and they locked eyes. She was almost out of the cab now, and outside something was roaring. He could feel it through the ground. And whatever was making that sound must be huge.

Going to die, he thought, and Stella knew that as well. He curled his finger around one of the rents in the cab's ceiling, desperate to hold Stella's gaze for as long as possible, but he was tugged out into the night.

Something crashed into the 4x4, knocking it aside. Eben felt his legs swing free of his attacker, and he heard a squeal as the truck spun and crushed it into the ice.

The snowplow! Lights glared on, blinding him and causing the attackers to hiss and pull back. He looked through the cab and saw Stella sitting on the ice, looking around in confusion. "Up!" he shouted.

Eben didn't wait to see whether she'd heard; there was no time. He kicked out blindly and crawled beneath the hood, pulling his way through elbow-deep snow toward the huge plow's side.

It reversed and drove forward again, and Eben heard a high-pitched squeal and scream. He emerged from beneath the 4x4 and saw Stella in the snow several feet away, looking away from him at where one of the creatures was being pinned against a wall. Its arms were flailing, legs kicking.

Beau Brower leaned down from the snowplow's cab, grasped Stella's hood and lifted her. "Get in!" he shouted, sitting back and giving it some more gas. The plow scraped along the wall, the trapped thing grinding into the crumbling brickwork. Its scream rose even higher, almost passing out of audible range.

Beau reversed and looked down at Eben. "Quick, goddamn it!"

Eben kicked out at a pair of feet that appeared to his left and leapt for the snowplow. He held on to the door handle and hauled himself in after Stella, head hitting her behind, an involuntary laugh escaping him. *Almost losing it now,* he thought. *Almost there, Eben.*

Beau floored it. Stella was in the cab, Eben's legs still kicking at fresh air as he tried to climb inside after her. Hands grabbed at his feet and he panicked, kicking and shouting, feeling his shoe connect with something solid. A squeal sounded behind him and he grinned as Stella pulled him all the way in. She reached across and pulled the door shut.

Eben sat up, panting, realizing that he'd lost both of his weapons. He glanced across at Stella, down at her hands . . . then back up to her face. Her eyes were wide and shocked, and looking at him as though she had never seen him before. He smiled, reached out quickly, and touched her face.

They roared down the street, Beau steering them along as though it was just another day at work.

"Got one of the bastards," he said. "Crushed it against the wall."

"Good," Stella said.

"Got up again." Beau stared through the windshield, switching on wipers to clear the snow that was falling heavier than ever.

Eben was wheezing, and he searched his parka pockets until he found his inhaler. Stella huddled close to him, shivering from fear and the cold.

"Thanks," Eben said. "Thanks, Beau. We were dead meat back there. They lifted the 4x4, rolled it onto its fucking head, and— Thanks."

"Who's gonna write me tickets if you get fragged?" he said.

"We've got to ditch this thing, Beau," Stella said. "It just calls them. They'll be following. I think they'll catch up."

"And go where?" Beau asked. He glanced back at them and Eben saw a haunted look in his eyes, belying the nonchalance he was trying to inject into his voice.

"We know a place," Eben said. He levered himself up and scanned to see where they were. "You see them following?" he asked.

"Don't think so."

"Right. Stop around the next corner."

Beau turned the corner and skidded to a halt, and Eben was the first to open the door. He glanced outside. Nothing. *If I don't go now, I never will,* he thought, and he jumped down into the snow. Stella and Beau landed behind him, and they both saw what Eben saw.

A few yards along the street, impaled on sticks driven into the ground, several heads stared at them with upturned eyes and lolling tongues.

"Holy—" Beau began.

"Not at all," Eben said. "Nowhere fucking near. Come on."

The three scurried into the crawl space beneath the building in front of them, leaving the decapitated citizens of Barrow to watch for the creatures that must surely follow.

DAY 1

IT WAS WELL AFTER MIDNIGHT, though Eben could only tell by looking at his watch. All sense of time had vanished. The Dark inevitably brought on disorientation, but today was worse than usual. As far as Eben could tell, daylight had vanished forever, and Barrow had fallen into endless night.

A breeze shushed up and down the town's streets, an occasional gunshot came from close or far away, and they heard other things in the night. Shouts, screams, cries, growls, howls. Things they could not place other than in nightmares.

Eben moved slowly, cautiously through the crawl space. Beau was directly behind him, and behind Beau came Stella, shivering from where the creatures had ripped off her parka. Eben had briefly thought of handing his own coat back to her, but he knew what sort of reaction that would get.

Beau carried his shotgun, the only weapon they had left. Not that it would do much good.

Just what the hell are they? Eben thought again, and yet again no answer was forthcoming. Thieves, terrorists, wild people, junkies, gangsters . . . nothing he thought of could account for what they were doing, and how. Nothing could allow for their strength, their apparent immunity from gunshots, and their teeth and eyes. *Long sharp teeth. Deep black eyes.* He shivered and looked around, certain for a second that they were being watched.

"What is it?" Beau hissed.

Eben waved a hand back at the big man, paused, went on.

"Sheriff!"

"Nothing," Eben whispered. "Being cautious." He glanced back at Beau, then past him at Stella. He could only make out her silhouette, but her head nodded and he guessed she was smiling.

They moved on, and every time they came to the edge of a house, they paused for a couple of minutes to look around. Snow fell and danced in the air, whipped up by little storms that seemed to be wandering Barrow at will. *Almost like the wild's already reclaimed the place,* Eben thought, but that was too unsettling to consider. Next he'd be seeing polar bears from the corner of his eye.

They waited until they were sure the coast was clear; no shadows moving where they should not, nothing watching from neighboring windows, no footsteps nearby or things crouching beside the buildings. Then they moved on, dashing across backyards and diving beneath the next building. Here and there they had to pry boards aside to get into the crawl spaces, but many of the timbers were rotten anyway, and any that were stubborn Beau could easily break. Where they could, they tried to lift the boards back into place from the inside.

Beneath one house Eben crawled through something wet and still vaguely warm. He looked up at the floorboards above his head and wondered who it was.

Finally reaching the house across the street from the Kelso place, the three of them hunkered down in the cold and looked across the snow. There were no footprints in the virgin surface, and that was a good sign. No bloodied snow, no burning cars to illuminate them, no heads stuck on spikes to guard the street. It almost looked normal. But no lights shone in any of the windows, and the house two doors from the Kelsos' had had all of its ground floor windows smashed. There were dark prints on the light paint beside one of the windows that may have been blood.

"We ready to do this?" Eben asked.

"I guess," Beau said.

"Absolutely." Stella was hugging herself now, pressed close to Beau's side while Eben scanned the street.

"No stopping for anything," Eben said.

The others nodded.

"On three." He counted one finger, two, then on three they ran like hell.

The deep snow muffled their footfalls, offering only crunches that would be swallowed by the cool air. Eben was wheezing again, and he wished he'd taken a hit from his inhaler. The Kelso place seemed far away.

Stella got there first. There was one heavy, wide board nailed across the front door, and she set to work on the nails with her car keys. "Coming out easy," she whispered as Eben stopped beside her. Beau faced the street, shotgun at the ready.

"Hopefully because the others have already arrived."

"Hope so."

Eben held the board steady while the last nail came out and moved it to one side to let Stella open the door.

"Not bolted, either," she said.

The three of them piled into the house, snow wafting in after them, and Eben held the board back in place while Stella slipped the nails back in. They went into their original holes, and she tapped them with the heel of her palm. They made no noise. Once the board was back in place they closed the front door.

They stood there gasping and breathing heavily from their tense journey across town. They had seen nothing since leaving the snowplow, but every step of the way Eben had known that whatever was wrong with their town was getting worse. In between gunshots and screams, the air of the town was haunted.

Now they listened for any signs of pursuit. Eben stood at the front door and peered through the spy hole, seeing only a snowscape beyond. Nothing moved. No one walked.

He backed away from the door and looked around. There was no sign of the house having been invaded by those things; everything was neat and tidy, just as the Kelsos had left it.

Stella came to him, opened his coat and held him tight, sharing his warmth. She shivered and he rested his cheek against her head. Beau looked at him, hefting his shotgun.

"We can't try the attic just yet," Eben said. "We've gotta make sure we didn't lead them here."

Beau nodded and moved to the window. He leaned forward and looked out between the curtain and wall without shifting the material. "Looks quiet to me," he said.

"Did when I looked," Eben said. "That's what bothers me."

Stella sighed and Eben held her tight.

Beau seemed to know that Eben and Stella needed this moment. He pretended they weren't there, moving from one window to the next all through the downstairs of the house. He never touched a curtain, and when he disappeared from view, Eben didn't even hear his footsteps. For such a big man, he could move gracefully.

Neither of them spoke. Stella's shivering soon stopped but she did not let go. Eben liked the smell of her. There was the sweat of exertion and fear, but beneath that her own scent that he remembered so well.

"Well, it took monsters and slaughter to get us even looking at each other again," Stella said.

Eben uttered a short, quiet laugh. "I'd have never known you were here if you hadn't missed that plane."

She pulled back from him then, looking up with

an expression he could not read. Angry? Sad? He still wasn't sure. Even after all these years, sometimes she was a stranger to him.

"We should go through the house, see what we can find that'll be of use." Stella went off looking for Beau and Eben sighed.

A few minutes later, the three of them met in the family room, each carrying whatever they had found that could be of use. Beau showed off a pair of kids' walkie-talkies, pressing the squelch buttons to hear static.

"Kids left something here. Probably pretty short range," he said, "but might come in handy."

Eben had raided the kitchen, finding a box and filling it with canned food and a propane heater from the pantry. He'd thrown in a few carving knives, too, though the thought of using them against those things out there had almost made him sick. There were matches and candles in a basket on the work surface, too, a familiar sight in a place where power cuts were a common fact of life.

Stella had found one of Mary Kelso's thick coats, and shined a weak flashlight at the floor. "Battery's going, but it'll last for a while. And I found this in the master bedroom." She produced a pistol and box of ammunition, handing them to Eben. "Sheriff?"

Eben smiled and shoved the gun into his holster. "Lot of good it'll do," he said.

"Better than fuck all," Beau said. "Maybe a shot in

the right place'll do them. Put one through their eye, how can they see?"

"Have you shot any yet, Beau?"

"Nope. Ran a couple of the fuckers over, though." He looked away, troubled.

"They got up again, right?" Stella asked.

Beau frowned.

Something thudded against the porch outside. Eben actually heard the door rattle in its frame and he drew the pistol.

"Loaded?" he whispered.

"Damned if I know," Stella said.

"Excellent."

Beau crept forward, putting himself and his shotgun between the two of them and the front door. They remained like that for a minute or two, listening hard for any other sound. Then Beau crept forward and put his eye to the peephole. He sighed.

"Snow slipped from the roof," he said.

"Damn." Eben relaxed and felt his arms and shoulders unclenching. He was exhausted, he realized, physically shattered and mentally drained. "Let's get to the attic. The others may have heard us moving around down here."

"Gets my vote," Stella said.

They went upstairs, walking quietly because the silence was so intense. Wind whispered around the eaves, creaking timbers and rattling a loose pane of glass in one of the upstairs windows, but other than that they heard nothing but their own footfalls. The stairs were uncarpeted. Halfway up, Eben stopped and pointed the weakening flashlight down at the tread before him; there was a smudge of dirt and a small puddle of water. He pointed up, nodded, and they continued up to the landing.

It took them two trips around the upstairs before they spotted the trapdoor in the landing ceiling. "It's hidden well," Eben said. He tapped on the wall with his knuckles. "It's us!"

"Eben!" Stella said. "What if—"

A square shape appeared in the ceiling, the trapdoor moved back, and a ladder dropped gently to the floor.

Eben placed his foot on the first rung and pointed the pistol at the square of darkness. There was a pause, loaded with the promise of violence, and then a face appeared from the gloom.

"Carter," Stella said.

Carter sighed and slumped to the floor above them. "Thank God it's you," he said. "We've been listening to you stalking around down there for hours."

"Only been here fifteen minutes," Beau said.

Carter nodded and beckoned them up. "Beau, it *seemed* like hours."

Marlow returned to the police station to wrap up some unfinished business.

He took two of his pack with him, leading them like a hunter with dogs in tow. Marlow sniffed the air and then walked straight in, exuding the arrogance of a conquering warlord. Nothing could damage him, nothing here was his equal. He was tall and proud, and decorated with his victims' blood.

The human servant still hung from the cuffs chaining him to his cell bars. His wrists were bloodied from where he had been trying to work himself free. Marlow sniffed and grimaced at the stink. The two with him crept forward and Marlow spat at them in their own ancient language. They held back, taking station in shadows at the corners of the room.

He hated speaking in the cattle's voice, but sometimes it was necessary. "Wake." The language was unfamiliar in his mouth, and it sounded deep and thick.

The human's head rolled back, his eyes opened and his mouth broke into a grin. "You came for me!"

"I came," Marlow said, "to ask about the vehicles. And the guns. And the other aspects of your task which remain unfinished."

"I . . ." The human frowned, the smile turning into a grimace as he glanced around the cell as if for help. "I was hungry. And thirsty. And—"

"And you wanted to revel in the pitiful power you thought you had."

"No."

With inhuman strength, Marlow tore the cell door from its hinges and moved inside. The prisoner gasped, amazed, and laughter came from the darkness of the ruined office. The tall creature went to him and held his hair, moving his head this way and that.

"You're hurt."

"It's nothing," the human said.

"True. Hush now. We'll take care of you." Marlow twisted the man's head around until it faced the rear of his cell. Bones crunched, skin split, blood flowed, and Marlow backed away from the smell.

"The things they believe," Marlow murmured.

The two vampires came forward again, obsidian eyes glittering.

Marlow shook his head and growled to them. They nodded and backed away, retreating from the office and leaving the servant's blood to freeze.

"Leave him for the others," Marlow ordered. "Some meat is just too tainted." Then he went back out into the night.

First they made sure there were no openings in the roof space, shining the flashlight at the floor to shield its light and feeling along the walls at the gable ends and where the sloping roof met the floor. There was a window at one end and they covered it over, using tape liberated from the kitchen to hold the torn cardboard in place. And when they were confident that light within could not be seen from outside, they lit the propane heater and huddled around its glow.

Eben and Stella sat close, arms and legs touching. Jake sat on Eben's other side, resting his head against his brother's shoulder and snoozing. And the other wretched survivors also sat together, enjoying the companionship and warmth as the space slowly heated up.

Denise stared at her mobile phone as though doing so would bring in a signal.

Doug mumbled to himself, shaking his head, eyes wide, still staring down at the weapon between his feet as though it had purposely let him down.

Wilson nursed his sleeping father, Lucy and Carter chatted quietly, and Beau sat in a far corner, shotgun over his legs and eyes filled with discomfort. Eben glanced across at him and smiled, but Beau looked away.

"I think Beau's had enough of people for one day," he whispered to Stella.

She nodded. "He should wear one of those T-shirts, *Do I look like a fucking people person?"*

"Got us out of a scrape."

"Yep. Saved our ass."

"Asses."

"Don't get all grammatical on me, Eben."

He laughed softly and found it enjoyable. It used muscles that had grown stiff in the cold. "Great hide-out," he said louder. "How'd you know about this place, Denise?"

"Does it matter?" Denise said after an uncomfortable pause.

Eben shrugged. "Just want to know the odds of someone else knowing about it, too."

"Right," Denise said, looking around the small space. "Well . . . um. Unlikely. Charlie hid me up here once. When his wife came home early from work."

A few nods, another embarrassed silence, and then Stella said, "Glad he did."

"Yeah," Lucy said.

Denise offered a tentative smile, then went back to staring at her mobile.

Eben closed his eyes and tried thinking their problem through. It was painful. Everywhere he looked in his mind's eye he saw the people of Barrow lying slaughtered. And all the chances of escape and rescue were hopeless. The relay station was down, which meant that none of the phones or radios would work. No one was due to come to Barrow until the end of the thirty days of the Dark. No planes flew overhead this far north, and if they did there wouldn't be much to see.

"We're stuck here, aren't we?" Stella whispered, as though she'd been reading his mind.

"I think so, yes."

Jake had stirred and was staring at the propane heater. "How long will these canisters last?"

"Maybe a week," Eben said. "Maybe a little longer." *But probably not even that long,* he thought. Maybe if Kelso had kept them fully charged it would last a week, but Kelso always left when the long night came, missed most of the bad storms, and he wasn't one to prepare for the harsh conditions that could exist up here. Kelso was the sort to rely on others for help. So maybe a week, but probably less.

"We should conserve it," Stella said. "The roof of this place will be insulated; once it's warmed up it'll stay warm. Especially with all of us up here."

"But what happens when it *does* run out?" Jake asked.

"Then we find more," Eben said.

"And maybe those people will give up and go somewhere else before then," Lucy said, but Eben could see that she did not believe that for a minute.

"Where are they going to go, exactly?" Doug said. "They won't just up and leave. They must have come here for a reason, something . . ." He trailed off, shaking his head.

"I don't think they really are people," Wilson said.

Jake nodded, kneeling up and becoming more animated. "I saw them! When they attacked Grandma Helen they . . . bit her." He frowned at the memory, looking into the dark corners of the attic. "Like they wanted her blood. They're like . . . vampires, y'know?"

"Vampires don't exist, Jake," Stella said.

"I know that!" he said, turning on Stella. For a moment Eben saw a spark of anger in his brother's eyes—*don't talk to me like I'm a little kid!* And for that moment, he was prouder of Jake than he ever had been before.

"Vampires!" Carter scoffed. "Fuck's sake."

"Some of them had, like, fangs," Jake continued. He stared into those shadows again, and Eben would have given anything to be able to take those memories away from him. Jake would have them forever, live them every night and fear them every day. He reached out and squeezed his brother's shoulder.

"Maybe they *think* they're vampires," Stella said. Eben shot her a look but she chose not to notice.

"Maybe they filed their teeth down, and they're some sort of cult. I've read about them, they like to pretend they need blood to survive. Live in the dark, all that shit. All posturing and posing."

"Posturing and posing?" Eben said slowly. He pulled away from Stella and stood.

She shook her head. "I know, I didn't—"

"Lot more than fucking posturing going on here," Carter said.

"Right," Beau agreed.

"They don't fall when you shoot them!" Doug said, and Eben heard the first shred of hysteria in his voice. "You *shoot* them, they *keep coming!* They're no cult, they're something . . . *else!*"

"Hell, shoot me, I don't fall," Beau said, and Eben flashed him a brief smile. *We need that,* he thought. *Bit of humor. Make us remember who we are.*

"Right," Eben said. "Just because they're stubborn as Beau doesn't make them supernatural."

"Then what are they?" Carter asked.

"Right now, I don't care what they are," Eben said. Standing, he had taken control of the conversation. Now that they were still and relatively calm, he didn't want panic settling in, and that was always a danger. Panic, hysteria, those could be their undoing. "I just care about what we do about them."

"There won't be any help for a month," Denise said. "Can we live up here for a month?" She seemed to be asking this of her phone, but her words silenced everyone for a few loaded seconds.

"Ohhh God. We're going to die," Doug said, his voice almost a whimper.

"We can't last up here that long!" Lucy cried.

"Can it, and keep your voices down!" Eben hissed. "Damn it, we've come this far. Start thinking negative now and we *won't* survive, I can guarantee that. They surprised us, took away our defenses and our means of calling for help, and that in itself shows that they have their weak spots, doesn't it? It shows that they *are* vulnerable." He looked around the assembled group and really didn't like what he saw. Some of them refused to meet his eyes, others—Doug, Denise—were just starting to slip over the edge.

"We have food," Stella said.

Eben nodded. "Right! We have food. I brought some up, but the Kelsos have got a full pantry downstairs. We'll check it out, ration it to last four weeks. Use the heater in small bursts. Sleep in shifts. Then we talk about the next step." He paused, and when no one disagreed he went on with more confidence. "We have two big advantages over those fuckers. First, we know Barrow. Second, we know cold. We're Alaskans, and we live here for a reason: because nobody else can."

"Yeah," Stella said, and she ruffled Jake's hair. He pretended to slap her hand away but Eben saw his smile, and that lifted Eben's heart.

"We'll get through this," he said.

"I say we go out and fight," Beau said from the corner.

"Don't be an ass, Beau," Lucy said, and a couple of people actually chuckled.

Eben looked at Beau. *Is this when he blows? Now, or later?* But the big man merely shrugged.

"We'll be torn to pieces!" Doug blurted out. "Guts ripped out, heads stuck on fucking sticks!"

They all fell silent again for a while, and the quiet was beginning to feel uncomfortable again when Stella cleared the air.

"So, this guy walks into a bar . . ."

DAY 3

THEY BROUGHT UP FOOD from the Kelso kitchen and set about working out how much they had to eat per day. There were canned goods, potato chips, dried meats, several huge tins of cookies, and frozen milk. Not as much as Eben had hoped, but it wasn't starvation rations either. Besides, secretly he was pretty certain they'd never be here that long.

Something was bound to go wrong.

"What're you thinking?" Stella said, startling him. He'd cut a small flap in the cardboard they'd used to cover the window, and he was sitting there with a blanket covering his head, staring out. The snow had stopped a couple of hours before, the sky clearing to show a glorious array of stars and a half-moon. The streets were fresh with starlight, and if he was outside it would be almost bright enough to read. They were also silent. In over an hour, he had seen absolutely no sign of movement and heard nothing.

He folded the cardboard shut and sat back against the wall. "Just watching."

"Yeah, right."

"My phone just died!" Denise said, and it was as if she'd lost a friend. "Anyone got a charger?"

"Yeah, I stopped to pick one up when I was fleeing those blood-drinking freaks," Doug said.

"What's the point anyway?" Lucy asked. "No reception. No signal."

"There's always a chance," Denise said, but her comment was met with silence. They'd talked about this, even discussed getting out to the cell tower, trying to fix it up and send a signal from there. But Eben had been there and seen the damage. And he had no doubts about how thorough these things would be in their destruction.

"Does anybody in town have, like, a ham radio or something?" Denise pressed.

"Larry Cooper had one," Carter replied, "but he moved to Dillingham. Even if we could radio someone, they can't get to us."

Eben closed his eyes and felt Stella sitting down next to him. More contact; he liked that. Jake was asleep, the others were resting or talking quietly among themselves, and Eben could think of no better way to rest than by sitting here with Stella. He sighed.

"Guess it's good you didn't want kids, huh?" Stella said quietly. And with one comment, as ever, she shot the moment down.

"Damn it, Stella—" Eben said, pushing himself up.

"Eben—"

Maybe she'd said it without thinking, just a throwaway remark, and maybe she was right. If they'd had kids, then they would be involved in all of this as well. Eben had lost enough friends and family in one night to last a lifetime. But *damn it . . .*

And they were not the only ones feeling the pressure.

"Where's Catherine?" Isaac said, his voice far too loud.

"Mom died a long time ago, Dad," Wilson said, kneeling beside his father and tenderly touching his shoulders. Isaac mumbled something else, but Wilson whispered his fears back to sleep.

"Warmer over here with the rest of us!" Lucy said, casting her voice across to Beau.

"I'm okay," Beau said. Lucy crawled toward him and he raised his hands, pressed back against the wall. "*Really!* Really, Lucy . . . I'm better on the perimeter."

Eben glanced back at Stella, she was standing and reaching for him, and then the loud crash came from outside.

They all froze. Eben glanced around at everyone—wide-eyed, motionless, like a store of statues. Then Beau stood slowly in the far corner, and Eben thought, *I'm damn glad we have him with us.*

"Lights out," he said. "Everyone quiet and still." He turned back to the peephole, bent the cardboard, and he and Stella looked out.

Across the street and a couple of houses down, a front door had been ripped from its hinges. It lay in two broken pieces in the snow. A downstairs window smashed, curtains billowed out, and even this far away they could hear further sounds of destruction.

Stella turned and spoke. "They're ransacking the Clarks' place."

"Maybe they'll go through *every* house," Beau said. "I would. Flush out survivors."

Eben whispered, still looking from the peephole. "It'll take them a few days to get through all the houses." *Although the speed they're working there, maybe not,* he thought. The windows upstairs had been smashed now, and he was sure he'd seen snow dancing on the roof as tiles were bumped from the inside. More bad news he didn't feel like sharing.

"If they're searching that well, they'll rip through the boarded-up places, too," Lucy said.

Doug crawled toward Eben, knees thumping on the uncarpeted timber floor.

"Doug!" Eben hissed.

"We have to move!" Doug said quietly. Panic was evident in his voice, his stance, and eyes. "We have to get somewhere safer, away from here."

"And when do you suggest we do that?" Eben whispered. He glanced back through the peephole. The Clarks' house had fallen silent again, but he was sure the creatures were still in there. The place didn't look empty.

"Now!" Lucy said. "We go now, while we still have the strength!"

"No," Stella said. "Until we have some way to stop them, it's suicide!"

"It's suicide to stay," Doug said. Lucy nodded, egging him on. "We can wait here till they find us and kill us all, or we can run like hell. Some of us won't make it, but that's better than just waiting here to die!"

"Doug—" Eben began, but the big man was in his stride now, and behind Lucy's mumbled approval even Carter seemed to be in agreement.

"You may be the Sheriff, but I can't see what you've done so far that—"

"Back off, Doug," Jake said. He moved between Doug and Eben, small and slight but exuding a quiet strength.

Doug shook his head and sighed. "Come on Jake, I didn't really mean that. But your brother can't tell us all what to do! I say we run, and—"

"Then you might want to wait a few more days, lose a little weight so you won't be bringing up the rear."

Doug gasped, stood, and Eben thought he was going to back down.

But then his lips pursed and he slapped Jake hard across the face.

Things moved quickly, quietly, and with such silent violence that it was almost balletic. Eben rose and darted across the attic, feeling Stella's hand brush his leg as she reached out to stop him. Doug looked up from where Jake had fallen, obviously anticipating Eben's reaction, but the look of shock at what he had done was not enough to change things. Eben powered into him, one clenched fist sinking into the big man's gut. The other hand clasped Doug's throat, fingers digging in, squeezing, and as they went down Eben did his best to lessen the impact on the floor.

Doug wasn't fighting, and Eben was almost sorry.

"First," Eben said, "you *ever* lay a hand on my brother again and I'll feed you to those things myself. Second, Doug . . . start a fight, any of us, and the noise will get us all killed a lot faster. Got that?"

Doug nodded.

Eben squeezed harder, just for a second. "*Got* that?"

"Yeah," Doug said. "Sorry, Eben. Jake."

Eben released Doug and stood, turning back to make sure Jake was okay. He needn't have worried; his brother was already standing again, tonguing his swelling cheek. His eyes were strong and defiant.

Eben smiled and nodded, and he could almost see Jake's chest swelling.

"Stella?" Eben said.

She knew his meaning straightaway. She turned back to the window, opened the peephole and sat there for a few long seconds. Then she turned back to Eben and shrugged. "Looks all clear to me."

"The Clarks' place?"

"I think they're still in there. Saw a shape moving past one of the windows."

Eben sighed and looked down at his feet, willing his racing heart to ease up. His chest was tight, breath thin and pained, and he took a puff of his inhaler. *Almost out,* he thought. *But keep going like this, I won't have to worry about that. Could have given us away then. If we'd fallen awkwardly, knocked the propane heater over, spilled a pile of cans . . .* It did not bear thinking about. He almost wanted to turn around and slug Doug another one, he was so angry.

They'd only been here a short time, and already tempers were fraying. Four weeks up here? He glanced across at Beau, back in the corner nursing his shotgun. Beau's expression echoed his own thoughts: this won't work.

"Okay everyone," he said. "It's true. We can't stay here. Once those things get to this house, we're finished. We could last days or even weeks here, or it could end tomorrow. But ultimately we need to be somewhere safe."

"Where?" Carter said.

"Said it yourself back in the diner: the Utilidor. We get there, we can last the month."

Carter frowned. "But as *you* said, it's way out past the edge of town. How the hell do we make it out there?"

"We wait for the next snowstorm to give us cover." Eben glanced around at all of them, seeing half a dozen reasons why this would never work. "Next blizzard, we'll be ready."

DAY 6

WAITING FOR THE SNOW to come . . .

It wasn't something they usually had to wait very long for in Barrow, but now every minute felt like an hour, every hour a day. Two days after their arrival in the attic, there had been a teasing flurry, but it came to nothing. A day later, the sky turned leaden and heavy, the air stilled, but nothing came. It cleared again that night, and the moon and stars shone mockingly down.

Stella and Eben had sat close together for the whole time, but they could not talk. This made Stella sad—there was so much to say, and she knew that Eben felt this as well, but even when they sat touching there was a gulf between them. Perhaps the proximity of so many other people made it too difficult to say anything meaningful. She clung to that excuse, at least. But she also guessed that if she and Eben had been the only two survivors in the whole of Barrow, breaking their silence even then would have been close to impossible.

Maybe when this is over, she thought. *When those things have gone, and if we're still alive, maybe we'll talk. Maybe I'll talk. Maybe.*

Jake kept looking at her as if he was expecting something from her. She knew what. *You and my brother belong together,* his look said. Stella smiled at him and wondered how the hell Eben had never noticed how sensitive and damned grown up his little brother had become.

So they waited, and sometimes they talked without saying very much.

They waited for the snow to come.

Because when it did finally start to fall again, they would leave this place. And seeking somewhere safer was going to be a very dangerous game.

Every night, Jake dreamed of his grandma. When he did finally get to sleep she would be there waiting for him, strong and brave and suffering her cancer in silence.

He knew that she hadn't even told his mom about it, and to begin with that had felt strange. He knew, his mom didn't. But Grandma had been very specific about that, and the secrecy and shared knowledge had brought them much closer together.

Once, Grandma had told Jake that it was for him and Eben that she was fighting hardest. *I want to be a great-grandmother,* she had said. And her eyes clouded then, almost tearful, because of Stella and Eben.

So she would be waiting for him, and it was always when she came to tell him that the cancer had gone that the vampires attacked. Awake, Jake had trouble believing that's what they were, but in his dreams they were so real, and there was never any doubt. Fearsome, manic, monstrous things with teeth that ripped skin and flesh and scored bone. They looked like humans with sharks' mouths, though there was nothing human about their behavior.

He saw Grandma ripped apart almost every night, and somehow he never screamed himself awake.

In those last moments, when sleep and nightmare bled away, Jake swore blind that he would have his revenge.

They fell into an uneasy routine.

They slept in shifts, ate together, and always went down to the toilet in pairs. Bathroom visits were what worried Eben the most; the hatch would stay up, the pipes behind the toilet were opened to flush into the sewer below, and Beau stood guard at the top of the stairs with his shotgun. People moving around always gave the risk of someone making a mistake: slamming a door, tripping, dropping the toilet seat.

It would only take one mistake to be noticed.

Up in the attic, despite everything that had happened and the danger they were still in, boredom touched them with its numbing hand. They'd whisper songs, play word games, tell jokes, but physical inactivity seemed to aggravate their minds. They needed more to occupy themselves, other than the memories of what had happened and the fear of what was to come.

When the routine broke, it was almost with a sigh of relief.

Even after only a few days in the attic, hearing another human voice shocked them all.

"Hello!" it called. It was a woman shouting somewhere in the distance, her voice sharp, echoes muffled by the deep snow.

"Everyone!" Eben whispered. "We all stay quiet. We keep hidden. Got it?"

Stella noticed Eben looking across at Beau, and Beau stood beside the trapdoor with his shotgun pointing down. *Is it now?* she thought. *Is this when everything changes?* And suddenly she was terrified, afraid of going out there or of those things coming in here. She looked back on the last few awkward, uncomfortable days, and suddenly she didn't want anything to change.

"Stella," Eben said. They went to the window together, and Stella eased back the cardboard.

"Hello! Someone!"

"Getting closer," Stella said.

"You think they've gone?" Lucy asked behind them. "Maybe those things have gone and the survivors are coming out, looking for others?"

"One way to find out," Doug said.

Stella and Eben looked back together as the big man stood.

"Sit down and keep quiet," Eben said.

Stella expected Doug to bluster and curse, but instead he did just as the Sheriff had said. *Eben's holding us together,* she thought. *There's something in him that people respect.*

They turned back to the window.

"We should be so lucky," Eben whispered.

Stella only nodded. She could see nothing out there, only the view they'd become used to. Another house farther along the street had been ransacked two days before, but there seemed no reason or pattern to the creatures' actions. Eben had said he was pretty sure they'd not found anyone in there.

And then there was movement. Someone stumbled into view from behind a building, staggering through the snow and obviously distressed. Stella recognized her instantly. "That's Kirsten Toomey."

"Kirsten?" Denise said from behind them. "How is she? Is she hurt, is she—"

Eben tensed. "Everyone *quiet!*"

Stella watched Kirsten wandering the street, and she knew the young woman must have recently emerged from somewhere. Her clothing was torn and tattered, her face either bruised or dirty, and she was not wearing a coat. If she hadn't been inside until very recently, she'd have been dead from the cold.

"Hello, *anyone!*" she shouted. She looked desperate, scanning windows and twisting her hands together.

"She's just looking for a sign of life," Stella said.

Eben grunted. "But what's she doing out there? If

she's survived this long, she must know . . ." He froze then, and Stella was certain that he was still holding his breath.

"Someone! Anyone!" Kirsten called.

Carter appeared beside Stella, looking over her shoulder. "We need to bring her in before they find her."

"No," Eben said.

"What?"

"I said no."

"Please!" Kirsten called.

"Eben, we can't just leave her out there," Stella said, but she already knew that Eben had seen more than them. He wouldn't abandon someone to their fate, not now. Not unless he had good reason.

"The rooftops," he said quietly.

Stella and Carter looked.

On the opposite side of the road shapes drifted across the rooftops, stalking Kirsten, leaping the spaces between houses and landing without a sound. They did not even disturb the heavy snow lying on the sloped roofs. It was almost as if they really were only shadows.

"They're using her," Carter said.

Stella's breath caught in her throat. "Bait."

"What's happening?" Denise asked.

Stella turned around and told them all.

"We have to do something," Denise said.

Carter and Eben turned away from the peephole and faced the others. They all fell silent, knowing what *should* be done but not knowing how to do it.

"We can't just leave her," Carter said quietly.

"You saw them," Eben said.

Stella's mind raced but everything it worked on was bad. She felt a tightness in her chest, a tension waiting to break. She was sick to her heart.

Beau made to open the trapdoor. "The hell with that," he said.

Eben stood, startling Stella with his sudden movement. "If anyone's heading out, it's me."

"Not alone," Stella said.

Beau looked from Eben to Stella, back again. "Fine. We'll make it a party."

Stella hugged on her coat, and she felt the silence of stares. *They all know I could be going out there to die.*

"Look, protecting this attic is the first priority," Eben said.

"We can't just leave—" Lucy began, but Eben cut in.

"We're not leaving her, Lucy. We're going to try. But these things have been at her already, they're *using* her, and I'm just saying . . ." He shook his head and pulled Stella to one side.

"Stella, these people need hope. You're much better at that sort of thing than I am, you know that." In the semidarkness his eyes twinkled, and she could smell the fear on his breath. She'd smelled it before, on the day she left. It made her want to hold him and push him away at the same time, but right now she knew that he was talking sense.

Stella nodded. "Yeah. You're right." Eben smiled at her, checked his pistol and turned to Beau.

"So let's go," Beau said.

Eben shook his head. "Beau, it's my job to keep you all safe—"

"Hell of a job you've been doing," Doug muttered, and Eben sent him a withering glare.

"Beau," Stella cut in, "Eben's taking the pistol we found downstairs, but we need the bigger weapon here. We need *you* here. That's what he's trying to say."

Beau looked from Stella to Eben, then down at the trapdoor by his feet. Then he looked up again and nodded. "I'll not move an inch from here," he said.

"Thanks, Beau," Eben said. He glanced back at Stella and smiled. *Told you you're better with people,* that smile said, and Stella pursed her lips and shrugged.

"Be careful," she said.

Eben turned away, lowered the stepladder and left the attic. Stella's last view of him was as a shadow moving off along the Kelsos' landing. *Is that how I'll remember him? I should have said more. Should have told him more, all that time we've had up here to talk without saying anything, I should have told him* more!

Doug uttered a short, bitter laugh and shook his head, and Stella was on him in a second. Her fury and anger rose, her grief and desperation, and before her in this man she saw every reason why they would not survive. She shoved him with both hands. He took a startled couple of steps back.

"I hear another slam at Eben from you, I'll throw you to those things myself. Got it?"

"I . . . I thought you and he were—"

"Thinking, Doug. That's where it all goes awry for you."

When she turned around, Jake was already at the peephole. She joined him and they watched in silence, dreading the burst of noise and violence that could come at any second.

Eben was terrified. Those things could be anywhere; on the roofs, stalking the land between houses, in the crawl spaces underneath. They could be sitting in windows waiting for careless survivors to walk by, or hiding in the abandoned vehicles staggered here and there along the street. Perhaps they had even buried themselves in snowdrifts, waiting there cold and silent for days until they smelled the meat or felt the heat of a body walking nearby. He had no idea. So he could move out there to the best of his ability—slow, cautious—or he could admit defeat and return to the attic.

Even then he might be followed.

Perhaps they had seen him already.

He waited a block from the Kelso house, crouched in a crawl space and listening hard for Kirsten's voice. He constantly scanned the narrow band of rooftop he could see from here, but it appeared to be still and silent. Perhaps they had moved on.

How the hell do I get her away when they're watching her every move? he thought. There were no answers, only the niggling, persistent voice in his head that said, *This is madness, this is madness.* He had no plan, and if he thought about it in too much detail, he had no hope.

In the distance, Kirsten's voice called out again.

Eben shook his head, looked both ways, and broke cover.

Kirsten rounded a corner and the vampires were waiting for her.

She gasped and swayed on the spot. Her brain was telling her to *run, run!* but her legs would not move. The vampires turned as one and looked at her. She stumbled forward to meet them.

"I tried," she gasped.

The ones she thought of as the animals circled her as she closed in, moving so silently through the snow that they may as well have been ghosts. The tall one—the one that had spoken to her, their leader?—waited for her. He drew her in like a moth lured inexorably toward the flame.

"Please, I tried," she pleaded. "There's nobody."

She'd seen them attack friends, neighbors, tearing out throats and drinking blood. She knew what they were. In a way that helped her carry on, because now it felt as though she was living in a dream. A *nightmare.* Very little was real anymore. Kirsten was aware that she was losing her mind, but she welcomed the increasing buffer that gave her against sickening reality.

"*Please.* There's nobody left. They'd have helped me if there was, they'd have come out. *Please, God.*"

“God?” the tall one finally growled. “Show her how God answers prayer.”

Kirsten did not even sense the movement beside her. A shape passed across her face and her cheek was opened, blood gushing into the snow at her feet. She gasped and looked around, watching a vampire backing silently away with hunger in its eyes.

“I helped,” she said, finally able to cry. “I did what you asked.”

“You did,” the tall one said.

Another shape came in, and another, and every time she spun around, there was a fresh cut on her face, a gash on her stomach, a chunk of flesh ripped from her arm. She tried to scream, but found she could not. The breath was stuck in her, the scream, hidden inside where sweet reality had long since fled.

The tall one’s grotesque voice cut in, and she thought he was talking to the thin female vampire that sat at his feet. “And the Lord God said, ‘Ye shall eat the flesh of the mighty, and drink the blood of the princes of the earth.’ And so we do what we must.”

I’m going to die, Kirsten thought. The snow around her was speckled red and growing redder by the second. *I’m going to die here and . . .*

Finally, she thought she might be able to scream.

But before she could open her mouth, the tall one nodded to the vampire at his feet, and she leapt at Kirsten and took her throat.

• • •

Eben pressed himself against the wall, watching the creatures take the girl down and leap on her in a frenzy of feeding.

He panted, desperate to get away but unable to move.

I didn't do a thing, he thought. *I couldn't help, couldn't save her. Useless.*

Kirsten's final moments were a spray of red in the middle of the street. Eben felt pinned against the wall by the sight, every second imprinting itself on his memory.

Got to move.

One of the creatures looked up and shook its head, long tongue snaking out to pick fleshy scraps from its skin.

Jake is right. They really are *vampires.*

The tall one standing to one side looked around, and for a moment, Eben thought he'd been seen. His heart stuttered, his blood chilled, and when the thing looked away he sank down beneath the house.

If it saw me, they'll be here in seconds. He held the pistol out before him . . . briefly considered putting it to his own head. Better to go out that way.

But there was no movement, no sight or sound of pursuit, and after a few seconds he crawled away.

Eben moved for ten minutes, using crawl spaces where he could, hiding in the cover of snowbanks or fences where he could not. He went in the general direction of the Kelso house, though he was consciously trying to take a random route back. If he was caught, he didn't want his final movements to give away the location of the others.

His breath became heavy around the Riis place. He leaned against the piled dogsleds in the backyard and tried to regulate his breathing, chest tight and vision starting to swim. He took a shot from his inhaler, knowing that it was very close to running out.

Calm down, he thought, *take it easy, take it slow*. But he found he could not. Not after seeing what happened to Kirsten, and not with the possibility that he would be discovered at any second.

Taking raking, painful breaths, he stood to push himself away from the sleds.

"Eben," a voice whispered.

Eben froze and looked around. His own breath? Imagination? He glanced up at the rooftops, spotting no shadows with eyes.

"Eben," the voice said again, and this time he placed it. He moved to the back of the yard and looked down at the crawl space beneath the house. John Riis lay there, face pale and bloodied, his eyes swelled almost shut.

"John!" Eben said. "How long have you been out here?"

John reached out from beneath the house and his arms struck the moonlight. He clasped on to the snowy ground and, as if hauling on the light itself, slid himself out into the yard. "I . . . I'm not sure . . ."

Eben went to help, then stopped after a couple of steps. Riis still hadn't looked up. "Where's Ally?"

"They took her, Eben. They slashed me up . . . I watched them take her . . . couldn't do a thing."

"When was this?"

John shook his head and started to push himself upright. Eben could make out the wounds on his arms now, dark rents in his flesh where his jacket had been torn open and blood had dried. For a second Jake's voice echoed in his mind—*Vampires!*—but then John staggered and reached out for support, and Eben went to him.

"Hang on, we'll get you to safety."

"I'm so hungry," John said, and it was something about his voice that gave Eben pause. His hand closed around Eben's wrist, and it was cold. John hopped a couple of times to maintain balance, one foot flopping uselessly, and then he looked up. *"Starving."*

In the moonlight, John Riis's eyes were black as coal.

He opened his mouth and flicked his tongue at the air. His teeth looked unnaturally large in the silvery light, gums shrunk back and lips split from dehydration.

He tugged at Eben's arm, pulling him closer, but Eben punched him in the stomach. The two fell apart, Eben slipping on ice and going down. The gun flew from his hand and he heard a dull *thud* as it buried itself somewhere in the snow.

John stumbled back against his dogsleds, gasping, staggering again as his broken leg started to fold beneath him. But his face had changed now to something feral and vicious, and driven by an unimaginable hunger he came at Eben again.

Eben turned to run. It was not cowardice; it was barely even planned. But this thing coming at him no longer looked at all like John Riis. It was terror that drove Eben now, pure and simple.

He ran from the Riises' yard and into their neighbors', and it was here that something buried in the snow tripped him up. He went sprawling, clasping on to the chain of a child's swing to prevent himself from falling all the way. *If I'm down, I'm out,* he thought. The chain held, and his momentum swung him around to face John as, impossible as it might have seemed with his mangled leg, John charged again.

The swing twisted as the two men grappled with each other, Riis's teeth slamming shut inches from Eben's face. The Sheriff thought of reasoning, pleading, but there was nothing in John's eyes now that offered any hope of a peaceful outcome—his expression flickered from savagery to bewilderment, but his attack was remorseless.

Eben's breath was growing more raspy, and again his vision began to swim. He coughed, pushed at John, trying to untangle himself from the swing's chain, but somehow they were both caught. John leaned forward again, mouth wide and aiming for Eben's throat.

Eben looked around desperately for something to use as a weapon. The swing chain was pulled taut—no hope there—but then he spotted a pile of firewood and an ax against the side of the house. Just within his grasp . . . but he'd have to let go of John to reach out.

He butted his head forward and connected with John's nose. There was a crunch, John let out a strange whine, and then Eben let go and leapt for the ax.

John roared and fell forward, mouth open and teeth aiming for Eben's stomach.

Eben grabbed the ax and gave it one heavy twist. It slipped from the wood and he went with the motion, spinning around and letting the heavy metal head carve into John. It struck his shoulder and he gasped. Black blood pulsed from the wound.

Eben kicked him off and stood, free now of the swing's chains, ax held by his side.

"Ebennnnn," John growled, and Eben raised the ax and stepped in again. This time the blade buried itself in John's right cheek, shattering his eye socket and flipping his head back.

Eben pulled the ax free, groaned, and swung it again, and again.

John crawled and mewled until Eben cut off his head.

Eben sat back against the woodpile, trying not to see the corpse that he had just made headless. He groped for his inhaler, taking a double blast and knowing for sure it was the last dose. He threw it into the snow and rested his head back, looking at the sky and trying to see things clearer up there. But the stars shone with ancient indifference, and the moon merely revealed him to anyone who may have been looking.

I just killed John Riis, he thought. But the lie in that thought was plain. He'd killed the thing that *used to be* John Riis.

It didn't help.

Eben rose and rooted around in the snow for the pistol. It took him a couple of minutes to find it, his hands freezing up. He didn't spare the corpse another glance as he headed straight for the Kelso place now. If he was followed, so be it. He was sick of the company of the dead.

Stella saw him first. She nodded to Beau and they opened the door together, helping Eben inside after he swept his tracks away. He was panting hard. And there was blood, black and sticky in the weak light.

"Lost . . . my . . . gun," he said.

"Wouldn'ta done any good," Beau said.

"They're *everywhere*. And . . . John Riis. Was one of them."

"How did you stop him?" Stella asked, but she already knew the answer would be a bad one. She had been scanning Eben for wounds but found none. The blood was not his.

Eben raised the ax. "Nothing lives without a head."

Stella saw the burgeoning panic in his eyes and knew she had to put it down. "You had to," she said. "You *had* to, Eben. You can't leave us all alone."

• • •

Marlow stood above the remains of John Riis. He kicked at the torso, then found the head half-buried in a snowdrift. He picked it up by the hair, opened one of its eyes, and then pricked his finger on one of Riis's fangs.

"No!" he shouted, heaving the head away into the darkness. "Who turned this one?"

Iris cowered before him, but Marlow would not hurt her. She had never left his side. He enjoyed being her teacher.

He drew her head beside his own and whispered into her ear, *"Who would dare?"*

DAY 12

STILL WAITING FOR THE SNOW . . .

"Twelve days without a blizzard. Damn record for Barrow." Eben sat back from the peephole and looked around the attic.

He'd told them what he'd done to John Riis. There had been no alternative, and he had to explain the sticky black blood on his clothes and face somehow. They'd asked him lots of questions and listened in horror to his replies, never questioning or doubting anything he said.

And since then, things seemed to have changed.

Instead of some of the survivors—Doug especially—turning against him for killing one of their own, Eben had the sense that his leadership of the little band was sealed. It was nothing to do with him being a sheriff, or being the one who went out to try to save Kirsten.

He'd been blooded. It was as simple as that.

That hadn't ended the squabbling or the tensions, the stress or the frequent announcements that they were all going to die, this was hopeless, they'd be found and taken out there just like Kirsten Toomey . . . but it did make things more comfortable. Eben spoke, the others listened. As a sheriff he'd always commanded a certain amount of respect from those who knew him well.

Now, as well as the Sheriff, he was a vampire killer.

The food was running low. They'd all known that for a couple of days, but no one had mentioned it outright. It didn't need saying, just as none of them complained about the cramped sleeping conditions or the stink of the Kelsos' bathroom since the pipes froze three days before. It was a fact that they would have to deal with when the time came . . . and that time was getting close.

"You sure you don't want the last bit?" Jake asked Stella. He was scooping the final dregs of deviled ham from a can.

Stella smiled and shook her head. "Hate the stuff."

"I used to like the little devil on these cans. Eben?" Jake offered.

Eben shook his head. "Couldn't eat another thing. That half can of plum tomatoes did me in."

Jake nodded, offered a weak smile, and chewed.

"They didn't show up till sundown," Stella said, repeating what had already been suggested and discussed a dozen times before. "Maybe they really can't stand the light. So we wait it out until daylight's back. It's only two and a half weeks."

Denise laughed nervously. "Yeah, that's all."

"And now, as I'm sure everyone's noticed, the fucking food's running out. We can't hold out without food!" Doug said. Eben had been watching him for the last couple of days, aware that the big man could cause real trouble if he so wished. So far he'd held, but Eben knew that he was very close to snapping.

"What about other houses?" Lucy asked. "People must've left something behind."

Eben stood, shaking his head. "Too risky, running back and forth out there. Besides, they could be hiding and living on it themselves, and we break in somewhere, we're liable to get shot. We've spoken about this before. There were a hundred and fifty-two folks left in town; Chuck Moore, Carroll Trumbull, the Kobayashis. We're not the only ones left."

"We've seen no evidence of that," Doug said.

"Because they're hiding themselves well," Eben said. "We *can't* be the only ones left." He stared at Doug until the other man looked away.

Behind him Stella went to the peephole and looked out. Eben knew what she was thinking. *Out there, hiding in attic rooms, hidey-holes beneath the floors, families, parents with dead kids, kids who'd seen their parents taken and killed . . .*

"Snow?" he asked. Stella shook her head without turning around.

"Okay," Eben said quietly. *Okay,* he thought. *Maybe now's the time.* "I've done this." He took out his pad of traffic tickets and flicked it open.

"Not gonna write me up again, Eben?" Beau said. He'd gone almost whole days without speaking since being here, and Eben was glad to hear his voice.

"Always got a few for you, Beau. But this one's special. Come and see." Beau stood from his position beyond the trapdoor, stretched and came over, still nursing his shotgun. Jake had tried to persuade him to take some garlic paste they'd found and smear it around the barrel, so that the shot could pick it up on the way out. Beau hadn't even responded. Even after what had happened—what Eben had seen and told them about—the idea of supernatural creatures having invaded Barrow still seemed vaguely preposterous.

"What is it?" Carter asked.

Eben laid the pad down and smoothed out the page. "Map. Before too long there'll be a blizzard, and when it happens we need to be ready. We just need to walk. Look, see here . . . Barrow was laid out with functionality in mind. Each lot in town's twenty-five feet wide. The general store's eleven lots east. So under cover of snow, we get there for food and medical supplies, then head fourteen lots north to the edge of town, and a bit of open ground to the Utilidor."

The others gathered around, absorbing the plan, and Eben could almost hear their gears churning.

"We know this town," he continued. "We can walk it blindfolded. We just have to wait for the weather we've lived with since we were born."

"If it ever comes," Doug said.

"It'll come. It always does."

The others stirred, some still looking at the map, others glancing at Eben and nodding. *They think it's a good plan,* he thought.

Stella touched his arm and inclined her head toward the peephole. He shrugged: *What?*

She shook her head.

When they reached the covered window she sat down next to him, held his arm and leaned in close.

"Hey. You know how you told me you could never be a dad?" she whispered. "Bullshit. The way you look out for these people—they're grateful to you."

Eben shrugged. "I've never quit on anybody. My job."

"No, it isn't."

Eben pulled back and looked down at Stella. "What do you mean?"

"This isn't a civilized town anymore, Eben. Things have changed. This is survival."

"I'm still the Sheriff." He leaned back into Stella, and as he felt the laugh brewing at his dramatic statement, so too he felt her shoulder shaking. They laughed together, and when Jake came over they couldn't tell him why.

DAY 13

EBEN WAS AT THE PEEPHOLE when he heard the roar. He held his breath, heard it again and glanced around. No one else had noticed.

"Stella," he said. She came to him and waited for bad news. He shrugged. "Something out there. Sounds like an animal, in the distance."

"What sort of animal?"

"Well . . ." He looked out again at the snowy landscape that had not changed for days. Nothing moved, no shadows shifted, and the town glowed with reflected moonlight.

"What, Eben?"

"I think it might have been a bear."

"Bear?" Doug said. He'd overheard, and Eben closed his eyes and silently cursed.

The others stirred, looking at Eben and Stella and waiting for them to say more.

"I heard something, that's all," Eben said.

"Polar bear?" Beau asked.

Doug scoffed. "Hasn't been a polar bear seen in town for years."

"Maybe it smelled the blood?" Jake suggested, and they fell quiet at that, all thinking their own thoughts.

"Barrow's quieter than it's ever been," Eben said. "The derricks haven't been working for almost three weeks, all the lights are out, and . . ."

"Meat," Stella said.

Eben nodded. "Yeah. Maybe Jake's right and it smelled blood."

Doug shrugged. "So? What good does it do us?"

Eben smiled, and inside he enjoyed a sick satisfaction at the doleful expression on Doug's face. "Nothing at all, Doug. No good at all."

Next time they heard the roar, it came from much closer, and a few minutes later the polar bear ambled into view from between two houses. It walked into the middle of the street and looked around, sniffing the air, the ground, staring at the shadows of the unfamiliar landscape.

"Jesus," Stella said. "It's huge. Never seen one this close before."

"A male," Eben said.

Stella gasped and grabbed Eben's leg. "There. The roof of the Clarks' place."

Eben looked, scanning the shadows and watching for movement. "I can't see anything."

"Something shifted."

The bear turned ponderously toward them and started walking again.

Eben saw the movement this time. "Two of them," he said.

"What's happening?" Carter squatted behind them, the others sitting close by. They'd all heard the bear's roar that time, but the spy hole was only big enough for two at any one time.

"Bear's outside," Eben said. The bear paused thirty feet away and sniffed at the air again.

"Oh shit, what if it smells us?" Stella whispered.

Eben looked from the bear, to the Clarks' roof and back again.

"Can't you shoot it?" Carter asked.

Eben shook his head. "They're outside too."

"Oh fuck," Carter said, voice lowered. "They're using it. Following to see if it finds fresh meat."

Eben watched the shadows move closer to the edge of the roof, and it was then that he noticed another shadow slinking between houses on his right, coming closer along the street with every heartbeat. "Don't think so," he said.

"Cat and mouse," Stella said.

Eben nodded.

"You can't be serious," Lucy said from behind them. "Against a polar bear?"

"Let me see!" Jake said, scampering across the floor.

"No, Jake—" Eben said, but Stella had already moved aside. His brother joined him at the peephole and held his breath when he saw the scene outside.

"It's beautiful," he whispered, and Eben nodded

because it was. He'd seen bears several times before, but never this close and this clearly. He knew that they were unpredictable and often very dangerous, but there was a natural grace and power about this animal that was humbling.

The bear looked directly at them. Even in the starlight, it was close enough for Eben to see its nostrils flare and close as it picked up their scent.

"Shit," he whispered.

The bear roared, and the shadows leapt from the Clarks' roof.

"It knows we're here," Jake said. He turned around and whispered again to the others, and Eben heard them shifting, standing, starting to panic.

"Wait!" he whispered. "Still and quiet."

"But it—" Jake said.

"It doesn't matter. Look."

Three vampires stood around the bear, spaced evenly so that it could only see two of them at any one time. They circled, crouched down low, hands held out, dragging spidery shadows across the snow behind them. The bear seemed confused to begin with, turning this way and that as it tried to keep track of these audacious people teasing it. Then it roared and stood on its hind legs.

"It's *huge!*" Jake gushed.

Eben had never seen one doing this before. It must have been twelve feet tall, easily twice the height of the things circling it, and a glimmer of hope lit up his insides. *If it just takes one or two of them, that'll be one or two less looking for us,* he thought. He could not imagine even three vampires taking down this magnificent animal.

It roared again, teeth long and glistening, claws on its huge hands catching the moonlight.

A shadow darted in and slashed at the polar bear's rump. It growled and blood splashed the snow behind it. It fell to all fours again and turned around, lashing out with one paw, but the vampire had already retreated.

As it turned another vampire moved in, slashing at its side. The bear kicked out behind it, hitting only air. It turned again, charging for its attacker but finding nothing.

"Where'd it go?" Jake asked.

Eben pointed. "Roof."

As the bear noticed the shape moving on the roof above it, the other two streaked in from either side, striking at its yellow coat and turning it red in long, livid streaks. The bear roared again, in pain this time, and spun on its attackers. One was already away, but the other fell as it tried to run, the long sleeve of its coat tangled in the bear's claws.

Here we go, Eben thought.

"Tear its head off," Stella said from where she was watching over his shoulder.

The bear stood on the struggling shape and looked around, steam snorting from its nostrils. The snow around it was spattered red and it sniffed at one of the bloody streaks, evidently confused.

"Come *on!*" Jake whispered.

The vampire started struggling. The bear sniffed at its head, lifted its paw and turned it over.

The vampire lunged, slashing across the bear's face with both hands, claws slicing rough red lines through fur and into flesh. The bear roared, reared up on its hind legs and fell again . . . missing the vampire by inches.

The others came in, circling the creature while their companion crawled away. Then the three of them began taking turns moving in, slashing, and backing away. The bear stumbled around in a circle, striking out here and there but never quite catching any of them. It would start to charge, be struck from behind, turn and charge and find itself under attack from behind again. It bellowed in pain and frustration, trampling the bloody snow until it formed a wide stain across the street.

And it was weakening.

The breath plumed from its nostrils in great clouds.

Blood streaked its yellow fur and dripped from its underside.

The vampires were calling to one another now, strange grunts and growls that appeared to be a language. Eben had heard it before, watching them circling Kirsten and taking orders from the tall vampire that he was sure must be their leader.

"Their own language," he said. "Christ, how old are these things?"

"I don't want to watch this anymore," Stella said. Jake went with her, leaving Eben alone to view the polar bear's demise. He did not want to watch it either, not really, but he felt compelled, and somewhere deep down he thought it only right that he witness this grand creature's unnatural end.

They did not finish it as quickly as they could have. *Cat and mouse,* Eben thought again, watching the vampires dart in and out, slashing, taking chunks of flesh and fur away with their taloned hands.

The bear's roars grew weaker and more despairing, and when it fell onto its side in the bloodied snow, Eben knew that it was finished. No last-minute reprieve, no final burst of energy that would enable it to pin down a vampire and rip off its head.

In the end, two of the vampires held the still breathing animal down while the other went at its neck with its hands. Blood and fur flew, and a minute later they dragged its head away from its body.

They left it like that in the middle of the road. They didn't even feed. They'd killed it for sport, three things that looked like people but were not against the strongest, most vicious hunter stalking the Arctic.

Eben closed the peephole, lowered the blanket across the cardboard, and turned around.

For a while, nobody met his gaze.

DAY 14

Stella was in Seattle, eating lunch at one of the harbor restaurants where the fish were so fresh they almost swam onto your plate. She thought Eben was with her, but every time she looked around he seemed to have disappeared. So she ate, feeling her husband's presence with every mouthful, and wondered where he was.

The sun streamed through the glass wall that faced out over the harbor. There were more people sitting on the balcony outside, and many of the heavy glass doors had been left open. The smell of the sea wafted in. The presentation of food on her plate was gorgeous. But where was Eben?

She glanced around again, dropped her napkin, and ducked down to pick it up.

Eben was under their table. He was crying, and as soon as she saw him, she heard the sobs as well. He seemed to be cowering from something. Where the sun touched him—arm, neck, right cheek—his skin was a bright, lobster red. It even seemed to be smoking.

Stella reached out in concern, and when she touched Eben, his mouth opened and he squealed.

What the fuck was that?

His head turned, squealing again as though all his bone joints needed oiling.

Stella opened her eyes to darkness.

She looked around for a panicked couple of seconds, trying to remember where she was and what was happening. Even when she did focus, the panic did not go away.

In the light thrown out by the heater, she saw Wilson creeping across the attic, trying to be quiet but obviously also attempting to move quickly. The trapdoor was open, the white-painted underside catching the meager light.

Wilson climbed down the ladder without looking back. Stella stood and glanced around quickly. Everyone else seemed to be asleep, even Beau, the self-appointed guardian of the trapdoor. Maybe Wilson was just going to the bathroom . . . but then she looked across and saw that Isaac was missing as well, and her blood ran cold.

She hurried to the trapdoor and started down.

"Dad!" she heard Wilson whisper. It was coming from the staircase.

"I'm walking to Wainwright. I went there as a boy. It'll be warmer there," the old man answered from the ground floor. He made no attempt to keep his voice down.

Stella jumped the last couple of steps and hurried to the staircase. Wilson was standing halfway down, and when he heard her he glanced back, desperation in his eyes.

"Wilson? I said I'm going to Wainright."

"Eighty miles there, Mr. Bulosan," Stella said quietly. She descended the staircase and stood beside Wilson.

Isaac was at the front door, hand on one of the bolts. He didn't even look at Stella, let alone register her voice.

"Wilson! Come on, we need to get out! Bring your mother, too."

Stella moved past Wilson and grabbed Isaac in a gentle bear hug. "You need to keep quiet," she whispered, "otherwise they'll know we're here." He started to struggle, and for an old man he was stronger than she had expected.

He reached for the door again and one of his fingers flicked the bolt. Metal struck wood. Stella tugged him hard, stumbling back toward Wilson who seemed to be shocked motionless. "You go out there and we'll all die," she said into his ear, not unkindly.

"No. *No.* I'll die if I stay in here!" Isaac said, voice louder than ever.

Stella looked at Wilson, imploring him to help. And at last he seemed able to move again, darting for the struggling pair and holding his father's head between his hands.

"Dad—"

"Let me *out*!" Isaac almost shouted that time, and Stella clasped a hand over his mouth, expecting to be bitten at any moment.

"Dad, this can't help," Wilson said.

Isaac froze, then went limp in Stella's arms. He started to cry. Relieved though she was that he'd stopped shouting, she wasn't sure which sound she liked the least.

"I'm sorry," he whispered. "Jesus, just look at me. I'm sorry."

"It's all right, Dad. We're all . . ."

"Just stay quiet, Mr. Bulosan," Stella said. "We'll get you back upstairs where it's warm."

"Can I use the bathroom first?"

Stella let the old man go. "Use the one down here," she whispered. "But remember you can't flush. The noise. We'll just open the valve afterward."

"Where is it?"

Jesus, can't you smell it? she thought. "Over there." She pointed at the door beside the boarded glass window in the hallway.

Wilson guided his father to the door, opened it and then closed it again quietly. He slid down the wall, drained. His eyes were locked on Stella. *Expecting a reprimand?* she wondered. *Damn, he's doing his best by his father, trying to make sure the helpless old man isn't killed by those monstrous things, and right now he seems frightened of a few harsh words from me?*

"What are the odds we would make it this long?" she said. The words encouraged her as well as Wilson. "We're ahead of the curve."

He shrugged. "Every day they need more food. They'll be back. Just looking forward to the next blizzard. Getting out of here. Hey, you think Kelso will—"

They both heard the sound from the bathroom, a sliding, rasping noise. Wilson tapped on the door, barely a touch. "Dad?"

No answer. He turned back to Stella. "I think—"

She nudged him aside, pulled her driver's license from her pocket and slipped it between the bathroom door and frame. She played with it, sliding it up and down, hand always on the handle. It took maybe half a minute, but it felt like hours.

When she got the door unlocked, moonlight streamed through the open window. The bathroom was empty.

Wilson turned for the front door.

Stella grabbed his arm. "Wait! You can't just rush out there!"

"He's my *father!*" Wilson hissed.

"He'll get us all killed!"

Wilson shrugged and pulled loose, going for the bolts on the front door again. Stella grabbed for his sweater, got a handful, and then he spun around and punched her on the side of her head.

She went down, shocked and surprised and feeling the throb of pain already reaching down her jaw and into her neck. She tried to stand, but dizziness made her pause.

The door was hanging open. She was aware of that, but she still couldn't force herself to close it. *Slugged me a good one,* she thought, and for an instant she was back eating fish in Seattle. This time she knew that

Eben was beneath her table, and the knowledge was disquieting.

Then she saw Eben hurrying downstairs, the ax he'd used to kill John Riis swinging by his side. He went straight to the front door and pushed it shut.

"What happened?" he asked.

"Oh, I'm fine thanks." Stella sat up, head swimming.

"Where's Wilson?"

"Out there. Isaac took off, said he was walking to Wainwright." She stood and held on to Eben's arm. "Wilson slugged me one." She closed her eyes and leaned into Eben for a full minute, enjoying the closeness and welcoming his arm as it encircled her shoulders.

"Okay now?" he asked. She nodded.

Eben went to lock the front door when it started to open of its own accord.

Stella froze, but Eben was already moving, grabbing her arm and dragging her sideways into the bathroom Isaac had so recently vacated. He pushed the door closed, leaving a crack through which to see. He watched. Then his eyes opened wide.

Stella heard slow, heavy footsteps on the timber floor.

Eben glanced sideways at her, pointing. From the fear in his eyes, she knew what was out there. She had never seen him so scared.

He held out his left hand to warn her back and raised the ax in his right. His breathing was fast, shallow, harsh, and she almost wanted to nudge him and tell him to shut up. But then she remembered that he'd used the last of his inhaler days ago. *Not now,* she thought. *Don't have an attack now*. She saw his eyes close as he concentrated on controlling his breathing, then snap open again when something creaked outside.

It was an interior door opening. The cold had frozen condensation on its hinges, and ice crackled as the thing out there forced it.

Eben put his eye to the crack and glanced across at Stella. *Kitchen,* he mouthed.

Stella looked around. The window that Isaac had fled through was still open, the freezing air quickly filling the tight space of the bathroom, and she strained to hear any noises from outside as well as within. Isaac and Wilson had fled out there only before this thing came into the house. Perhaps they were dead already.

A sudden racket from beyond the bathroom door made her jump. Wood broke, metal things clashed and scattered to the floor. Eben leaned down and cupped his hand around her ear. "It's smashing up the kitchen."

"What do we do?" she whispered.

"Hope it goes." The bleakness in his voice, the simple statement that there *was* no hope unless the thing left, chilled her to the bone. Eben stood before her with an ax in one hand and the other now holding the pistol, but he was utterly terrified.

The noise from the kitchen ceased, and then she heard the creak of floorboards again. The footsteps came closer. Something sniffed, an animalistic sound like a dog snuffling at the ground. And then, more terrible than anything that had come before, a sound that can only have been a chuckle.

"Dad!" Wilson called, somewhere in the distance.

The thing outside grunted.

Eben pulled back from the door, pistol raised. Stella stood beside him, ready to fight with him if and when the moment came.

For a second or two, there was complete silence. And then Wilson called again, and with another grunt the thing burst back through the front door and crunched away across the snow.

Stella let out a held breath and stood on the bathtub edge, looking cautiously from the window. She saw something dark and fleeting disappear along the street—*so far, so quickly!*—and then there was silence once again.

"Fuck," Eben said. He sat down on the lowered toilet seat, holstered the pistol and lay the ax across his thighs. "Fuck."

"Wilson," Stella said. "Isaac." But she already knew.

"They're dead," Eben said.

"Maybe not. Maybe they're—"

"Isaac is probably stumbling about in the snow, maybe lying under a house if he's come to his senses. Wilson is out there shouting for him. Being careful, maybe. But calling. Unarmed. They're dead, Stella. There's nothing we can do for them, and I'm not going to take the same risk I took for Kirsten."

"Eben—"

"There are people here I have to look after," he said, then he looked up at her, his eyes haunted by dreams and ideas she could not comprehend. "Jake, and you."

They waited in the freezing cold of the bathroom for another five minutes. They did not hear Wilson calling again, nor any other noises. At least it seemed that theirs had been a quiet death, and hopefully quicker than the polar bear's.

As they left and Stella reached up to carefully close the window, she noticed that it had started to snow again. "Snow," she said.

Eben nodded. "Time to move."

Perhaps things were about to start going their way.

Eben helped Stella back up the ladder and closed the trapdoor. He made sure the blanket was thrown across it before nodding back at Lucy. She lit their lamp, illuminating concerned, frightened faces. Everyone was awake by now. And they all knew that something was wrong.

"Must've crept past me," Beau said. He was standing stiff and awkward across the trapdoor from Eben, clasping the shotgun as though he'd never let it go again.

"No one's to blame," Eben said.

"What happened to them?" Lucy asked.

"They're dead."

"You saw it?"

Eben shook his head.

"Then they might still be out there!" Jake said.

Eben sent him a withering look. "Keep your voice down! One was in the house—there's no guarantee it won't come back."

"Why did it leave?" Carter asked.

"It heard Wilson calling for his father," Stella said. "He sounded a street or two away. There's that, at least."

"There's also footprints in the snow," Eben said.

"Oh yes," Stella said, offering a smile which did nothing to melt the iciness of the attic. "It's started snowing."

Jake darted to the peephole and glanced out. "Coming down quite heavy."

"Then it's time to go," Beau said.

"No," Denise said, and even in one word Eben heard sanity slipping. "No, not now, not yet, I'm not ready, and we can't go unless I'm ready."

"None of us is ready," Eben said, unable to find the calming tone he sought.

"Stay close," Stella said to the frightened girl. "We're all in this together."

"So . . . so was Wilson and . . . and his father." Denise was sobbing now, and Eben was afraid her sobs would turn into wailing. It wouldn't take much. God knew it was a miracle nobody had gone insane before now. They all trod an icy edge, with sheer drops on either side. And he was doing his best to make sure they all kept their footing, because if one fell, everyone else would follow.

"I should have stopped him," Stella said quietly.

Eben leaned into her, forehead against forehead. "Hard to keep a guy from taking care of his own."

"Fuck!" Jake fell back from the peephole, pushing with his hands and feet to get away from the window as quickly as possible. "Quiet!" he hissed. "Quiet!" He looked to Eben, the terror evident in his eyes.

Beau knelt and trained the shotgun on the covered window, Eben drew the pistol, and then they heard the scratching sounds above them. Eben switched off the propane heater, the weak light filtering away to nothing.

"Everyone cover up," he whispered. They lay down, pulling blankets over themselves, struggling against fear and panic to keep still.

The scrabbling, scratching sound crossed the roof from front to back, then paused.

"What did you see?" Eben breathed to Jake.

His brother moved close enough for Eben to smell his breath. "Shadow from the roof. Moving." As if to confirm, the scratching noise began again, coming from two locations this time, then another. The three things moved back and forth across the roof and Eben thought, *Maybe they can smell us, we haven't washed properly for two weeks, or hear our heartbeats, or sense the heat from the heater . . .*

The survivors remained motionless for some time, listening to the scratching sounds moving back and forth across the roof, and at any second Eben expected the window to smash, the trapdoor to burst open, a hole to appear in the roof. There would be shooting and hacking with the ax, and then there would be screaming.

But if the creatures did know they were inside, they were biding their time. After a few minutes, the scratching noises stopped. Ten minutes later, Eben moved carefully to the peephole and looked outside.

It was snowing so heavily that he could barely see the far side of the street. Maybe there were things hiding close by, but even if there were, he wouldn't be able to spot them.

"Can't see anything," he whispered, and behind him someone started chuckling.

Eben spun around, hand going for his gun. But it was only Doug. The big man was sitting beside the cooling heater, shoulders shifting as the chuckles came from deep within his chest. They grew louder and his face broke into a helpless grin.

"Doug, what the fuck?" Eben's breath was light and pained, rasping in his throat.

Doug kept laughing.

Stella was by his side, hand flat against his chest. "Take it easy, Eben. No more inhaler. Do they have them in the store?"

Eben nodded. Doug's laughter grew louder. The others looked at him in alarm, and Beau moved forward until he was standing behind the seated man.

"Shhh," Denise hissed. Doug only laughed harder.

"Have you lost it?" Lucy said.

Eben shrugged Stella's hand from his chest and walked to Doug, grabbing him by the lapels of his jacket, lifting him up, smelling his sour body odor and stale breath as the man giggled in his face. He pulled

Doug close, almost pressing nose to nose. "What are you laughing at?" he asked.

Doug continued the hysterics, and he was crying now, maniacal tears that flowed freely.

"What the *fuck* are you laughing at?" Eben said, and he closed his eyes because he knew he was talking too loud. He let go and Doug fell to the floor, and when the big man continued laughing Eben fell on him, striking out and connecting one fist with his jaw.

"Shut up, shut up, *shut up*!" He pulled his hand back, ready to punch again, and Doug's laughter faded away like an echo.

Beau and Stella grabbed Eben's hand and pulled him to his feet. Beau's arm remained across Eben's chest, gentle but firm. "Too much noise," Beau said.

Doug stood. He was still crying, but they were different tears now. They diluted the thin dribble of blood at the corner of his mouth.

The others stared at Eben, shocked.

"I'm sorry," Doug said. "I . . . I just . . ."

Eben shook his head and looked down at his feet. *Damn it!*

"Eben, I'm sorry, I'll try to do better."

Eben could not look up. If he did, he wasn't sure what he'd do. His breathing was raspy and uneven, and the violence had already drained him.

"You all right?" Stella whispered.

"I will be." Eben looked around, meeting everyone's gaze and trying to let them know that he was still there.

He took a step toward Doug, and no one seemed to think he was going to strike out again. "Sorry, Doug," he said.

Doug nodded.

Eben looked at Beau, who was standing back at his station next to the trapdoor. "Beau?"

Beau nodded. "Time to blow this joint."

DAY 15

MARLOW STARED DOWN at the two humans. He had known that they and several others were hiding here for two days, and now it was time to let Iris take them.

The male had shot him. Pulled a pistol and put a round through Marlow's chest.

Marlow grinned as he ripped the gun from the man's hand. "You and your loyalty," he growled in the cattle's language. "Keeping your friends hidden? We'll find them, too. You were made for nothing but pain. And we are made only of hunger."

The man started to say something but Marlow ignored him. He lifted him easily with one hand, held him against the wall, picked up a poker from the fireplace and drove it through the human's chest. Its location approximated the wound in his own torso. Such poetic justice amused Marlow.

The man screamed, but the vampire grabbed his chin and turned his head to the woman on the floor. "Watch," he said. And then he nodded to Iris.

The female vampire closed in on the woman, held

her down and began snapping her fingers. One by one. And the woman screamed.

Marlow let go of the man's chin, because he knew that he would watch on his own now.

There was an old record player in the corner, a disc on its turntable, and Marlow delicately touched one of his claws to the grooves. The music he heard was a composition of agony, and blood.

They gathered around the heater, taking what comfort they could from the fading heat before they had to go out into the snow. They had raided the Kelsos' wardrobes and dressed as snugly as possible, and every one of them was armed with something from the kitchen—knives, scissors, corkscrew. Eben knew that nothing would do any good against those things, but if it made people feel better then that in itself could help. They needed confidence, not a sense of doom.

"We head to the store for food and supplies," he said. "Then if the storm holds out, we use it to cover us getting out to the Utilidor."

"You really think we can make it?" Doug said. Even now, there was still a hint of surliness to his voice. Eben did not bite.

"You can't see a foot out there. The whiteout will cover our tracks, if we leave now. Who knows what those things heard or sensed when they were on the roof? They could be on their way back with others."

"They knew we were here, they'd have come in on their own," Beau said.

Eben shook his head. "We can't take that chance. And maybe Wilson or Isaac . . ."

"They'd never tell," Lucy said.

"They might not have any choice." Eben tried not to think about what he'd seen happening to Kirsten. These things were capable of anything, extremes of torture he probably couldn't even imagine. And Isaac, God bless him, wasn't the most altogether person there was to begin with.

The others fell silent for a while, shocked perhaps, scared.

"How do we get into the Utilidor?" Carter said. "It's locked tight, and hell if I know where my keys are."

Eben frowned and sat back, mentally cursing himself for not thinking of that before.

"Great," Doug said. "We make it all the way out there, then freeze to death because we can't get inside."

"Haven't heard you come up with anything better," Denise said.

Doug simpered, glancing from one person to the next as if waiting for the next verbal attack.

Eben tried to ignore it all. They were tired, cranky, and scared. But Doug was right; they couldn't afford to go all the way out there, only to find—

Then he remembered his last trip there—which now seemed like it had been years earlier—checking out the ruined helicopter parts.

"Carter, that sewage pipe. The one the twins were fixing? Where does that lead?"

"Yeah!" Carter said. "It's shut off from the rest of the

town, and it'll lead straight underground and inside the plant."

"We crawl through a sewage pipe?" Lucy asked.

"Big enough to walk through," Carter said.

"And be glad you'll be alive to smell it," Eben added. "Now listen, once we're out there, *no stopping*. There's no fighting these things; we have to move. The only chance we have is to run and hide."

He looked from face to face, trying to project a confidence he did not feel. "Any questions?"

"Plenty," Jake said. Denise actually raised a chuckle.

Eben smiled grimly. "Okay then. Time to move."

They gathered in the darkened kitchen of the Kelso home, cupboards now bare and utility drawer stripped of everything sharp. The only source of light was Eben's flashlight. He used it sparingly, covering it with a square of torn wool to diminish the glow. At the back door, he shined it briefly at the lock as he worked with the heavy knife, prying the lock out of the wood with squeals of protesting screws. The damn door had been double-locked from the inside, and of course no key could be found.

"Too loud," Carter whispered.

"Still better than going out the front door," Eben heard Jake say. Good boy. He had a sense of survival about him. And for that Eben was glad.

The lock came away after a few minutes of careful destruction. Eben placed it on the countertop beside the door and clicked off the flashlight. "Few boards across the doorway," he said. "We'll push off just enough to get out, then replace them."

"Why bother?" Doug said, louder than Eben would have liked.

"They might think it was only Wilson and Isaac living here," Stella said. "If they even know where they came from. No need to advertise our existence."

Eben raised his ax in his right hand and pulled the door open with his left. A waft of windblown snow came in, but beyond the porch he could see little.

"Whiteout," he whispered. Then he turned to the others and repeated the word.

"Good," Carter said.

"Great," Beau said. "And I get the week off work."

Eben chortled, surprised that he could, and then he and Stella worked off a couple of the clumsily nailed boards across the door. Thankfully Kelso had used nails, not screws.

"You first," he said to Beau. Beau slipped through the door, shotgun raised, and moved sideways along the porch, keeping low. "Now everyone else."

They left the relative safety of the Kelso house—their home for more than two weeks—and ventured out into the blizzard.

It was a true whiteout. The wind howled around the backyard, whipping snow horizontally against their faces, into their eyes, up their nostrils. It seemed that however well they'd wrapped up, still the snow found its way through their defenses, melting cold against their skin. There was no order to the snowfall; it was a riot of white. When flakes did hit the ground, they were whipped up again, and drifts were quickly building against the wall of the house. Within an hour or two, the landscape of the town would be completely changed; walk-throughs blocked, roads impassable, roofs heavy with snow and creaking beneath the additional weight. And there, Eben knew, lay their advantage. Because he and the others had been here long enough to know the town, however it looked.

He led the way from the house, heading east toward the store. Behind him came Jake, Carter, Doug, Lucy, and Denise, then bringing up the rear were Beau and Stella, walking side by side. He glanced back every few seconds, just making out Beau's hulking shape through the storm, and the pressure he felt was massive. *I'm looking after them,* he kept thinking. *Forget the badge I'm still wearing, I've become their leader and protector. No pay raise. No danger money or special training. Nothing in my fucking contract that mentions vampires.* He smiled into the scarf he had tied around his face as a mask, still trying to keep his breathing calm. *Get to the store, a huge puff from an inhaler, feel loads better.*

They left the Kelsos' yard, crossed an area of open ground and then came up against the next house. Eben led them immediately into the crawl space, which was thankfully mostly free of snow and open all around. There was barely any light, but he risked using the flashlight in brief flashes to show their way.

Denise stumbled a few times and Carter helped

her along. Doug grumbled about the cold, the frozen ground on his hands and knees, the fucking pointlessness of what they were doing. But he did so quietly. Even in his arrogance, he had seemed to acknowledge how much danger they were all in out here in the open.

They found a body beneath one of the houses. Eben gasped when he nudged it. He couldn't identify who it was—the face had been ripped off—and the remains were frozen solid, almost inhuman. He told Jake and asked him to pass the news along the line, and they all crawled past the dead person. To begin with, Eben wanted to keep the flashlight turned off, but then he imagined Stella crawling past the body just as it started to move, turn, opening the ruined maw of its mouth. So he stayed beside the corpse and lit everyone's way, ax clasped in one hand.

As Beau and Stella passed, he considered taking the body's head from its shoulders. But he could not face it. So he turned and crawled back along the line, pausing at the edge of the crawl space and staring out into the whiteout.

In the distance, beyond the wind whistling around the eaves, they all heard the howls of things less natural.

Marlow could not help screeching, even though he knew it still scared Iris. Such fury, such rage, such power she was still not quite used to. But she was getting better.

He hated the snow . . .

It took his sight, hid the humans away . . .

So he screamed again.

Eben lost any concept of how much time had passed. They moved, hid, moved again, never seeing anything that offered a threat but feeling it all around. The howls continued, mostly in the distance. Eben didn't like them. They were angry and sounded as if they were on the warpath. But they came no closer, and if they were inspired by Wilson's and Isaac's certain capture, it seemed for now at least that the Kelso home was still safe.

But that did not lessen the danger of being caught.

When Eben realized they were passing directly in front of the store, the sense of relief was so intense that he slumped down into the snow. Jake knelt beside him and whispered in his ear. "We're there."

Eben nodded, and the two of them crawled up the steps to the store's front porch together.

They all gathered there, ready to open the door and go inside. The snow had blown up here as well, and Eben looked down at the tracks they had made on the boarded porch.

"Can't do anything about that," Stella said. "Few minutes and the wind will have blown it away."

He nodded. *Can't account for everything,* he thought. *There's far too much left to chance.*

"I want candy," Beau growled, and someone—Denise or Lucy—laughed.

Eben's breath was becoming raspier than ever, so he

said nothing in response. Stella's hand on his shoulder told him that she knew.

The store door was still unlocked. Beau went first once more, shotgun pointing ahead.

Once they were all inside, Eben leaned against the door to shut it against the wind. The sudden silence was heavenly. He watched from the window, not able to see much in the snowstorm and terrified that something would come snarling, drooling, snapping from the whiteout.

"Hey," Stella said. She was on his left, and Jake appeared on his right. "You got us here."

"Cool," Jake said.

"Fucking freezing," Eben said, the rasp in his voice surprising even him.

"Need to get your stuff."

He nodded. "Can't stay too long." He turned around to address the others. "Use the flashlights sparingly. We all know the layout of the store, so let's feel our way around. Beau, Lucy, Denise, Doug: you grab all the canned goods you can. Stella and Carter, propane and batteries. Jake: medical supplies. I'm getting axes and bear traps. You have two minutes. Let's go."

They split up and circulated around the store, not even Doug complaining at the tasks set. They had all heard the urgency in Eben's tone and the pain in his voice.

Jake grabbed Eben's hand and the two of them went left for two aisles, then right again to the medical shelves. Eben flicked on the flashlight and pointed it at the floor, and by its weak glow he saw the rack of boxed inhalers. Jake had already taken one and torn it from the packaging, and Eben grabbed it and puffed greedily. *Aahhh. Oh thank God.* He smiled at Jake, shoved several more into his pocket and went on, leaving his brother to gather more supplies.

All around the store he heard the rustling, knocks, and scrapes of people trying to keep quiet in the dark. He worked his way to the back, flicked the flashlight on briefly and picked up three bear traps and a couple of long-handled axes. *God knows what we'll end up doing with these,* he thought. The idea of preparing the Utilidor for a ten-day siege was not something he wanted to dwell on right then.

Denise, Beau, and Lucy were collecting a couple of cases of Ensure, while Doug stuffed his pockets with Oreos. He chuckled. "Told my wife I wouldn't live on these while she was gone."

"She'll cut you some slack," Denise said.

"Yeah." Doug ripped open one packet and shoved a couple into his mouth, chewing with an expression of delight on his face. In the weak reflected light from Denise's flashlight, it made him look almost devilish.

"We need to hurry," Lucy said.

And then they heard the sobbing.

All four of them paused in what they were doing, tilting their heads, listening, trying to make out where it was coming from. Lucy looked at Denise to make sure she hadn't started crying. Beau glanced at Doug, still not trusting him after his outburst in the attic. The sound was muffled, obviously weak, and it came from the rear of the store.

Beau was the first to move. He lifted his shotgun and edged toward the doors that led back into the storeroom. The others followed.

"Who can that be?" Denise whispered, but Lucy touched her arm and shook her head.

Beau pushed open the door with one foot, flicked on his flashlight and entered the storeroom. The walls were lined with shelves, many of them empty, and in one corner lay a pile of opened wrappers, empty water bottles, and the obvious glint of glass.

Closer, a whiskey bottle lay smashed across the floor, the smell permeating the air.

In the center of the room, her back to them, crouched a little girl, who looked like she was sobbing over the body of the man before her.

"That's Tommy Melanson," Denise said. "Oh honey, you need to come with . . ."

The girl turned, and the light glinted from the blood spread across her mouth, chin, and cheeks. Her eyes were black. Tommy Melanson was doing the real sobbing, and he whimpered again as the little girl spoke.

"I'm done playing with this one," she said matter-of-factly. She plunged the fingers of her left hand into the terrible wounds at his throat, placed her left foot against his chin and pushed.

His head ripped off with a terrible sound; tearing, the whoosh of air, a single groan.

The girl looked at them again. "You want to play with me now?"

Beau moved first. He raised the shotgun, but the girl lashed out with unnatural speed and knocked it from his hands. It skittered across the concrete floor and disappeared beneath one of the shelving stacks.

Denise and Doug backed away. Lucy stumbled over her own feet and went down. Doug reached for her flailing arm and pulled, her weight barely slowing him at all.

At the door, Doug leaned to one side and grabbed a shovel propped against the store wall.

The little girl giggled.

"In the back!" Denise called. Eben knew instantly that something was very wrong.

Should have checked the store.

He dropped the bear traps and brandished one long-handled ax.

Stupid of me!

Doug was dragging Lucy along the floor, and Eben couldn't make out whether or not she was hurt.

Where the fuck is Beau?

Beau appeared then, thrown violently back through the store doors to land in a pile against a cereal display. The boxes collapsed around him, and Eben saw the store doors opening again.

He ran forward and swung the ax at head height. But he'd never expected a kid.

The blade passed inches above her head and then she

was on him, spitting and growling and clawing at his coat, knocking him back, ax spinning from his hands as he brought them up to protect his neck. The girl's teeth were clacking together inches from his face. She dribbled blood.

Stella darted in from the left, grabbed the girl from Eben's chest and used her momentum to turn and fling her away down an aisle.

Several flashlights were dropped, casting beams of light here and there like searchlights. Eben saw Doug and Denise rushing away along an aisle, heading for the front door. "Don't go out!" he tried to shout, but the breath had been knocked from him and it came as a whisper. *It's all falling apart,* he thought.

The girl was already back on her feet, but Carter came in from a side aisle brandishing a flashlight and a bottle of something in his other hand. The girl hissed at the sudden glare in her eyes, and Carter sprayed bleach into her face.

She shrieked, spat, and lunged for Carter, but he side-stepped her hands and stumbled back toward Eben.

Eben plucked the pistol from his holster and aimed, but then thought of the noise the shot would make. The door was shut, yes, and the wind and snow outside would camouflage the shot from a ways away . . . but if more of those things were close, they would home in on it like moths to a flame.

"Help me!" Carter screamed as the girl jumped and ripped off his cap and hood. He sprayed more, but she squinted and went for his face.

Eben swatted her across the head with his revolver. Her cheek and nose opened up, gushing black blood, and she hissed, turning on him. He threw the pistol back at Carter and grabbed the girl's upper arms, pushing her back against the shelves, leaning back so that he avoided her gnashing teeth as she lunged at him again and again. Her feet kicked for his gut and groin and he turned sideways, taking the impacts on his hip and thigh.

"Fuck's sake!" he said. He looked around desperately. Beau was still on the floor, stirring and holding his head. Lucy, Denise, and Doug were nowhere to be seen. Stella was trying to stop Carter from firing the pistol. "The ax!" he said. "Somebody!"

The girl was wriggling like a snake, amazingly strong for a child so small, spitting blood and doing her very, very best to open the veins on Eben's neck and drink from him. "She's getting loose, someone hurry and—"

The ax blade flashed past his face and buried itself deep in the girl's head. The sound was horrible, the sudden silence even worse.

Eben dropped the still twitching body and turned to see who had saved him.

Jake stood frozen in the fading beam of a flashlight, hands still fisted even though he no longer held the ax. He was staring at the body of the girl as though nothing else existed.

Eben went to his brother and held him, turning so that Jake no longer had to see the corpse. "Hey," he said, feeling the boy beginning to shake. Glancing up he saw Doug, Lucy, and Denise appear at the end of the aisle, close to the front window.

"Where the hell were you?" he said, bristling at the fact they had run instead of helping.

Doug looked uncomfortable. "I thought we should start off with the food in case you . . ." He glanced at the girl's corpse, his meaning obvious. *In case you lost.*

"She's just a girl," Jake whispered in Eben's ear, and such pain in the voice of someone so young almost broke his heart.

"Not anymore," Stella said. She hugged both Eben and Jake, and together they felt like a family.

A few minutes later, Eben stood at the rear of the store, recovering the bear traps and axes he'd dropped. None of them wanted to retrieve the ax from the girl's skull.

No one had said very much since it happened. Jake was with Stella, holding hands and shivering. Beau had told him what a good job he'd done, saving his brother like that, and the boy seemed in control. *Stronger than I've ever given him credit for,* Eben thought. But the brutality of what had happened would surely leave yet another scar.

Carter emerged from the storeroom to face them, scarf wrapped around his head where the girl's nails had scratched him. "It pulled Tom's head off before it attacked us," he said, shocked.

"I saw," Beau said. "Looked very intentional, like maybe she was teasing us."

"Or maybe it's not all out of bloodthirst," Stella said.

Beau nodded. "Right. Could be . . . they want to keep their numbers down? Don't want to . . . 'turn' anyone else into one of them? Don't want to make competition for themselves? I don't know."

"Who was she?" Denise asked. "Some girl they just turned—or one of them? Does anybody recognize her?"

They all shook their heads; no one recognized her. "She was one of theirs," Jake breathed, and Eben was glad at the relief in his voice.

"It. Not her," Eben said.

Lucy trotted from the front of the store. "The white-out's over."

Eben closed his eyes and sighed. And yet again he thought, *It's all falling apart.*

"This is bad," Eben whispered to himself. He was so close to the glass that his breath condensed there, freezing almost as soon as it touched. He backed away, cursing his clumsiness. "Real bad."

Outside, the air was almost free of snow. It was clear and crisp, and Eben could see wisps of errant clouds drifting away to the east. Barrow was a whole new place again, given fresh contours and landscape by the windblown snow. He recognized some of the stores across the road purely by instinct, but some of the drifts blown against buildings were huge, and the road itself had vanished beneath an even white blanket. He reckoned it was a foot deep, at least. And as for the paths and spaces between buildings . . . some of those now seemed impassable. The survivors knew the town well, yes. But they also knew that its geography was subject to constant change.

"We need to decide what to do," Stella said. She'd appeared at his side without him hearing, and his heart leapt.

He smiled grimly. "Don't see what we *can* do if it stays like this."

"Doesn't mean we can't talk about it." She squeezed his arm and turned to go deeper into the store.

"How's Jake?" Eben asked.

Stella turned, and he saw the dreadful pity in her eyes. She was almost crying. "I really don't know, Eben. He's strong, and he saved your life. For now that's enough. But do you think he'll ever be free of that little girl's face?"

"She wasn't a girl," he said, but it sounded weak and hopeless.

"We don't know what she was."

He sighed. And when Stella turned to walk away he called her back one more time. "Stella?"

She turned, head cocked awaiting the next question.

"Glad you're here."

For a second her expression didn't change, and then she burst out laughing. "I'm not!"

Eben laughed with her, and together they walked to the rear of the store.

The others were already there, huddled behind a bank of shelving where they would be invisible from the front door and window. There were better hiding places, but they were tainted now by death. This would do.

There was a low-level mumbling that stopped as soon as Eben and Stella approached.

"It's bad, isn't it?" asked Carter.

Eben nodded. "Not a flake in the sky. Must have stopped in a matter of minutes."

"It's a blessing we were inside when it stopped," Stella said, and Eben thought, *Good girl. Keep them positive.*

"So what the hell do we do now?" Doug said. "Sit here and play with ourselves?"

"A charming image," Denise muttered. Doug glared at her, but the young woman was staring at her hand, as though still holding her useless mobile phone. Eben noticed that her thumb was even moving, sending an impossible text to someone unknown. *Perhaps this is how some pray to God,* he thought.

"Eben?" Beau asked.

Eben and Stella sat down among them. Eben didn't like them all looking up at him—made him feel too responsible. And he felt bad enough as it was. He took another puff from his inhaler, glanced around at them all as they watched him, then closed his eyes and breathed evenly for a few seconds.

"First," he said, "I'm sure they'll be watching the store, if not all the time then at frequent intervals. We can't afford to get trapped in here. And maybe they'll start to wonder where the one we killed is."

"The girl?" Doug asked, and Eben could have punched him dead center in his fat mug.

"The thing," Jake answered. He stared at Eben, who offered his brother a brief smile that meant so much.

"Utilidor's too far without cover," Beau said.

"Yeah," Eben agreed. "Too much open ground."

There was silence for a second or two, then Carter spoke up. "Could we make it back to your station if somebody created a diversion?"

"When you say someone . . . ?" Eben started, already knowing his old friend was making the offer.

"What sort of diversion?" Lucy asked.

Carter frowned, seeming to concentrate on something that wouldn't come. He worried at the bandage around his head, rubbing his scratches through the material.

We're lost here, Eben thought. *None of us can think of a thing*. "We could set fire to a building," he said.

Carter shrugged. "Could draw a few of them."

"One of us running in the opposite direction?" Doug said.

"You volunteering?" Eben asked, biting his tongue too late.

"Well . . ." Doug said, his bulky frame shaking in consternation. "Just a fucking idea."

"Hey," Stella said. Her voice was quiet, but it held a note of excitement that urged them all to look at her. "These things can't survive the sun, right?"

Doug held up his hands. "How do we know that?"

"Well, they're . . . vampires." The word seemed to stick in Stella's mouth, but no one even smiled when she spoke it.

"Just because something stopped Bela Lugosi doesn't mean it'll stop these things," Beau said. "We don't know the rules."

Stella persisted. "So why would they use that Stranger to cut us off for the duration of the Dark, unless it's the only time they can feed? We're isolated here, sure, so why choose now instead of any other time?"

"Okay," Eben said, "but even if that's true, how does it help us?"

"What if we brought the sun early?" Stella glared at him, urging him to see. He didn't.

"Like how, exactly?" Denise said.

Stella smiled. "Helen had that medicinal marijuana operation at home."

"Yeah!" Jake said. "And she used an ultraviolet lamp to grow the stuff!"

Stella nodded. "I can run for her place, let them follow me, then fry them with the sunlamp while the rest of you beat it to the Sheriff's station."

They sat in stunned silence for a few seconds, until Eben broke it. "Simple," he said. "And it might just work. But I can run faster."

"What if it *doesn't* work?" Jake asked, suddenly losing his enthusiasm for the idea.

"Insanity," Denise said, not even looking up from her hand.

Doug looked back and forth, Carter sat with his eyes closed, and Beau nursed his shotgun and stared at Stella.

"It *has* to work," Stella said. "There's no other way of

thinking." She tapped a couple of gas canisters leaning against the wall behind her. "Eben, take these with you when—"

"I can run faster," Eben said again.

"Bullshit," Jake said. "I weigh less than you, and I know Grandma's house better than either of you."

"No fucking way," Eben said, glancing across at his brother. "Not after this. Not after today. You're fifteen. Forget it."

Jake stood, a young boy towering over his older brother. "I'm fifteen, right. You've got a wife, Eben. And people who need you to help them out of here."

Eben stood as well and leaned in close. He could smell the fear on his brother's breath, and see his own reflected in Jake's eyes. "I saw you with that ax," he whispered, and everyone could hear. "Saw what it did to that thing's head. You think you're up to doing that three or four more times?"

Jake glared back at him but the strength in his eyes was gone. It broke Eben's heart, but gladdened it as well to save his brother from so much risk.

"You don't even think this plan'll work," Stella said. "Do you, Eben?"

"But you do, right?"

Stella opened her mouth, could not speak, and nodded instead.

Eben smiled. "Look, who's the Sheriff here, and who's the desk-jockey bureaucrat from Anchorage? I'm making the run, and I'll see you at the station."

Stella could not find it in herself to smile, but she

handed Eben the walkie-talkie. "You'll need to start her jenny first," she said.

"It's in her side yard by the woodpile," Jake said. "Then head in the back door; the pot's growing in the laundry room."

"See you soon," Stella said, and there was an urgency in her voice that made him want to hold her. But all eyes were on them. And somehow, holding her would feel too much like saying good-bye.

Eben stood at the store's front door for a few heartbeats, and every second that went by made it harder to leave. He didn't turn around to speak to anyone, though he felt their eyes on his back. He just surveyed the scene before him, lit by moon- and starlight so that it was almost bright enough to read.

Hardly any cover.

A whole new landscape.

He hefted the ax in his hand, stepped forward and let the door swing shut behind him.

He was out now, exposed, and he scanned the rooftops for signs of movement. There was nothing, but as his gaze passed across the shadows, he wondered whether those things were motionless in there, watching him and wondering what he was doing. If so, he couldn't give them any hints that there were others in the store. No backward glances, no muttered prayers.

From now on, there was only him and the snow.

Eben moved off quickly. To begin with, he considered heading along the middle of the street, giving the vampires plenty of opportunity to spot and follow him. But he had to grace them with some intelligence; they would know that he was revealing his whereabouts on purpose. So he kept to the shadows, working his way along the footpaths across the fronts of the buildings, and here and there he grunted or knocked the ax against a canopy support post. Many of the paths had been smothered with snow, and where he could not go through he went around. He passed a humped shape that could only have been a car, tattered black metal showing through. It had burned recently enough to have retained adequate heat to ward off the worst of the snow.

He thought about looking inside, but he knew he wouldn't like anything he found.

Eben wanted to be noticed, but he didn't want to be attacked. Not yet. Losing himself to these things out here in the snow would doom Jake, Stella, and the others when they finally broke cover. *We didn't talk about how long they should wait,* he thought. *We didn't plan nearly enough.* A sense of desperation pressed down on him, crushing him onward against a terrible feeling of hopelessness.

He knew the way, even through the landscape altered by the blizzard. But things felt different here now. Barrow had changed. It was a dead place haunted by survivors, rather than a living place haunted by the dead. He wondered whether the town would ever be a good place again.

• • •

Helen's house was small and unassuming, one of a dozen on her street that looked almost identical. There were a few aesthetic differences, but not many. Barrowites rarely stamped their personality on the outsides of their homes, because the harsh climate was always too eager to tear it away again. But Eben recognized the half-fallen fence that separated his grandmother's backyard from the house next door. And he also knew the curtains that wafted, impaled, around the broken front window.

They could have gone in, he thought. *Who knows what pot means to them? Maybe they enjoy smoking it. Maybe they smelled it and tore it all up, smashed up the place afterwards, and they* must *have heard me or seen me by now, must have.*

He hung back from the house for a few seconds, looking behind him at the snowbound road, then up at the shadowy rooftops. He could see nothing, but he had a definite sense now of being watched. *Maybe just because I'm expecting it so much,* he thought, but his skin crawled and the hairs on the back of his neck bristled.

Eben darted into Helen's yard, glancing constantly at the house in case one of those things was already inside. He tucked the ax into his belt and lifted the lid on the generator cover, sighing with relief when he saw that it was still in one piece. *And why would they smash it up?* he thought. *They've killed most of Barrow, why smash the place up?*

But such questions humanized these things. Perhaps they needed no reason.

He shook his head, looked around again and then

pressed the starter button on the generator. Wincing against the expected noise. Shoulders slumping when nothing happened.

"No," Eben whispered. He felt whatever was watching him coming closer. Maybe he smelled or heard it, or sensed it with some other animal instinct long since faded in humans.

He checked the fuel level of the generator: fine. He primed the starter motor, turned the valve to give it more fuel, and pressed the button again.

A scrape, a chug, a roar and the generator whirred to life. The sound was almost painful against the snow-dampened silence, and Eben backed away from the generator as it puffed diesel fumes into the still night air. He plucked the ax from his belt and went for the back door.

It was locked. He shoved it with his shoulder, almost grinned at his caution and then kicked at the handle. It took three loud impacts of his foot against timber before it gave and the stop splintered, door smashing open against the wall. He clicked on his flashlight, hurried inside and pushed the door closed behind him, not bothering with the lock. *No point,* he thought. *Want them inside anyway.*

His breath suddenly started coming in short, raspy gasps, and as he paused to dig the inhaler from his pocket, he thought he heard something outside.

A howl, perhaps. Or maybe just the metal workings of the generator getting used to each other again.

He moved through to the laundry room. The plants

were laid out in a dozen trays, all of them wilted and dead now, and it was a sudden stark reminder of Helen's murder. He thought of her face, her strength, her quiet laugh. The cancer was taking her anyway, she had made no secret of that. Even though she was fighting her hardest, she had always told him that it would get her in the end. But at least there was some dignity in that. It was a cruel disease, but Helen had been using all her strength and will against it. These things, though . . . there had been no defense, and no fight.

Eben felt overcome with a wave of sadness. And then anger.

"Fuckers," he whispered.

A long, bulky ultraviolet lamp hung above the trays, and the last person to have touched this was Helen.

"You fuckers." He rested his finger against the on/off switch and thought of her touching it, giving light and life to the plants that would help ease the agony of her disease. She had been a very proud woman, stalwart and unfussy. They had ripped her apart. Jake had started talking a few times about what he'd seen in the station—the things coming in and going at Helen—but he had never been able to finish. Eben suspected that it was something the boy would never get over, whether he buried it or blurted it out. Some things cannot be forgotten, and some things shouldn't.

"For you, Helen," Eben said, and he closed his eyes and flicked on the light. Even through closed eyelids the illumination was harsh and oh so welcome. He smiled, opening his eyes slightly, and he swore that he'd never take light for granted again.

The light flooded the laundry room. Eben breathed in deeply, catching just a hint of the dead plants' scent. If this light could no longer aid Helen's pain relief, perhaps it could mete out pain in revenge.

It took longer than he thought before they came in.

Eben turned off the lamp after a couple of minutes, switched on the flashlight and propped it on one of the trays of dead plants. It threw his shadow against the curtained window, and he moved left and right as if tending the plants. He did not go out of his way to make noise, but neither was he purposely quiet.

They must *have followed me,* he thought several times as the minutes ticked by. He turned the light on again, let it glare for a few seconds and then turned it off.

Maybe they're weak, he thought. *Maybe most of them have gone.*

And then he heard a thump from outside, like something heavy dropping into the snow.

He held his breath and froze, exhaling slowly so that his hearing was at its best.

Something creaked elsewhere in the house. Perhaps it had been upstairs, though he wasn't sure. He thought of his grandmother's house, quickly doing a mental walk-through of the upstairs: stairs, landing, main bedroom, spare room, bathroom. There were a few places where he knew there were creaks, and one of them—

A door slammed. It was farther away than the door he had entered through, probably at the front of the house. Whatever had come in would be several seconds away, he could hear its feet now, hear a rattle as what sounded like claws scratched at the timber floor with every footfall.

Bits of Helen beneath those claws, he thought, and he hefted the cumbersome lamp and aimed it at the laundry room door.

The footfalls stopped. *Just outside the door.* Eben tried to calm his breathing but it was raspy again, the tension and fear bringing on another bout of asthma. *It's just outside the door, and now I know what a condemned man feels when he's facing the gallows.*

The flashlight beam flickered, making shadows of the dead plants dance against the wall.

Seconds left to live . . . he thought. And in those seconds—before the door smashed open and night poured into the room to take him—Eben thought of so many things he had left unsaid.

She waited for ten minutes after Eben left. Every one of those minutes, Stella lived in fear of hearing the animals shriek of something attacking in the distance; howls, growls, the raw ripping of tender flesh. And every minute that went by without those sounds coming made her think that their plan really could work.

If the creatures followed Eben . . . if they took the bait.

After ten minutes, she decided that the time had

come to move. She turned to the people gathered behind her, all of them carrying food supplies, medicine, or weapons. Jake and Carter were at the front, Doug, Denise, and Lucy behind them, and a few steps to the rear, Beau nursed his shotgun and stared at her. She caught his eyes and nodded grimly, and he raised the shotgun higher.

"Fast," she said. "And quiet. Eben may have drawn some of them, but probably not all."

"Stupid fucking plan," Doug said, and Stella glared at him.

"Eben's run out there to save your sorry skin, Doug," she said. "Don't let me think you're not grateful, not for a second."

"Let's go," Jake said. "I never see this store again, it'll be too soon."

They went. Beau came to the front, eased the door open and stepped outside. He looked around for a few seconds, then turned and nodded.

Stella held the door open as the others dashed past her and headed left, passing between the high snowbank beside the road and the store's façade. Doug was last to leave, arms hugging several bags of food to his chest, and Stella closed the door quietly and followed him.

"It's like daylight out here," he said.

Stella leaned forward and nudged him between the shoulder blades with the head of the ax. He turned, she stepped closer and pressed her mouth to his ear. "Shut the fuck up, or next time I'll swing."

Doug glared at her, anger and confusion vying on his face.

Stella nodded past him at where the others were moving ahead. They were silent, the only sound the soft crunch of their feet in the fresh snow. There was little they could do about that.

I don't want him between me and them, she thought. *I don't like being cut off from Jake.*

Doug sighed, nodded, and moved on, and before following, Stella glanced back over her shoulder in the direction Eben had taken. *Please God, he's okay,* she thought. But her faith was shaky at best, and the silent prayer felt hollow.

Stella followed after Doug. They moved well to begin with, keeping low and quiet. They kept a few paces between each other, and Stella found that a depressing indication of what they were all expecting to happen: if the person in front of them went down, they didn't want to be close enough for the creature to get them, too.

Doug was clumsy and noisy, breath wheezing, and every few seconds he glanced around as if expecting Stella to really bury the ax in his back.

She had decided days ago that Doug was not a survivor. Everyone else here had some sort of trait that served them well, whether it was Beau's independence, Denise's difficulty in believing what was happening, or Eben's raw courage. But Doug had nothing. He criticized every decision made, when he could come up with no better ideas himself. He displayed bluster and arrogance to cover his lack of courage and humility. There was no subtlety about him. Even now, walking through the snow and facing death any second, it seemed more as though he was on a forced march.

Stella felt like telling him that if she was going to kill him, she'd have done so days ago. But there, too, lay Doug's fault. If he really was afraid that there was a chance she'd do it, then he had a lot to learn about sticking together.

Beau led them past several houses, across a narrow street, through a couple of crawl spaces. Stella could taste the tension, but with every step they took there was also the sense that maybe they really were doing the right thing. If the vampires had seen them, surely they would have struck by now? Out in the open when they crossed the road, perhaps, or on the snowed-in walkway before they'd come under the houses.

Five minutes later they emerged from another crawl space and found themselves two blocks from the police station. *Damn,* she thought, *we might just make it.*

And then Doug stumbled and dropped his armful of food.

Bags split, cans rattled together, and the food buried itself in fresh snow.

Stella winced. *Could be worse.*

That was before Doug shouted, "Fuck it!"

Beau and the others spun around, the big driver half raising his shotgun before he saw what had irked Doug so much. He caught Stella's eye and she frowned, looking around to see who or what had heard Doug's curse.

Doug froze, turned slowly, eyebrows raised in a silent apology.

Stella looked at him and blinked.

The vampire slid from the roof of the house and fell on Doug.

The sudden burst of violence was stunning, devastating, and for a couple of seconds, Stella could not react. The creature was a blur of limbs and gnashing teeth, and the white they had been working through quickly turned red. Clothes tore, flesh ripped, bones cracked, and the growls of the attacker were countered only by the grunts of the attacked.

Stella tipped back and fell into the snow. The ax dropped from her hand and she felt for it frantically, unable to take her eyes from the gruesome, unbelievable scene before her.

The attack was so vicious that Doug had no chance to utter anything other than another grunt and a low, gentle whistle that could have been air escaping opened lungs.

Beau appeared beyond the flailing monster. He raised the shotgun, face calm but eyes wide, and Stella waved her hand at him. He saw her, she shook her head, and then he nodded understanding and backed quickly away.

Stella pushed herself up the snowbank behind her, quickly reaching its summit and tumbling back onto the more level snow on the road.

Now, she could only hear Doug's death.

She crouched low and ran for thirty paces. When she reached a cut-through she ducked inside, glancing quickly to the left and right before emerging onto the footpath. The others were already disappearing around a corner to her right, and to her left she saw Doug, splayed in the dark snow, his body only twitching now as the thing that had killed him buried its face in his neck and dined on his blood.

She weighed the ax in her hand and tried to fight down the guilt that had already hit her. *Should have tried to help,* she thought. Against all logic the idea remained as she ran after the others. *Should have tried to help.*

As she rounded the corner, the vampire that had killed Doug keened, a long, high sound that resembled nothing she had ever heard before.

Three minutes later, she tumbled through the front door of the police station. Beau eased it shut behind her, leaving it open an inch so that he could look out.

"Not safe here," he whispered.

"They'll think we've run. They won't believe we'll hide so close to where they got Doug."

"You can't know that."

She shook her head, panting from exertion and fear. "None of us know anything."

A series of howls rose up all across Barrow, answering the creature that had killed Doug or perhaps calling the others somewhere else.

Eben, Stella thought. And she reached into her pocket for the walkie-talkie.

• • •

The laundry room door and frame shattered, and even though Eben had been expecting it, he was shocked. One of the creatures simply flowed into the room, limbs and body seemingly floating on air, and it was almost on him before Eben clicked on the lamp.

The room flooded with light from the UV lamp, and the creature shrieked. It stopped instantly, crouching down to the floor as though to escape the light. Its hands—hooked and clawed—drew back to cover its eyes. It turned its head away and the shriek continued, rising into a piercing scream.

Eben smelled burning. *Good. Take that, fucker.* He glanced at the covered window and the shattered door, and then advanced a couple of steps toward the cowering beast. Smoke rose from its hair, face, and hands, and there was a sickly sizzling noise like bacon frying. He checked his balance and then kicked out, striking one of the thing's hands away from its face. It—*she*—looked at him, eyes filled with hate and hunger and an animalistic fury that made him quiver. Then its eyes misted, and as the eyelids closed, they ruptured and steamed away on its charred face.

Eben backed away, panting hard, wheezing, startled by the devastating effect of the light.

There was movement at the door and another shape came into the room. It reached for the cowering, smoking creature and pulled, hauling it—*Her? Can I call it her?*—from the room.

Eben's hand slipped on the light and knocked it off,

returning the room to the subdued light from his flashlight, and the thing in the doorway paused.

It was tall, bald, brutal, and yet exuding control and composure, the same alpha male vampire he had seen taunting Kirsten Toomey. And it was intelligent. He could see that in its eyes, stance, and stare. These things did not hunt and kill on instinct; everything they did was calculated.

It looked at him. Marking him. Hating him.

Eben switched the UV lamp back on and aimed it at the door, but the thing was gone, dragging its screaming companion with it.

A door slammed, snow crunched, and Eben risked lifting a corner of the window curtain. The tall vampire was out there, looking down at the thing huddled at his feet in the snow. Ice seemed to bring it no comfort; smoke rose in the moonlight, and the injured vampire twisted and writhed in agony, as though the light were still scorching into its flesh.

The tall creature bent down and gently touched its face. It grew still for a moment, and Eben strained to hear a guttural, deep rumble that must have been talking. There was a tenderness in its voice, and he hated hearing that. It touched the wounded vampire's face and ran its nails gently over the bubbled skin, and he despised seeing that as well. It gave them a compassion which he could not afford to believe in.

The tall vampire then clasped the injured creature's head and ripped it from its shoulders.

It turned and looked at the window, seeming to know that Eben watched. Then it snarled, mouth going wide to display a range of teeth that would have put a shark to shame.

Eben was frozen by both fear and fascination, hardly believing what he was seeing. The tall thing placed the head gently beside the motionless body, never taking its eyes from Helen's house, and when several more shadows appeared, it hissed at them, pointing directly at the window.

Eben ripped the curtain aside, placed the long lamp against the glass and turned it on.

There were more hisses and growls, but nothing like the scream from that first creature. He tried to see past the lamp but reflected light hid his view. And then he heard the sound of wood splintering. As he backed away from the window, nudging a trestle table covered with Helen's dead plants, the lamp flickered.

Eben's walkie-talkie suddenly clicked into life. *"Eben, we're safe."* Stella, quick and quiet in case the noise would give him away.

Eben dropped the lamp just as it went out for good. He lifted the walkie-talkie. "That's good. The lamp worked, but they've just trashed the generator. I'm making a run for it." He turned, fled the laundry room, and sprinted for the front of the house.

"I'm making a run for it," Eben said, and then he went quiet.

Oh Jesus, no! Stella looked around at the others. Denise had closed her eyes, Lucy turned away, and Carter shook his head. "He's not dead yet," Stella whispered, but it felt so unconvincing.

"Damn right he ain't." Beau reached for the walkie-talkie and Stella handed it over, seeing the determination in his eyes.

The big man clicked the button and spoke. "I'll give you a shot, Sheriff. Break out and tear for Rogers Avenue. Run for where the trencher's parked up."

"Brakes are jammed on that thing," Eben returned, voice jumpy and low, obviously running and trying to stay quiet at the same time.

"What I've got in mind don't need brakes. Just go." He clicked off and Eben did not reply.

"Beau?" Stella said.

"He don't have much time," Beau said. He grabbed a couple of bear traps, tucked his shotgun beneath one arm, and headed for the door.

"Beau, what are you doing?"

He shrugged. "Got a plan. Eben's done his bit as decoy, and he's needed here more'n I am." He smiled, his face unused to the expression. "I'm going out to get him."

"What can you do to help?" Carter asked.

"More out there than I'm doing in here. Don't worry, I don't aim on dyin' *just* yet."

Stella nodded, wanting to say *thanks* but not really knowing how.

Beau waited by the front door for a beat, glanced back, and then disappeared out into the moonlit night.

• • •

Eben ran. It was all there was to do.

He still carried the ax, but in the light of what he had seen—the tall vampire twisting its companion's head from its shoulders, those eyes, those *teeth*—it felt like wielding a wooden spoon to defend against a polar bear. There would be no standing and fighting, not here and now. Later perhaps, if there *was* a later and if it really was the final alternative. But while he still had breath, he could run, and while he could run, he could hide. And there, perhaps, lay hope.

He burst from Helen's front door and went straight across the street, climbing the snowbanks and plunging into the darkness between the two houses facing hers. Every second, every step he expected a shadow to come alive and fall upon him. The effort it took to run instead of curl up into a terrified ball was immense, but it was also strangely thrilling as well. *Just discovered a new extreme sport,* he thought.

As he passed between the two houses, he heard the destruction coming from Helen's home. The vampires were breaking in and through the building, searching for him, perhaps sniffing out his trail. Once they realized that he had not gone to ground, they would be after him. A heartbeat, maybe a few seconds and then they would come, and he was still several blocks from Rogers Avenue.

He remembered that the house on his left had kept dogs, and he shouldered their yard gate open. The dogs weren't in their outdoor kennel *(dead, they were probably all dead),* but he ran through their compound, kicking up the snow there in an effort to mask his odor with theirs. He exited the rear of the yard and crossed a lane, climbing across the tops of several parked trucks, leaping a walkway, scrambling over a fence, and rolling to a stop against a nearby shed.

He took a quick puff from his inhaler, then scurried across the yard and entered the crawl space beneath the house.

There were no sounds of pursuit, but that could be bad as well as good. Silence could mean that they had lost him; it could also mean that they knew exactly where he was and were stalking him, like cats toying with a mouse, or vampires playing with a bear. The image did nothing to calm his nerves.

Rogers Avenue, he thought. *Whatever you've got in mind, Beau, I hope it's good.*

Eben ran on, moving as quickly and cautiously as he could. No point in creeping, no point in hiding. They *knew* he was out here and they'd search until they found him. Rogers Avenue, that's all he had now. That and Stella and Jake, the two people he loved more than life itself. They kept him going. Jake swinging that ax and becoming a man, and Stella . . . Stella leaving. All the quarrels, all those arguments, and right now, as he ran for his life through the snow, Eben could not recall what many of them had been about. Kids, yes, that was the big one; their difference of opinion about becoming parents. But really, much of what drove Stella away had been more trivial than that. Small things which they had both exaggerated into major arguments. Minor transgressions of the ever stricter rules by which they had been conducting their relationship. All so pointless, all so foolish in the light of real life. Or real death.

He saw a sign for Rogers Avenue and followed the arrow, crossing the road and hiding for a moment behind a snowbank. Some places he trod virgin snow, but here and there he'd crossed sets of footprints. He couldn't tell who or what had made them, but he clung to the hope that there were other survivors still hiding out here as well.

Maybe they were watching him even now, pitying him and waiting for the kill.

He turned left at the next intersection, and after a dozen steps he changed his mind and turned back. *Where the fuck is Rogers Avenue?* Back at the intersection he went straight on, crossing the road quickly and slipping over the snowbank, following a walkway that led past a couple of shops. They'd had their windows smashed and contents strewn over the pavement, but the recent snowfall had hidden most of it. He walked on carefully; a broken ankle now would be fate laughing at him.

He paused before the next house and looked around. Taking a puff on his inhaler again, knowing he was using too much, Eben felt a rising sense of panic.

In his own town, he suddenly felt lost. He'd been here for a long time, but looking across the street he could not place the house he was staring at. He *recog-*

nized it, but could not *place* it. It could be to the east of Rogers Avenue or the west, he just wasn't sure.

Not a damn tree in sight, Stella had said the first time she came to Barrow. *Who the hell named it an avenue?* And as if conjured by his increasingly desperate thoughts, Stella's voice crackled through on the walkie-talkie.

"Eben, where are you?"

"You know," he answered, "I haven't got a fucking clue."

"Beau's out there somewhere, I don't know what—"

"I can't come back," Eben said quietly. "They might be following me."

"Are they?" Stella asked, and even over the walkie-talkie Eben could hear the tension in her voice.

"Don't know," Eben said. "Maybe. It's quiet. Not calling to each other. Maybe they all know where I am and they're just waiting."

"Eben . . ."

"Stella, there's so much—" Something grumbled in the distance, a low, meaty growl coming from Eben's left. "Hang on," he whispered. He lay against the snowbank, staring over its top into the street beyond.

There they were, gathered at the intersection, seven of them, and the tall one from Helen's house was there. It was staring directly at Eben.

Eben slid the walkie-talkie into his pocket and grabbed his ax. He guessed the running was over. Now, sooner than he thought, was the time to stand and fight. *Stella,* he thought. *So much more I wanted to say. We'd hardly even begun.*

And then the growl he'd heard rose and turned into a roar.

The huge trencher burst out from between two buildings, scattering shards of wood and chunks of ice, and thumped down onto the intersection. Beau was at the wheel. Eben was sure he was grinning.

The chain saw on its extendable arm was whirring, a silvery blur in the moonlight, and Beau revved the motor and skidded the trencher into a sideways slide. The chain saw caught one of the vampires across the chest and ripped right through. Blood, bone, and meat sprayed through the air, and for a second the moon was red.

"Holy fuck," Eben muttered.

"Who's next?!" he heard Beau roar. Vampires howled and raged, and Beau's sudden laughter seemed to spur them on even more.

For a second, Eben was torn. He could go to help Beau . . . but really, what help could he offer? One man with an ax? Or he could take advantage of the situation and do just what Beau obviously intended: *run*. And perhaps, with good luck and fate smiling at him, he could make it back to the station.

He took one more look at the battle taking place at the Rogers Avenue crossroads, then turned and fled.

Beau, he thought, *God bless you*. Eben thought the snow had started again, but then he realized that he was seeing Barrow through tears.

• • •

Beau turned the wheel and aimed at another vampire.

"Quick bastards," he muttered as the shadows slipped aside. He floored the gas and spun the wheel, skidding the trencher in a circle around the intersection, and the chain saw caught one of them across the arm. Blood misted the air again and the thing squealed. Beau laughed. "Like that?" he shouted. "Come here, I got plenty more!"

The feel of the trencher changed and Beau glanced into the rearview mirror. One of the things had leapt up onto the bed and was stalking quickly toward him, legs splayed and arms held out for balance. He nodded. Good. Let it come.

Beau turned the wheel with one hand and grabbed the shotgun across his waist with the other.

Just as the vampire behind him launched itself at the back window, it stepped in one of the bear traps he'd set. The jaws clamped around its leg—Beau heard the meaty *chunk* even in the cab—and the thing tumbled over the side of the vehicle, howling.

"Ha! Fuck face!" Beau slammed the trencher into reverse, gears grinding and objecting with a squeal, and then backed up. He felt it rise as one of the treads ran over the floored vampire, and he pressed on the gas. A shower of tattered clothing and flesh spewed across the snow in front of the vehicle, and the thing trapped beneath finally stopped screaming.

Beau glanced in the mirror again, saw other shapes jumping onto the truck's bed, and then in the distance behind them, he saw a shadow hurrying away between houses. Just a fleeting glimpse—one shadow moving to the next, barely touched by moonlight—but Beau knew who it was. He'd taken enough parking tickets from Eben to know how the Sheriff moved.

"Okay you shits, let's go for a ride." Beau aimed the trencher along Rogers Avenue and gave it some gas.

Two vampires jumped onto the hood, teeth bared and hands fisted as they punched at the windshield. Beau dropped the shotgun onto his lap and gripped the wheel, twisting left and right as far and fast as he could. The trencher fishtailed. The vampires held on, punching at the glass and starring it with their fists. A few more like that, Beau knew, and they'd be in. If only he still had brakes . . .

He turned the wheel again, farther this time, and one of the creatures slipped and tumbled forward, swinging on the chain saw arm and catching its leg in the spinning teeth. It shrieked as it disappeared from view, but Beau did not feel the vehicle run over this one. He looked in the mirror and saw it standing awkwardly, the snow around its feet turning red as one leg gushed blood. Then it launched itself at the trencher, climbing back up into the bed.

Other shapes swarmed over the truck now, and Beau heard the satisfying crack of another bear trap snapping shut.

He gave it more gas and careened around a corner, sliding across the road and impacting against a high snowbank. The seat belt strained against his chest and hip and he cringed, but smiled again when he saw several shapes skidding from the truck to land in the snow. He turned the wheel to the right and pressed the accelerator, spinning the truck and sending the chain saw slashing across the top of the snowbank. White turned red again.

"Yes! Welcome to Barrow, you ugly fucks. Top of the world!"

He accelerated along the street, feeling the weight of the truck changing as several vampires jumped aboard once more. The windshield shattered and a face leered in at him, long hair plastered across its cheeks by a splash of blood.

"Evenin'!" Beau said, and he thrust the shotgun against the thing's right eye and pulled the trigger. The vampire flipped back and disappeared from the hood.

Others were battering at the glass behind him now, and the bear traps were used up. He glanced in the mirror and saw the glass rupture. He leaned forward just quickly enough to avoid a swipe from a viciously clawed hand, rested the shotgun back across his shoulder, and fired. A creature screamed behind him, the truck jumped, and Beau swung the wheel left and right again. Some shadows fell, but others leapt to take their place.

The chain saw whirred in the moonlight, throwing silvery reflections across the shattered windshield.

Beau pumped the shotgun and fired at a head appearing above the front of the hood. Metal squealed and tore, the thing's face disappeared in a haze of blood, but then it rose again, long teeth glaring white in the mess of flesh and bone.

"Okay," Beau said. "Nearly there." He pumped the gun again, fired over his shoulder, and spun the wheel. "I'll show you how welcoming Barrow can be!" he shouted.

More shapes leapt at the trencher, hands and faces appeared at the shattered windshield, but Beau looked past them to make sure he was steering in the right direction.

He was. The Admiralty Bay Hotel loomed ahead, a place where he'd used to drink but which had banned him several years ago. Well, now he was back. And it was going to be carnage.

Beau leapt to the side, lying across the seat as the truck drove into the hotel. He felt the sudden jolt as it jumped the steps, then the crushing impact as it struck the main doors. He cried out at the noise of destruction around him—shattering glass, splintering wood, crushing masonry. Walls fell, ceilings caved in, and the smell of diesel and blood was sickeningly rich.

The truck came to a standstill. Beau looked up at the windshield. For a second he thought this was it—there were things stretching in for him, sharp things ready to cut and slice—but then he realized they were only broken boards and glass shards. He sat up slowly, picked up the shotgun and the box of flares he'd tucked beneath the seat and kicked the door open.

He slid from the truck, clambered over a pile of tattered floorboards and came to a stop leaning against the hotel's reception desk. He didn't waste time looking for the vampires . . . he knew they were there somewhere.

He pumped the shotgun, but it was empty. Figured.

A pile of broken timber erupted as two vampires stood, both battered and bloody. One of them had almost lost an arm to the chain saw, and the other's face was a mess of blood and broken bone. They both let loose with inhuman screams and showed him their teeth.

"Yeah?" Beau said. He growled back. His heart was beating fast, hands shaking as he opened the box and plucked out a flare.

More vampires emerged from the ruins, two of them dragging bear traps behind them. They looked like people, really, but my God they were so different. Beau couldn't hold back a laugh. "What the hell do you *look like?*" he said, and the monsters snarled at him. "Yeah, yeah, growl away," he said quietly.

He sighed. So this was it.

"Well fuck it, it's been a good life," he said as he lit the flare. "Come on."

They came.

Beau dropped the flare into the box.

Eben heard the explosion and immediately ducked into a shop doorway. He looked back the way he had come, witnessing the glow of fire above the town. "Beau," he whispered.

The only slight comfort he could find was the knowledge that maybe Beau had taken a few of those bastards with him.

Eben looked around cautiously for a minute, making sure none of the shadows moved. He could hear the roar of flames—it seemed to be coming from the hotel, so the inferno would have plenty of fuel—and the light from the fire threw darkness into sharper relief. The moonlight had been superseded. Exhausted, he felt that he could stay here for a while, slip into a sleep from which maybe he would not wake. That would be so easy. Let sweet dreams come to sweep away the nightmares he had lived and continued to live.

He closed his eyes, but the darkness was still there. *I'm so cold,* Eben thought, and it went deeper than the snow and ice.

He opened his eyes and bit his lip. The pain was not as stimulating as he'd hoped.

As certain as he could be that he had not been followed, Eben made his way to the station.

From outside it looked quiet and deserted. He hoped it was not. Eben went to the door and tried the handle, and of course it was locked. *Can't bang. They'll be watching, won't they?* He reached for the walkie-talkie, and then the door opened and Stella was there with Jake. They reached for him as he fell and caught him under the arms, hauling him inside silently and closing the door behind him, Stella watching from behind the blinds, Jake staring at her urgently until she turned around, shook her head and then looked down at Eben.

Stella, he tried to say, but he could not speak. He thought it instead, and with her name came a flood of warmth and love that he had not felt for a long, long time.

She was crying as she knelt down beside him. He sat up and reached for her, and their embrace was hard and painful. A good pain. One that made Eben feel alive, and as he crushed Stella tighter to him he knew that she was taking as much comfort from this as him.

"Come back and live with me in Barrow," he whispered.

"No fucking way," she answered, and they both laughed quietly as they cried.

After a minute Eben pulled back and looked at Stella. "Beau," he said.

She nodded sadly. "And Doug."

"Damn."

"But you're here because of Beau, and we're here because of you," Jake said. He was smiling, an expression that Eben liked on his brother's face.

"What're you grinning at?" Stella asked.

Jake looked from Eben to Stella and back again. "You make a nice couple."

"Watch it," Eben said, and Jake laughed and came to help him stand.

"Need to sort out the supplies," Stella said.

"Then get to the Utilidor," Eben added.

"The lamp worked?"

Eben nodded. "It did."

"Wow," Jake said. "We might make it yet."

Eben thought, *I've lived a lifetime this night already*. But he smiled and nodded, and together the three of them went through to the main office to join the others.

Marlow stood outside the burning hotel and watched the flames. It was as near to sunlight as he would ever see, and fire had always fascinated him.

Another shape stumbled out and rolled in the snow. It stood, shivering and hissing, and Marlow could not even recognize who it was.

He growled in disgust. "One man and he did this to you?" he said in his ancient language. The vampires around him—charred and wounded—knew better than to respond.

Marlow's own arm was slashed from where the chain saw had flashed at him. The bleeding had already ended, and he felt the maddening itch of knitting flesh. By the time this fire had burned out, the wound would be healed, but he always kept the scars. His scars were his history, and sometimes he looked at them and dreamed of older times, lost places.

Another shape stumbled from the ruins of the hotel, and even Marlow felt a moment of surprise. *Him!* The man fell down the shattered steps and lay groaning in the snow, steam rising from the charred flesh of his face and neck.

Marlow walked quickly to the downed man. He used the cattle's language again, simply because he liked to tease them before they died. Especially this one.

"When a man meets a force he can't destroy, he destroys himself instead." He placed his foot flat against the side of the dying man's head. "What a plague you are." He pushed. Hard.

As he turned and walked away, Marlow wiped his foot in the snow. "There's at least one other," he said. "Find him."

Lucy and Denise were sorting through the supplies they'd managed to bring with them. They looked up and broke into smiles as Eben entered, and Denise gave him a hug. She sobbed once, then managed to smile again.

"You're a sight for sore eyes," she said.

"If I look as bad as I feel, I don't believe that for an instant."

"Beau?" Lucy asked, but Eben could already hear the knowledge in her voice.

"He went a way of his own choosing," Eben said.

"We heard the explosion."

"I think it was the hotel. I saw him cut one of those things in half with the trencher. Heard his shotgun blasting away. Went on for at least five minutes." He shook his head, pressing his lips tight.

"Brave," Lucy said.

"He was," Eben said. "He was brave." He scanned

the room, then looked across at the cell. The Stranger had gone from the bars. "Where's *he?*"

"Dead," Stella said. "Head twisted almost off."

"So they came here again." Eben saw the blanket-covered shape on the cot in the cell.

Stella nodded. "I took him down. Wasn't nice to look at. Afraid we can't do much about the smell."

They've been here twice already, Eben thought. *Maybe we'll be safe here for a while. Maybe.*

"I think we should stay here for a bit," he said. "Eat, get strong."

"And wait for the snow again?" Jake asked.

Eben nodded. "For a while, yeah. But if it doesn't come in the next couple of days, I think we should make a go for the Utilidor anyway." He glanced across at Carter, huddled in the corner with his hood pulled up over his head. "Carter?"

"Asleep," Denise said. "That thing in the store really shook him up, I think."

"He's not the only one." Jake rooted absently through the goods laid out on Eben's old desk.

"They're monsters, Jake," Eben said. "I saw more of them out there, and I'm sure of that. They look human, but they're not. They've got the shape of people, but too many teeth for their mouths. Claws, talons. They're killing things, that's all. Sunlight burns them."

"Garlic and crosses?" Jake asked.

Eben shrugged. "Who knows? The stories must come from somewhere."

"I heard they can't cross running water either," Jake said, and Eben was glad his brother's mind was elsewhere again. Not dwelling on that girl-thing, the ax, her head . . .

"Does it matter?" Lucy asked. "There's only six of us left."

"That's why we stay here," Eben said. "Take time to come to our senses again." He thought of Beau driving the trencher, heard the gleeful defiance in his voice. "Besides which, they know about me now. They'll be looking. So we lay low."

"Well if that's the case, I think we should get rid of that." Lucy nodded at the cell where the covered body of the Stranger lay. "Stinks marginally worse now than when he was alive."

"Waiting room?" Jake suggested.

Stella nodded. "Good idea. Lucy, Denise, you want to help me and Jake?"

Jake glanced across at Eben as if expecting his brother to protest. But Eben only nodded grimly and sat down at his desk.

While the others dragged the body through, Eben assessed their supplies. There wasn't much. Some food—enough to last a few days, maybe. A few big batteries for the flashlights, a pathetic-looking pile of knives and choppers from the Kelsos' kitchen, some candles and matches. Jake had also brought a bag of medical supplies, at least half of which was comprised of Eben's inhalers.

We could take one of those, he thought, *and somehow make some garlic spray*. He burst into a sudden fit of giggles. "Ridiculous," he muttered.

"What is?" Carter asked.

Eben sat up, startled. He hadn't realized his friend was awake. "Me," he said. "Saw those things kill a fucking polar bear, and here I am thinking of spraying garlic at them."

"Hmm," Carter said.

"You think it would work?"

Carter was quiet for a few seconds, still huddled in the corner. "Don't know," he said at last.

Eben's laughter trailed away.

"How desperate are we?" Lucy asked. "Six of us left, and how desperate we are."

Once again Carter took a few seconds to answer, and when he did it started with a long sigh. "Lucy," he said. "Soon there'll just be five."

Eben started a quick mental count, but by the time he reached two, he knew what his old friend meant. *Oh no, does it never end?*

Carter stood slowly and lowered his hood.

And then Eben knew for sure, and he'd probably known back in the store the second that girl-vampire died.

Carter's eyes were black, his skin pale, the scratches on his face swollen, puffy and pink. *"Five of us left,"* he said, his voice lower than Eben had ever heard it before.

The others came back into the room and spread out along the wall, gasping and cursing.

Carter was sweating and trembling, and though his eyes were black, they still somehow exuded the fear he obviously felt.

Eben handed Stella the pistol and hefted the ax. Stella stepped away from him so that Carter would not be able to attack them both at the same time. Jake and the others remained backed against the far wall, leaving Carter alone, abandoned in his corner.

"I'm sorry," Carter said.

"How long ago?" Denise said.

"The girl in the store. I changed—so thirsty now, so *hungry*. What do you think, do those things live forever?"

"It's not living," Eben said.

Carter flinched. "What is? Making a living from the snow and ice? Is that really living, Eben?" His face was still drawn and frightened, but Eben didn't like the tone of mockery he heard creeping into Carter's voice. *Any time now,* he thought. *He'll come for us any time now.*

"Carter—"

"Couldn't tell you—that photo's all I got left of my family. Martha took the kids to visit her mom . . . got hit by a drunk driver," Carter whispered. "I wanted to join them so much . . . couldn't bring myself to do it . . . but I know they're waiting for me. Don't let me change. There's not long left, Eben. I can feel it coming on, I can feel myself being driven down." He looked around at all of them, people who until seconds ago had been fellow survivors, and Eben wondered what he saw. Old friends backing away from him with a mixture of fear and pity on their faces?

Or meat?

"No," Stella said. "No, Carter. We can't—"

"You *must*!" he hissed.

"Carter, there must be a way," Eben began, but he heard the hopelessness in his own voice. There *was* a way and they all knew it.

"Only one," Carter said. He smiled at Eben, and did his teeth look different? Had his gums receded, teeth grown? "And really, it'll just make me one of many. Barrow's lost its head already, Eben."

Eben felt the wooden handle of the ax in his hand, sensed the grain of the wood and its new roughness. Not yet worn smooth by use. Barely blooded.

"We just can't do this," Stella said.

Eben looked at her and said, "He's told us what he wants." He didn't want to argue with her about this—with anyone—because that would not be right. Carter deserved better. He blinked once, slowly, then turned back to Carter. "Where?" he asked.

Carter looked around and nodded toward the kitchen door. His shaking was getting worse, and twin trails of blood ran from the corners of his eyes. *How appropriate,* Eben thought. *Being reborn as a vampire and crying blood.*

"No," Stella said again, but it was quiet this time, more an expression of astonishment rather than a plea.

Eben nodded and followed Carter into the kitchen.

He kept his eyes on the back of his old friend's neck. Held the ax at the ready. *Just in case,* he thought. *Just in case he wants to lure me in there to do away with me. He thinks I'm the strongest, so he'd want to take me first.*

When they reached the kitchen Carter turned back to him, crying and smiling at the same time, and Eben felt guilty for his shallow suspicions.

"Thank you, Eben," Carter said. And he knelt.

Stella went to Jake and held him close. Denise and Lucy sat beside each other against the cell bars, both looking at the kitchen door. They could all see the shadows moving in there and hear a few whispered words.

Stella still held the pistol in one hand.

She'd once watched the execution of one of the Baghdad hostages on the internet. It had been a strange curiosity that took her there, and also a sense that she needed to witness for herself what was going on. The news could tell of beheadings and shootings, but the brutal truth of what was happening could never be communicated with words. It had almost felt like a duty. To begin with, she had felt a moment of voyeuristic guilt, but then a sense of rightness, that by watching the poor man's dreadful death and feeling revolted and sickened, she was somehow giving it power.

So she had sat and watched, and as the inevitable moment drew closer, she'd started feeling sick. Her heart hammered, she perspired, and she'd felt queasy.

Afterwards, she had thought about what she'd seen for a long time.

This was a hundred times worse.

She knew that Eben was doing the right thing, but it felt so wrong. Carter was not a prisoner or hostage; he was a friend, someone they had all known for a long time.

Her heart thumped, and she felt it more because Jake had his head pressed against her chest.

The shadows in the kitchen stopped moving, the talking ended, and then came the appalling *thunk* as the ax did its work, and another *thunk,* and then a bump as Carter's head hit the floor.

Denise vomited, Lucy groaned, Jake went limp in Stella's hands, but Stella herself stood strong. Eben would be out soon. He would need her.

Eben emerged from the kitchen seconds later and shut the door behind him. He was still carrying the ax, though he had wiped the blade somewhere. *On Carter's clothes,* Stella thought. *He wiped it there because it was tainted blood*.

Eben walked across the office, head bowed and looking at none of them. He stopped by the door, leaning his head against the smashed frame and breathing deeply.

Stella nudged Jake to check if he was okay. He smiled at her weakly and leaned against Eben's desk, crossing his arms and looking into some unknown distance. Perhaps he was still seeing the girl-thing's skull cleaved by the ax . . . or maybe he was imagining what had happened to Carter. Either way, they were thoughts a boy his age should not have to suffer.

She walked across to Eben, touched his shoulder and leaned her head against his. His breathing did not change; he did not acknowledge that she was even there.

"Hey," she said. Words seemed suddenly so useless. "Hey, we can make it. We've got food and supplies, and we can make them stretch for two more weeks. We can—"

"Just stop it!" Eben said, low and fierce.

"Stop what? Stop hoping?" She backed away, his anger hot and sharp.

Eben looked up and she had never seen such haunted eyes. "The last hopeful idea took away three people I've known my whole damn life."

Stella reached for him, wanting to touch his face and take the pain, and perhaps allow him to cry. His eyes were strained and red, dry and sore. She wondered what he saw when he looked at her.

I'm so cold, she heard him say, and she frowned because she wasn't certain that he had actually spoken. *"You're cold?"* she asked.

"Don't think I'll ever be warm again."

When she touched his face he drew back and raised his hands, warning her off. He would not catch her gaze.

"You did something you had to do," she said. "Carter *asked* you."

"I cut off his head."

"Yes."

Eben nodded, searching for more words but finding none.

"I'm here," Stella said. "I'll be sorting the food. You come to me when you can."

Eben smiled, a gruesome grimace. "Thanks," he said.

Stella nodded and turned. Walking away from Eben was difficult, but she knew he needed to think. Later, hopefully, there would be plenty of time for talk.

I'm so cold, she heard him saying again in her head.

DAY 16

Stella was in her office back in Anchorage, completing a report on the computer and wondering why it was freezing. Eben kept popping into her mind and that was strange, because they had been apart for several years. Barrow was a distant memory.

Weird, she thought. *It's cold, like I was only there yesterday.*

She printed her report, addressed the envelope, and sealed it up.

The door opened and Eben walked in. He looked troubled and upset, his clothing was dirty and streaked with blood, and his eyes . . .

He was a haunted man.

Eben, Stella said.

I'm so cold, he said. *Stella, so cold.*

She stood from her chair and invited him to sit, but she could not bring herself to touch his face. She saw his reflection in her computer screen. His eyes were black.

• • •

Stella jerked awake and cried out, and a hand clapped across her mouth.

Eben.

"You okay?" he asked.

She nodded. "Bad dream." She looked around the office and everything flooded back in. Lucy, Denise, and Jake were sleeping. Eben moved away and took up position again at the window, glancing back to make sure she really was awake. She smiled and nodded, but he did not smile back.

She sat up and hugged her coat around her. *I'll never let him be like that,* she thought. *What he did to Carter I can do as well, and I will if it needs doing. I'll never let Eben become one of those things. I love him too much for that.*

The thought did not surprise her as much as it should.

"Coffee?" she asked, and he nodded without looking back. "See anything out there?"

"Nothing. No movement. I think the hotel's stopped burning."

Stella busied herself lighting the gas burner and making their drinks. "Lucky the whole town didn't go up," she said.

"Are we?"

Stella sighed. He'd been like this for hours. Distant, unreachable, and when she tried to talk he went quiet, listening but not responding. *It's not you,* he would say. *It's me. It's the idea that we're the only ones left, and I couldn't do anything to save anyone.*

You saved us, she would say.

And eventually, the thought that was really troubling him came to the fore. *For how long?* And when he said that, he had haunted eyes.

She took him the coffee and they sat watching from the window together.

DAY 20

EBEN TOOK THE LONGEST, most frequent watches. Stella and Jake sometimes persuaded him to sleep, but he felt responsible, and his place was at the window.

They were still waiting for the snow.

The five survivors shared long silences in the police station office. In the waiting room lay the body of the Stranger who had started all this. The smell was not too bad—it was very cold, and decomposition was slow. In the kitchen next to the office lay the corpse of their dead friend. The door remained closed, because none of them wanted to see what Eben had done.

They had taped blankets across the window so they could use a flashlight, none of them relishing sitting in complete darkness. There was a small gas stove that gave them meager warmth, and they ate cold food from cans. As he had done in the attic, Eben had fixed a second blanket across the window so that they could hide beneath it and keep watch on the street beyond.

Tonight it was still dark and deserted. The sky was clear and star speckled. The moon hung high and bright. Once he thought he saw movement, but stare as he did at where he'd seen it, the shadows refused to shift. He lowered the cover and looked again a few minutes later, but nothing seemed to have changed.

He was thinking about how much food they had left, how weak they were becoming, whether they should make a break for the Utilidor without a blizzard to cover their tracks, how Jake was taking it . . .

It had taken two strikes from the ax to part Carter's head from his body. If he'd swung it harder, made Carter lean his face against a table instead of kneel . . . but there was no point thinking like that. All he could see when he closed his eyes was that moment between the first strike and the next, when Carter's head tipped forward and the meat and bone of his neck opened up for view. He'd struck again quickly, but for those couple of seconds . . . he had no idea whether Carter had felt pain. Whether he'd even been conscious or aware when Eben struck down again and completed what he had begun.

If I'd swung harder, Eben thought, and he'd thought it a hundred times already.

He lifted the corner of the curtain again, trying to distract himself from these terrible ideas. It was good that the street remained still and quiet, but it was also unsettling. *Where are they?* he kept thinking. *Hiding, resting, searching?*

He could not even begin to hope that they had gone.

• • •

Later, as they ate canned peaches, they decided to wait for another couple of days. By then perhaps the snow would have begun again. The thought of making a break for it in the moonlight seemed less and less attractive to Eben, and he kept picturing that stretch of open area between the town and the Utilidor. It could easily become a killing ground.

DAY 21

EBEN WENT FOR FOOD.

They talked about it for a long time. There was a house a block away from the station that belonged to someone who had left for the duration of the Dark. Eben could slip across there, break in, and raid their pantry. Simple. They needed the food, and none of them had seen or heard any sign of the vampires for almost five days.

"Maybe they've gone," Lucy said, expressing the hope that Eben could not allow in himself.

"Or maybe they're asleep," Jake said.

"Whatever," Eben said. "We need to get food now, or on our way to the Utilidor. Can't rely on there being any food there, and we've got days to go."

Everyone was silent while that sank in.

He went from the back door of the station. Stella watched him go, and she and Jake waited just inside the door for a stressful ten minutes until he came back. He was carrying two bags of food, and something about him had changed.

Stella couldn't quite place what that was until he spoke.

"Someone's still alive," he said.

"In the house?" Stella asked.

"No. Across the street. Must have seen me. Come on." They hurried through to the office. Eben dropped the bags and went to the window, and the others switched off the flashlights and gathered around.

"There's a light," he said. "A few houses down the street, flashing Morse. Watch."

They watched for five minutes, and just when Stella started to think Eben had mistaken reflected moonlight for a light, they all saw the flash.

"My God," Stella said. "You're sure it's Morse?"

Eben nodded, then frowned. "Well . . . I think so. Give me a second, I'll try to read it."

The light continued flashing, and Eben's lips moved as he tried to read what the message was saying.

Realization hit Stella. Maybe the cold had slowed her thoughts, or fear had blinded her, but it suddenly struck her what they were seeing. "Jesus, that's the Kitka house!"

Eben watched the flashing for a few moments, then smiled. It felt good. "Yeah," he said. "And that's Billy."

"What's he saying?"

Eben ducked back into the office and grabbed a flashlight. Back at the window he shielded most of the face with his hand.

"Eben, you sure about this?" Stella asked, staring at the flashlight.

"It's worth the risk."

She considered for a moment, looked at the small flashing light again and nodded. "Of course it is," she said.

Eben flashed his own light a few times.

"What did you send?"

"I told him we see him."

The light over at the Kitka house paused for a few seconds then started again, and this time it seemed more determined.

Eben concentrated on what was being sent, wishing he had a bit of paper and a pencil to write the letters and words down. When it stopped, he sent Billy a quick flash, then he and Stella ducked back into the office again.

Jake, Denise, and Lucy were gathered around waiting for him.

"What?" Jake said.

"Can you read it?" Denise asked.

Eben nodded. "I got the gist. He said they tore through his house and he hid in the vents. They really smashed the place up, and he's trapped there now. Been there for a long time. He said he can see a lot of the town from up there. Hotel's completely burnt out."

"Peggy and the kids?" Lucy asked.

Eben shrugged. "He didn't mention them."

Lucy nodded, frowning.

"I have to go," Eben said.

"*We* go," Stella said. Eben turned to protest but then he saw her face, her eyes, and he realized she never wanted them to be apart again. It was a good feeling, and he nodded in return.

"I'll signal him, tell him what we're doing. He can let us know when it looks safe."

Eben waited at the window for half an hour before Billy sent him the signal: *Looks good*.

"Okay," he said to the others. Stella was already zipping up her coat and slipping the pistol into her pocket.

"What kind of shape can he be in?" Denise asked. "It's been a long time. If he's been trapped there since the beginning . . . I mean . . ."

"What, Denise?" Stella asked.

"He'd be dead," she said.

"Maybe he was trapped later, when they returned to the house," Eben said.

"Is that what he said?" Lucy asked.

Eben shrugged. "Not sure. My Morse isn't what it used to be."

Lucy frowned, staring at Eben as though urging him to change his mind.

"We're going, Lucy," Eben said.

She shook her head. "Damn it, Eben, it's just one more risk. It could expose us all. And I'll be honest with you, I'm not even convinced that's Billy over there."

Eben thought of all the things he could say, all the

anger he could throw her way. But he was more tired than he had ever been, and anger took energy. "Lucy, *I'm* sure. We're going." He looked at Stella. "Right?"

She nodded. "Right."

Eben hefted the ax and looked into the shiny blade. He saw his own face reflected in there, dark eyes and three weeks' beard growth giving him the look of a madman.

"Maybe he should stay where he is," Lucy said. "We'll be a lot safer here if he acts as our lookout."

"He's starving, Lucy," Stella said.

Lucy nodded. "Starving for what?"

"We don't have any choice," Stella said.

"Don't we?"

"Lucy," Eben said, leaning forward until he was looking directly into her eyes. He spoke very softly, but everyone there heard the rage simmering deep down. He didn't try to hide it. None of them could know how what he had done to Carter had affected him; he wasn't even sure himself, not yet. All he did know was that he was changed. And after this was over, if they survived, all of them would be very different people. "We're not losing anyone else."

She stared back at him for a few seconds and then nodded. "Okay Eben. You're the Sheriff."

He chuckled at that, and the others even managed to laugh with him. *Amazing what sheer terror, hopelessness, and agony can do to a sense of humor,* he thought. Jake handed him a can of Ensure.

"This'll help him get back," his brother said.

"We'll make a fortune in advertising after this," Eben

said, and the others laughed again. He touched Jake's shoulder and nodded to him. "You hold things together here."

Jake nodded, the smile slipping from his face. "You take care," he said.

Eben nodded. "Believe it."

He and Stella stood at the station's front door, waiting a few moments so that they became accustomed to the moonlight. She reached out and squeezed his hand and, surprised, he squeezed back.

Back out into my dead town, Eben thought.

He took a puff on his inhaler and opened the door.

They darted straight across the street, over a snowbank and into an alleyway. Nothing called or howled in the night. Eben looked back at the station and it appeared deserted, the door closed again, and the windows dark and still. Good. He didn't want the others giving themselves away in their desire to watch his and Stella's progress.

A breeze whispered along the street, raising a mist of snow and driving it like dust. Somewhere, a door creaked.

Stella's eyes snapped open and she reached for the pistol. Eben touched her hand and shook his head.

The creak came again and again, back and forth as the wind played around the corners of buildings. "Open door," he whispered.

Stella leaned in close and pressed her mouth to his ear. "They could be anywhere," she said. Damn, but even now Eben liked the feel of her lips against his skin.

"Then we should go," he said. "Fast and quiet."

They did. Stella broke cover first, choosing the clear street over the walkway, which was littered with smashed windows and piled snow. Eben sprinted after her, wincing at the crunching sounds their feet made in the snow, but preferring speed over stealth. If they were watching, they were watching, and there was little he and Stella had to combat that other than surprise.

Billy Kitka's front door was wedged open by a small bookcase fallen onto its side. Books lay scattered across the hallway like frozen dead birds. Eben went in first, ax held before him. He would not hesitate to use it. He'd wrapped his flashlight in stretched material and he flicked it on, casting the weak light around.

To call the place smashed up was an understatement. Furniture was wrecked, clothes lay scattered underfoot, and walls were holed. The staircase looked climbable, though a few of the steps had been broken apart, and Eben edged his way up slowly. Where he could, he kept to the edges to avoid creaks.

Stella followed him all the way. He felt her presence—it made him feel strong.

At any moment, he expected one of the vampires to come at him. Billy perhaps, or worse; one of his teenaged daughters, beautiful girls who would be turned ugly and sour by undeath. They would come while he was still on the stairs, he was sure. He was unbalanced there. He mounted the last step, went up onto the landing and paused, listening.

Stella shrugged. Neither of them could hear anything. Eben indicated the front bedroom and went in first, ax held across his chest.

The room was a mess, with furniture piled against one wall and the ceiling ripped down.

"Oh, Jesus," Stella gasped.

Eben froze, staring at what she had seen. Billy's wife Peggy and their two girls lay on the floor, dead. They were dressed in their nightclothes. Their skin was mostly pale, but darkened here and there where blood had collected after their deaths.

Eben went closer and played the flashlight beam across their bodies. His heart was hammering, ax held at the ready. As certain as he was that they were dead, he could not shake the image of their eyes snapping open as they rose to bring him down.

"Doesn't seem to be a mark on them," Eben whispered. He knelt beside Peggy and checked her neck and throat, looking for anything that could be teeth marks. Nothing. Then he noticed what he should have seen straightaway . . . her left eye. It was gone. "Fuck!"

"Eben?"

He glanced at the two girls, then stood and backed away. "They've all been shot," he said. "Straight through the head."

"So where's Billy?"

A groan came from behind the furniture piled against the wall.

Stella pointed the pistol.

"Here," Billy said weakly. "Eben? That you?"

"Billy!"

Eben signaled that Stella should stay back and keep the pistol pointed at the wall. Then he slid the ax into his belt and started shifting the piled junk aside. He worked slowly, not wanting to make any more noise than was necessary. With the wall revealed he saw Billy at last, crushed into one of the big air vents in the shattered wall.

He shined the flashlight at his deputy. Billy squinted.

"Open your eyes," Eben said.

"Eben . . ."

"Open them."

Billy's eyes opened a squint, then as they became accustomed to the low light, they opened a little more. Eben leaned in close, looked, and backed away.

"He's okay," he said to Stella. Her shoulders slumped and she relaxed, but she still held back as Eben hauled Billy from the wall.

Jesus, he stank. Billy definitely must have been there for a long time. Eben pulled out the can of Ensure and sat Billy against his hip, pressing it to his lips. He drank greedily.

"Peggy and the girls," Stella said.

Billy nodded. "Me. I . . . didn't want them to suffer. Not like the others. Not like everyone else."

What?! Eben gasped and closed his eyes, trying to imagine the scene. He snapped them open again. He was already haunted; no need to invite in more ghosts.

"Tried to shoot myself, too," Billy continued. "Fucking gun jammed. Shots brought them, I hid in the vents. They smashed the place up and I got trapped."

"When was this?" Eben asked. He looked up at Stella's amazed expression.

"A week. Ten days. Not sure. I've lost count of the hours."

"But your fucking *family,* Billy!"

Billy started sobbing, though there were no tears. Eben supposed he'd cried himself dry. *How the hell could he have done something like this?*

"I should have just stayed here," the deputy said. "Stayed here and died. Never should have signaled you. Almost didn't. But I was stuck in there, and I knew they were . . ." He glanced at his dead family and his eyes screwed tight. "They were here. And I just couldn't stand being alone with them anymore."

"Billy, I can't believe . . ." Stella began, and when Eben turned she was looking at the two dead girls. She was crying.

He grabbed Billy, knocking the can from his hand and hauling him to his feet. Billy's legs didn't work, so Eben held him upright as he shook him. "You have a family!" he said, voice rising. *Quiet,* he thought, *keep it quiet*. But the rage was on him now, and if Billy had been angry and defensive, maybe Eben would have let him be. But he only cried some more, stuttering something about how awful it had been for him, how alone he felt, and Eben's anger erupted like blood from a sliced artery.

"You have a fucking family, Billy, a *family,* and you never, *ever* hurt them, *ever!* You do whatever it fucking takes to make them safe, to protect them, and did you stand between them and the vampires? Did you even think of doing that?"

"Eben, keep it down," Stella whispered harshly.

"I saw what happened to people who stood," Billy said.

Eben nodded, shaking the crying man one more time. "Yes! They died protecting their families!" He dropped Billy and stood back, glancing at Stella's stern, worried face. The anger drained as quickly as it had come. "They didn't kill them themselves," he said. He sat on the upturned bed and held his head in his hands.

Billy lay where he had fallen, breath harsh in his throat. Eben's own breathing was getting wheezy again, and he concentrated on calming himself down. He could blame Billy—of course he could—but he wondered just how much of that rage was actually directed at himself.

He was, as they had told him a few minutes ago, the Sheriff after all.

"We should get back," Stella said.

"I'm not sure I can—" Billy began, and Eben lifted him and slung Billy's arm across his shoulders.

"You don't have to walk," he said. "Just hold on."

"Where are we going?"

"Back to the station, of course. Jake's there, with Denise and Lucy."

"Anyone else?"

"No," Eben said, and he briefly thought of those they had lost. "No one else."

"And once we're back?" Stella asked.

Eben shrugged. "Snow or no snow, I think it's time to move on," he said. "I can't live with the stink of death any longer."

The wind had picked up. When they came to rescue Billy thirty minutes before, there had been a slight breeze that set a few snowflakes dancing. Now the breeze was climbing toward a gale, and snow was whipping along the street like sand. It stung where it touched exposed skin, and Eben and the others had to squint their eyes almost shut to see anything at all. The sky was darkening as clouds came in from the north. The moon was hidden now, and only starlight lit their way.

Eben was glad. The noise would mask the sounds of their footsteps, and it looked as though snow was coming again.

Billy slung his arms over Stella's and Eben's shoulders, and between them they dragged the exhausted deputy across the street. Eben carried the ax in his right hand, and Stella lugged the pistol in her left. If anything came at them out of the night, they would not hear it until it was upon them.

They waited at the front door for a few seconds, expecting Jake to let them in. Nothing happened. *Must have seen us coming,* Eben thought. *He'd have been watch-*

ing. He tapped the door once with the ax, just in case, but still it remained closed.

He and Stella exchanged glances. He nodded at Billy and Stella took the deputy's full weight.

Eben opened the door and entered the station. It was darker than ever with no borrowed light from outside, but he resisted the temptation to switch on the flashlight. He made his way quickly through to the main office. All was quiet and still.

"It's me," he whispered. "Jake!" No answer.

Eben switched on the flashlight and cast its weak beam around. "Oh shit."

"What?" Stella asked. She'd hauled Billy in behind her, and now the three of them stood just inside the office door. The stench of death and decay was strong, and Eben wondered how they'd managed to live with it for the past few days.

"They've gone," he said.

"Look." Stella let Billy lean against the wall and went for the thing she had seen on the floor. "Walkie-talkie."

"Why would they leave that?"

"Dropped it?"

Eben knew they were both clutching at straws. The only thing that put his mind slightly at ease was that there was no sign of fresh blood, although many of the supplies he'd just brought over from next door still lay on his desk. They'd left in a rush, that much was obvious.

"Maybe they tried for the Utilidor?" Stella said.

"Without us?"

"Perhaps they thought they saw something . . . or *did* see something."

Eben nodded, tight lipped.

"What now?" Billy asked.

"Jake's my brother," Eben said. "I'm going to find him. Stella?"

She looked at him, eyes narrowing. *You even have to ask?*

Eben nodded. "Billy, we'll help you as much as we can. And we'll check every house on the way, just in case they've holed up somewhere else."

"The Utilidor is—" Billy began.

"Our best hope." Eben rooted around in the bags they'd brought from the store days before and found a small hand ax. He handed it to Billy. "Their heads. That's the way to kill them."

"You've killed some?"

Eben glanced at the kitchen's closed door and could not answer.

It was colder than ever when they left the station. Eben guessed they were feeling it more because they hadn't been eating properly—nothing cooked anyway—for over three weeks. The smell was too much of a risk. The three of them were wrapped up well, but Eben had only worn thin gloves so that he could maintain a good grip on the ax. His fingers were hurting already.

The wind was blowing and the sky was overcast, but it had not yet started to snow again. If and when it did, they could move faster, but with the weather like this they were doubly handicapped: they could not hear if anything approached, and they were clearly visible to anyone or anything that might be watching for them.

He wanted to hurry, but caution kept him slow. Billy, as well. He could shuffle along if he held on to Eben's shoulder, but he couldn't move very fast and, Eben suspected, he would not be able to go far.

We could leave him.

He hated the idea of doing that, but after seeing what Billy had done to his own family the thought was not as abhorrent as it should be. *Leave him in one of the houses, hidden away with a supply of food and a flashlight. Come and get him when this is all over.* But Billy was weak and devastated by what had happened. Helpless. There were five days until sunup. If left alone, Billy would be dead in two.

Eben led the way, Billy walking behind him with his hand on Eben's shoulder. Stella followed on a few paces behind Billy, and Eben could not help turning around every minute or so to check she was still there. Seconds after leaving the station he'd had the sudden conviction that they were being followed, and that the vampires would pick them off one by one, starting at the back. *So what do I do if next time I turn around she isn't there anymore?* But there was no answer to that; at least, nothing that gave any comfort. She *had* to be there, every time he looked. There was no other alternative.

If there were footprints in the snow, it was too dark

to see them. Or perhaps the wind had already wiped them from view, wafting loose snow around and dusting Barrow clean every few minutes. Eben looked up to the rooftops but saw no movement. He waited before traversing the spaces between houses, passing by front doors or crossing roads. He was constantly trying to second-guess where an attack would come, and he changed direction several times on a whim. He figured that if he surprised himself, maybe he could surprise them as well.

Billy and Stella never questioned his choice of route, and for that he was grateful. They trusted him.

It's a long way to the Utilidor, he kept thinking. *Anything could have happened to them.*

He was exhausted. Physically worn and emotionally shattered, Eben was relying on fear and dread to drive him on. His muscles felt wasted, his bones weak and cold, and his skin felt loose over his body. He reckoned he'd lost twenty pounds, and while he'd often felt that he could do with losing a bit of weight, this was not the way.

When Eben made the mistake, he knew instantly it would not have happened had he been sharper.

They walked out into the intersection and a vampire howled somewhere close by.

Stella froze and drew her gun. Until she knew where the noise was coming from, she didn't want to run, but Eben was already breaking left, taking Billy with him.

She glanced around quickly, then followed.

The howl came again, so close that she feared an attack at any second. Eben was almost dragging Billy, ducking into the crawl space beneath a house and looking back with terrified eyes.

Stella nodded that she was okay and went on her hands and knees to follow.

Had they been seen? That was the big question, and there was only one way to find out: wait and see. It was possible that the vampire had seen or found someone else—

Jake?

Stella's heart jumped, sending a cold shock through her chest. The darkness of the crawl space beckoned, but just for a second she almost went back out, ready to run and fight and do anything she could to ensure Jake's well-being. But getting herself killed was the last thing that would help.

"Where did it come from?" Eben whispered into her ear as she ducked beneath the house.

"No idea." She turned and looked out across the intersection. Damn it, they'd walked right out into the street without looking around! Right now she wasn't sure they could have done anything more cautiously, but if they'd given themselves away so foolishly, and the vampires came . . .

The futility of such a death struck at her. *I'm so cold,* Eben's voice whispered, and she almost turned to hug him. But the voice had only been in her head, and something about it made her want to move away from him, not closer.

"I think Billy's passed out," Eben said.

Stella nodded, shrugged.

"We'll have to stay here awhile," Eben continued.

"We need to keep still, and quiet," she said. "Watch."

The first vampire appeared a minute later, stalking along the middle of the street as if it owned the town. Its arms seemed too long, its head too small, and even beneath the wind she could hear it sniffing and snorting as it came. It had been a man once, but even though it still wore a man's clothes—black suit, white shirt stained dark with dried blood—it had lost all trace of humanity. Its bare feet crunched in the snow.

Almost where we were when we heard it howl, Stella thought. *Our footprints . . . if they're there, if it sees them . . .*

Eben clasped her arm, obviously thinking the same thing.

Stella nursed the gun. *Two bullets each for Billy and Eben, and if I still have time, there's one for me, too.* The thought shocked her, but there was a calming effect in it as well. It's what she had been thinking before: *I'll never let Eben become one of those things.* Now she applied it to all three of them. She hoped that, should the situation arise, she could be as brave as Carter.

The vampire paused and looked around, raising its head as though to sniff the air. It crouched down and examined the ground, then turned right and moved off in the opposite direction.

Stella sighed in relief.

Another inhuman howl broke through the wind, so close that it made Stella cringe and Eben dig his fingers into her arm. His grip was so tight that she almost cried out.

The vampire turned around . . . and looked straight at them.

Eben let go of Stella and moved forward, putting himself between her and the creature.

Something dropped onto the sidewalk directly in front of them—bare, muscled legs and the hem of a dirty white dress was all they could see.

We came straight to the house it was sitting on! Stella thought. *Like flies to the middle of a spider's web! Damn it, damn it . . .* She reached out and grabbed Eben's coat, hauling him back. He looked over his shoulder and shook his head, putting his finger to his lips and glaring at her.

The female vampire that had dropped from the house walked into the street, stopping when it reached the other creature. Its white dress was scorched in places and completely missing across its back. Maybe this one had met Beau.

They seemed to converse for some time, and neither of them looked toward Stella and Eben.

Can they really not know we're here?

And then another vampire arrived, and another, and Billy started to moan.

Stella turned and fell across the deputy. "Shut up!" she whispered, but he must have been unconscious or asleep because the moans grew louder. Something was chasing him through his nightmares; his dead family, perhaps. Ironic that if the chase persisted, they would get him killed for real.

Stella nudged him, harder, and when he would not wake she felt across his face in the dark, grabbed his lip between two fingers, and squeezed hard.

He gasped and sat up.

"Quiet!" Stella breathed into his ear. "They're here!" Panting, shaking, still Billy understood immediately.

Stella looked back out into the street. There were four of them now, and one of them seemed to be laughing. It looked so unnatural, these four monsters standing around like old friends shooting the breeze. She had to resist the temptation to start shooting as well. *Maybe I'd get two,* she thought. *Bullets in the head . . . maybe that would work.*

Eben grabbed her arm and pulled her close. "We should wait till they go, then get inside somewhere," he whispered. "I don't like the idea of moving when we know they're around."

Stella nodded, hating the fact that they would not be looking for Jake. "How long?"

Eben shrugged. "Until it feels safe."

"Right. Safe."

"You know what I mean."

They leaned together, sharing warmth and watching until the vampires parted and went their separate ways.

"Do you think they know we're here?" Stella asked quietly.

"If they do, why wait?"

"Playing with us?"

"Cat and mouse?" Eben asked.

Stella was quiet for a while, until the last of the vampires had disappeared from view along the street. She looked at Eben—just a silhouette in the darkness—and let out her held breath. "I think we were lucky," she said.

"Me too. Let's get into the house."

"How? I'm not too wild about going out there just yet." Stella stared out at the windswept street, seeing shifting shapes in every swirl of blown snow.

"We'll have to find the floor hatch."

"How do you know there is one?" she asked.

"This is the Collettas' house," Eben said. "Ben put one in for his dog."

Stella shook her head. She hadn't even realized whose house they had been hiding under. "You stay with Billy," she said. "I'll have a look around."

It took her five minutes to locate the floor hatch and another five to open it. Even in thick gloves her fingers were numb from the cold, and she was as quiet as she could be with the bolts. She was only thankful that the Collettas hadn't locked the hatch from the inside. *Why bother?* she thought. *They were probably still in the house when all this happened.*

And that meant that the Collettas' bodies would probably still be inside.

With the hatch open, Stella was suddenly in two minds about whether she really wanted to go in at all.

• • •

They found Ben Colletta in the hallway and bathroom. His body was in a bath filled with bloody water, protruding flesh pale and slick with death. His head was on the floor in the hallway, a few feet from the kitchen door. His mouth was still open and screaming. Stella found a towel in the kitchen and gently covered his head, staring into his open eyes until she could no longer see them.

Susan was in the living room, spread all around. They didn't go in to investigate further. The smell drove them back, and Eben shut the door as they retreated into the study. Here at least the smell was not too bad; the window had been broken, letting fresh air in and the stench of death out.

Billy sat in the swivel chair before the desk, eyes drooping. The light was very poor in here; the window was small, and the snow was getting heavier, blocking out moon- and starlight. Eben watched the deputy, concerned. *He'll slow us down,* he thought. But his musing no longer went any further than that. They'd lost too many people already.

"What now?" Stella asked.

"We sit and wait a bit," Eben said. "There were four of them out there that we saw. There may have been more. I don't like the idea of moving when they're so close."

"The snow's coming down heavier now."

He nodded. "That'll help."

There was silence for a couple of minutes before Stella broke it. "Eben, I'm sure he's okay."

"He's barely a teenager."

"He's grown up a lot this winter."

Eben snorted. "And what will it do to him, even if he does survive?" he asked. His brother now lived in a world where vampires were real. What would that do to his psyche? How would he cope? Would he ever trust anyone again, or believe anything that anyone said to him? *There's no such thing as monsters,* that's what children were told, and there weren't many of them who grew up and died with any cause to disbelieve.

"He's a strong boy," Stella said. "Stronger than you give him credit for."

"He saw his sick, elderly grandmother ripped to pieces by monsters that shouldn't exist."

"I know," she said. "I know. But he kept it together enough to save your life, didn't he? And it's still the Dark, Eben. It's always felt unreal at this time of year, and I'm not sure it's really hit him yet. We're still in the nightmare."

"And when the sun comes up?"

"That's the time to start worrying about him. About all of us."

"What about you, Stella? What do you think about all this?"

She glanced at Billy, then back at Eben. Her expression was vague and unreadable in the poor light. "I'm just living hour by hour," she said. "But good always comes from bad."

"What possible good—?" Eben began, but Stella moved closer to him and wrapped her arms around his neck. She pulled him close and pressed her cheek against his. They hugged each other tight, relishing each other's warmth and love, and Eben understood and agreed. Good from bad.

He looked at the window. *Hour by hour,* she'd said. For Eben, it was down to minute by minute. And any one could be their last.

DAY 26

THEY ENDED UP waiting there for a long time, because nothing felt safe anymore.

The snow had reduced to a flurry again, denying them the long blizzard they so desired. Eben was soon sorry for that, because it meant that they saw what happened to Paul Jayko.

Another dark scene for their blackest nightmare.

It was Stella who noticed movement across the street. "Look," she said. "Up at that roof junction, on the Jaykos' house. Something there."

Eben squinted through the broken window and nodded. "It's one of them," he said.

"What's it doing?"

"Wait, there's another!" There were two vampires on the roof of the house, crawling across it like giant crabs. One of them descended the façade, and whenever it came to a window it scratched with its claws, the unbearable screeching sound cutting through the wind.

"Fuck, I hate that noise," Billy said. He still sat in the chair but he'd wheeled it closer to the window to see.

"Keep it quiet!" Eben whispered.

"But—"

"We have no idea how well they can hear, smell, or see. They're not like us." He almost smiled at his understatement.

The two vampires crawled across the house like spiders trying to find their way into a closed nest. At every window, they scratched and tapped, then moved on. When one of them lowered itself onto the front deck it rattled the door handle and scurried away, scraping claws along the timber walling as it went. Eben was sure he heard a low chuckle as the creature climbed back onto the roof.

"What are they up to?" Stella said.

"Don't know," Eben replied. *Strange,* he thought. *They could get in if they wanted. Almost as if . . .*

"Cat and mouse again," Stella said. "Like they're teasing. Eben, you don't think the Jayko twins are inside, do you?"

"It's possible," he said. "House doesn't look smashed up. Maybe there are still some the vampires haven't been into yet."

"But why not?"

He shrugged in the dark. "Conserving food."

"Oh Jesus, Eben."

"You asked." And it was the only reason he could think of for the vampires having not smashed up the Jayko house yet. Maybe they'd known from the beginning that Paul and Xavier were still inside, and had decided to keep the twins for later. Let them think they were hiding, surviving, and all the while the vampires were keeping watch and anticipating the day when the Jaykos' time came.

"Look," Billy said.

One of the vampires had come down to the front door again, and as it reached for the handle, there was a burst of automatic gunfire. The door shattered, the vampire fell to the ground and thrashed in the street, and a shadow stood in the doorway and continued firing into the writhing shape.

"That's Paul," Stella said. His face had been illuminated by the strobe effect of the gunfire, and now he had stepped back into shadow once more.

The vampire rose to its hands and knees and scurried away like an injured dog.

"That would have stopped an elephant," Eben said.

"They'll go in after him now," Stella said. "Why doesn't he come out?"

The scene remained silent for a full minute, and in that time all three of them felt the almost unbearable expectation of further violence.

They heard a smash first, then several of the vampires howling and growling, and then the windows of the Jayko house were lit up with gunfire. Several long bursts at first, then a couple of shorter ones, and each burst was followed by a vampire's scream.

"He's hurting them," Billy said. "Maybe—"

"No," Eben said. "Bee stings would hurt you. But you'd still be able to run, and eat."

A shadow appeared in the front doorway, and for a couple of seconds, Paul Jayko was silhouetted as he fired back into the house. Then he fled out into the snow.

Perhaps they'd been expecting someone who looked confident in what they were doing. Someone with a plan. But Paul looked terrible. Thin, disheveled, eyes wide in the pale mask of his terror. He stumbled from his porch and fell down the steps, stood again and took off across the road intersection. He was carrying an automatic rifle in one hand and a pistol in the other.

One vampire burst from the house, another jumped from the roof, and the two converged on him.

Another shape came in from the right, almost too fast to see. Paul squeezed off a few rounds before the guns were ripped from his hands. A tall vampire held him around the neck and lifted him from the ground.

The other two vampires moved closer, but they were slowing.

The tall vampire hissed at them—an animal warning to stay away—and then it ripped out Paul's throat and buried its face in his neck.

"Fuckers," Stella said.

"We should be . . ." Billy began, trailing off as he realized there was nothing they could do.

Eben gripped the ax. The wooden handle was warm in his hand, the blade sharp. "I've seen that one before," he said. "The tall one killing Paul."

The vampire dropped Jayko's corpse to the ground and fell on it, clawed hands raking his chest as it tried to bury its face deeper into his neck. Blood spurted briefly across the snow, before the creature clasped its mouth over the ruptured artery.

"Maybe it's their chief, or something," Stella said.

Eben nodded. "Yeah, that's what I think, too." The other two vampires were squatting in the snow like wolves watching their alpha male feed. "Looks like they're waiting for the scraps."

"What about Xavier?" Billy asked.

Eben looked across at the Jayko house. It appeared empty and lifeless now, the remains of the front door swinging in the breeze. "I reckon Xavier's dead," he said.

Eben gestured that Stella and Billy should move away from the window, but he watched. He had to. He could not take his eyes from the vampires, because to do so was dangerous.

And seeing what they did to Paul Jayko, how they fed on him, ripped his head from his shoulders and kicked it away beneath his own house . . .

Eben was feeding his hate.

"They've gone," Eben said.

Stella looked up. "You're sure?"

He shook his head. "How can I be sure? But they finished with Paul then went their separate ways. The door to the Jayko house is still banging in the wind. And Paul's body has cooled enough for the fresh snow to start settling on it."

"Sure," Billy said. "No more blood."

"So what should we do?" Stella asked.

"You know what I *want* to do," Eben said. He was twitchy, eager for them to go back out and continue on their way to the Utilidor. The thought had crossed his mind once or twice that others in the town may have figured that it was a good place to hole up, and he was trying to hold down the pleasing idea that they would meet more Barrowites there. And perhaps Jake and the others had made it there already.

Or perhaps not.

"But what *should* we do?" Stella prompted.

"Stay for a while longer," Eben said. "Eat. I'll dig around in the kitchen. You wait here and keep watch. Billy, you try to sleep. Need you back on your feet as soon as you're able."

"I'll do my best, Eben."

"Good." And Eben couldn't help imagining Billy shooting his wife through the eye, then moving on to his teenaged daughters . . .

The kitchen had been ransacked. Cupboards were open, food containers spilled across the floor, crockery smashed, furniture splintered. He found a box of cereal that had one unopened packet and a bar of chocolate that had slid beneath one of the units. Little else. He took it back to the study and they gave Billy most of the chocolate, Stella and Eben sharing the dried cereal. It took a long time for Eben to eat, fragments sticking between his teeth and to the roof of his mouth. He wished they'd brought along some of the abandoned supplies from the station, but all his thoughts had been on Jake.

Still were.

• • •

Billy started snoring, so they had to wake him up.

"No sign of anything out there," Stella said. "Snow's coming down good and heavy again. Looks like it's settled in for a while, too."

"Good," Eben said. "I was starting to think they can control the damn weather." He nursed the ax on his lap, turning it this way and that so that the blade reflected the weak light.

"Eben, they may be there already, waiting for us."

He nodded. "Yeah, I hope so."

She looked from the window again, then back at Eben. "Shall we go?"

Eben stood, helped Billy to his feet and sniffed. "Never too soon for me," he said. "This place stinks."

He led the way past Ben's covered head and along the hallway, lifted the trapdoor and listened for any movement below the house. "We need to move fast," he said. "I've been thinking on this, and we can't afford to check every place between here and the Utilidor. We just need to get there. If Jake and the others haven't got there already, there must be a reason. And you're right, Stella. He's grown up a lot. He'll get there if he can, and if he can't . . ." He looked down at the square of darkness waiting to welcome them. "Well, if he can't, then it's probably already too late."

DAY 28

THE GIRL, GAIL, hid with her family. She was very scared, but her mom and dad said they'd look after her and her brother Larry.

They'd been in the hot water heater closet for hours now, ever since Dad heard something outside. Her legs were hurting and Larry cried sometimes, but her parents kept telling them they had to keep quiet.

"There's something out there," her mother said, again and again. Her voice sounded as though she wanted to cry as well.

And then they all heard the something, and even Larry shut up.

Floorboards creaked, and the thing whined on the other side of the door. Gail heard heavy breathing, too, grunting breaths like one of the Riises' sled dogs after a trip. Panting. And there was a smell, like bad meat.

Her mother pushed her deeper into the closet, shoving with her knee, and Gail reached up and tugged some of the tank insulation down around her face. If she couldn't see, if she couldn't hear, then maybe it meant everything would go away.

The door was ripped open. Larry was gone. Then her mother and father were gone, too, and though Gail squeezed her eyes closed, there was no escaping the sounds.

Screaming. Then whimpering.

And finally after that had stopped . . . feeding.

Another crawl space, another snowstorm, and Eben went first.

They had been moving for half an hour. The storm deadened echoes, but it also caused each sound they made to seem incredibly loud. Eben knocked the ax against a house stilt and they paused, waiting for the creatures to home in on them. Stella dropped her gun, Billy banged his knee and groaned, and every time they expected an attack at any second. But no vampires came, and they continued slowly but surely toward the Utilidor.

Eben knew that they would have a lot of open ground to cover once they reached the edge of town. He tried to put that from his mind, but it plagued him; the image of them rushing through the snow without any cover, dark specks against the virgin white, and anything looking that way was bound to see them.

He wondered how Jake, Lucy, and Denise would have crossed the snow plain without even the cover of a storm.

He heard something in the distance and froze. Billy crawled into him and grunted, and Eben reached back and squeezed the deputy's shoulder.

Stella was already motionless, pistol held out before her.

The sound came again, a wailing accompaniment to the wind. But it sounded so wretched that it must be human.

Eben scurried to the edge of the crawl space. This house had steps that led directly onto the sidewalk, and Eben slipped beneath the steps, looking both ways. Stella slid up beside him.

"What is it?" she said.

"Listen."

Billy appeared behind them. "It's crying," he said.

"You're sure?" Eben asked, straining to hear the sound again. The wind seemed determined to steal it away.

"I've heard enough to know," Billy said. "That's a girl crying. And it's getting closer."

"It'll be another trap," Eben said. "Like Kirsten Toomey." He shuddered at the memory of what he had seen them do to her, the tall vampire that seemed to be their leader and the others.

"Don't know for sure," Stella said.

"What happened to Kirsten?" Billy asked, but neither Eben nor Stella replied.

The voice came closer, distinct from the wind now, and the three of them waited to see who or what was making it.

Stella gasped. "There!" she said. "Gail Robbins! She's only a kid, Eben."

Gail hurried along the street, glancing behind her every few seconds and letting out a desperate, hopeless wail. The wind buffeted her, sweeping her long hair in twisted halos around her head, and she waved blown snow away from her eyes.

"Something's following her," Eben said. "Maybe tracking her, seeing if she leads it—"

"She's running from something," Stella said. "Look at her clothes. She's been surviving somewhere inside till recently, and now she's running."

Eben realized what Stella meant. Gail wore enough layers of clothes to bulk her out, and her boots were a couple of sizes too large. Her coat was wet across one shoulder. It could have been blood.

She was fifty feet away now, veering across the street so that she would pass a few feet from the foot of the steps they hid beneath. Eben imagined grabbing her, the scream it would cause, the risk it would mean taking . . .

And then he glanced back at Billy, picturing the deputy's wife and children dead by his own hand. Such a waste. A selfless act that Eben could only see as selfish, and Billy stared back at him with watery eyes.

"We can't just leave her," Billy said.

"Stella, you grab her, pull her in, and I'll cover her mouth."

"What about—?"

"We've got a few seconds. I'll scan the street, one word from me and you hold back. Got it?"

Stella nodded. Eben smiled briefly, then crawled forward so that he was viewing the street through the stairs' middle open riser.

Gail was a dozen steps away, stumbling their way blindly, and he could see now that the wetness on her coat was definitely blood. *Whose?* he wondered, but it was too late to worry about that right now. He looked past her, searching for any signs of pursuit. The street seemed clear, though shadows swayed here and there where snow flurries danced to the wind. The rooftops appeared empty of everything but snow. Houses and shops faced onto the street, all of them apparently abandoned, though any one of a dozen windows would offer a perfect place to watch what was about to happen.

Eben looked back at Stella. "We grab her and move!" he whispered.

She nodded without looking at him; all her attention was on the girl.

Eben's muscles tensed as he readied to throw himself back beneath the house.

The girl wailed again, a horrible sound that testified to unspeakable things. She slipped, stumbled, and found her feet, tears falling to the ground to freeze with the rest of Barrow.

Stella stood from beneath the house, grabbed the girl and pulled her down into the shadows. Eben crawled to them and put his hand over Gail's mouth, just as she opened it to scream. She bit, hard, and he thought *Oh fuck, oh shit, we were so fucking stupid!* He winced and raised the ax, but Stella knocked his arm aside.

"It's okay, honey," she said, "we're not like them, it's okay."

Eben pulled his bleeding hand away and looked down at the girl. Her human eyes flickered back and forth from Stella to him, and for a heartbeat he thought it really was going to work out.

But then Gail opened her mouth and screamed.

Stella leaned forward across her face, whispering into the girl's ear even as she pressed her own hand across her mouth.

Too fucking late, Eben thought, moving back beneath the stairs to look out onto the street. *We had our chance and now it's—*

The vampire was looking directly at him. Standing across the street and a couple of houses down, still as a scarecrow against the buffeting wind, he felt its obsidian eyes meet his and heard the gleeful howl.

Eben spun around. In that split second, he made a choice, and not knowing whether it was a good one or bad, he acted upon it. "Stella! We're seen! We'll meet where it's safe!" He didn't want to mention the Utilidor by name, just in case this thing could hear.

He grabbed Billy by the hand and pulled. "Come with me!"

He glanced through the stairs—the thing was running at them, loping on all fours like a long-legged dog—and then ran.

Billy stumbled along with him. Eben looked behind to make sure the vampire was following them and not going under the house; if that happened he'd turn around and fight, he'd *have* to.

"Run, Billy!" he said, and the vampire howled again.

Damn, it was fast! Eben wielded the ax, ready to turn and swing when the thing caught them.

Next time he looked around, Billy was gone.

He paused briefly, spotted Billy's shadow slipping between two buildings and the vampire stalking after him, and then he ran again.

Damn it Billy, you should have stayed with me! The vampire must have been hungry, Eben decided. It had gone for the weaker prey. Soon, hunger satiated again, it would come after Eben.

He ran along an alley, over a fence, through a backyard, up onto a storage shed, across the back of a car. Losing himself again, in the hope that the vampire would also lose him. His breath became raspy and shallow, but he couldn't afford to halt, not for a second.

Eben ran for five minutes before he heard the distant pistol shots. By then he had come too far to go back, and even if he did, he'd never find them in time.

Stella, he thought, *keep running, don't go down, don't be caught.* Yet all he could think of was his wife pressed into the snow by one of those things while their tall, bald leader bit chunks of meat and gristle from her throat.

The second Eben left, Stella turned and fled back beneath the house. She dragged Gail, still crying and moaning but now hopefully convinced that Stella was not going to slaughter her.

She hated leaving Eben; hated even more the memory of him running into the street, dragging Billy by the arm and exposing them both to the loping shadow that followed. She hadn't waited to see what happened. Eben's actions were largely for her, so she could not waste a heartbeat.

For those first few minutes, she expected the vampire to double back and come after them. She kept the gun clasped in one hand, holding the girl's hand with the other. They emerged from the crawl space and ran, keeping to the sidewalk where they could, ducking down so that the snowbank beside the road at least partially hid them.

She paused once, pulling Gail close and whispering to her, "Keep running, I'll never let you go." The girl cried some more, but at least she nodded, the first sign of understanding. Stella only glanced at the splash of blood across her shoulder. She could not even imagine what this little girl had seen, heard, and felt, and probably only recently. And now was not the time to find out.

She aimed for the edge of town and the Utilidor beyond. She considered breaking into a house and trying to hide, but that seemed more and more like a mistake. Paul Jayko had obviously tried that, and now he was a stain on a Barrow street. Gail's family, too. Stella could not shake the feeling that they were being watched every step of the way. Herded, like cattle. *Cat and mouse,* she thought again, and then she ran into the vampire.

It was a tall female, just emerging from the broken doorway of a house and carrying a head in its hand. Stella didn't look too closely at the head in case she recognized it. Blood still dripped from its ragged neck, dotting the snow red.

The vampire's eyes opened wide in surprise as Stella barreled into it.

She let go of Gail and brought the gun around, even as she fell on top of the vampire. The creature was already reacting, scratching out with dreadful claws and hissing in her face, the stench of old rot and fresh blood almost unbearable.

Stella moved her head quickly to one side, avoiding one slashing limb. *Seconds,* she thought, *that's all I have before this thing throws me off and—*

A jagged spike of wood smacked into the side of the vampire's head, and its eyes glittered briefly with shock.

Gail! Stella thought. *Good girl!* Then she pressed the pistol against the vampire's left eye and pulled the trigger.

The creature jerked below her, and sickly black blood erupted from the back of its head.

She fired twice into its right eye, once into its mouth, and three times through its neck, hoping to sever the spinal column. Then the creature's thrashing and flailing finally threw her off and she crawled away, still clasping the pistol.

"Please," Gail said. Stella grabbed her offered hand and they ran.

At the corner of the next street she risked a quick glance back. The vampire was on its hands and knees, blood still spewing from its shattered head and neck.

It turned its ruined face toward them, and Stella and Gail ran for their lives.

• • •

Eben reached the edge of town.

He paused only briefly, beside a truck that had obviously been parked in haste. The driver's door was open and dried blood was splashed on the inside of the window.

They had all been seen—there had been howling and gunshots—and he knew that this hunt would not end without a kill. He had no time to catch his breath and sneak around. Speed was all he had, and the hope that they hadn't tortured their destination from Billy as they killed him.

Before him lay a stretch of open ground blanketed in virgin snow, and beyond that the Utilidor. Its storage towers were pale giants against the sky, the flashing lights atop them darkened now, and there was no sign at all that anyone else had made it out this far. *There wouldn't be,* Eben thought. *Jake would have covered their tracks.* He took a puff from his inhaler and glanced back over his shoulder.

Behind him lay Barrow. He spared a final glance for the desolate, ruined town and then continued on.

Eben reached the Utilidor without incident. He felt alone and abandoned, and that was a good feeling. It made him realize how claustrophobic Barrow had been ever since the vampires attacked, a place of crowded rooms and huddled survivors, crawl spaces and secret hideaways. Now—at least for a time—he had only sky above him. The blizzard had settled and was blasting snow almost horizontally, and that was good as well.

Come on, Stella, he thought. *Come on.* He'd already imagined a dozen scenarios that would have allowed her time to fire the gun, but he could not end any of them positively. *Shoot them and they get up,* he remembered Beau saying. And that had been with a shotgun.

But they'd learned more since then. That they were vampires, for a start. Take their heads and they die.

Come on, Stella. Please.

He reached the pipe where the Jayko twins had been working last time he was here. Brushing snow from the maintenance hatch, he sighed with relief when he found the butterfly screws. *Thank fuck they didn't bolt it back on.* When he touched the first one it fell into the snow, held in place by nothing more than a blob of chewing gum.

Jake? He couldn't get his hopes up. It could have been anyone.

He ducked inside the pipe, carefully replaced the hatch from the inside and sat back. The weather was shut out, but he was about to make his way through a confined, dark, stinking place once again. He took out his flashlight and flicked it on, but almost straightaway the beam started to fade. He switched it off again, deciding to reserve it for when it was most needed.

Tempted to remain where he was—to rest, to sleep, to await Stella's arrival—Eben roused himself and headed off. The pipe smelled, but it was not as bad as he had expected. This was the dried sewage smell of old Barrow, not the death stench of the new.

To begin with he was almost doubled over, the pipe

hardly four feet in diameter. But the farther he went toward the Utilidor's main building, the larger the pipe grew, until he found that he could stand upright as long as he walked along the center of the pipe.

And the farther he went, the louder the whirring noise became. He edged forward, feeling with his feet to make sure the pipe didn't end with a vertical drop. There was a heavy vibration from ahead, and he knew that at some point this pipe must feed into the Muffin Monster. He only hoped there was a way out before that happened.

Within another hundred steps, the pipe was vibrating, metal creaking, the hidden machine humming and clanking, and Eben decided he needed the flashlight. Clicking it on, he saw the open shaft almost directly before him. He looked down at the whirring blades of the Muffin Monster ten feet below.

It was maybe a four-foot shaft. He'd have to jump.

He bit the flashlight between his teeth, squatted down, readied himself, then leapt.

As his feet touched the other side shadows moved directly before him, emerging from the walls and reaching out to shove him back, down into those metal chomping blades that would dice him in a second.

He didn't even have time to shout before the hand grasped his belt and pulled.

"Eben!" Jake's voice was high with relief, and as Eben's mouth opened and his flashlight dropped, he saw the tears of joy on his brother's face.

They hugged, squeezing each other breathless. Lucy

and Denise stood behind Jake. They smiled at Eben apologetically.

"Sorry we nearly diced you," Denise said.

"Sure," Eben said. Lucy had turned on a flashlight and pointed it at the floor, and in the reflected light they all looked pale, bedraggled, and in need of some serious food and sleep. But they were *alive* and that simple, amazing fact showed in their eyes.

Eben's tears came, and for a foolish second he tried to stop them.

"Hey," Jake said, hugging him. Then, voice uncertain, he asked, "Stella?"

"She's not here?" Eben said.

Jake shook his head and the others' faces fell.

"Oh Jesus, then she's still out there. She had Gail Robbins with her. We were seen, we got split up."

"Did you find Billy and his family?"

"Only Billy. But he ran from me, and I don't think . . ." He trailed off, not needing to say more. "What happened to you?"

"Something came in," Jake said. "We heard the front door open, then Lucy heard something sniffing around in the waiting room."

"That guy's body?" Eben said.

Jake nodded. "Yeah. And I guessed that if those things killed him and left him handcuffed to the bars . . ."

"Then they'd wonder what he was doing in the waiting room."

"Right. So we left. And . . ."

"Don't worry," Eben said, knowing what Jake was going to say.

"I dropped the walkie-talkie," his brother said, tears brimming in his eyes again. "I should have warned you not to come back, but I dropped it when we were getting out of there. We panicked. I'm sorry, Eben."

Eben shook his head. "I'm not. You guys are alive, and we grabbed the walkie-talkie. Stella has it."

"She does?"

Eben nodded, and in their silence he heard the fear over what would happen next. When they tried Eben's walkie-talkie, would she answer?

"Come on," Jake said. "We've found a place to hole up for a while. We can talk more there."

"Food and water?" Eben asked.

Lucy shrugged. "A little."

Eben nodded. "Better than none at all."

They walked for a couple of minutes and emerged into a corridor that ran around the waist of one of the storage towers. There were windows here, and Eben went straight to one and looked out. Snow swirled at the glass, a thousand tiny ghosts trying to gain access. He couldn't even see the edge of the Utilidor forecourt.

He pulled out his walkie-talkie, hoping against hope that wherever she was, Stella would have hers switched on. "Stella? Come in, Stella, where are you?"

There was no response.

"We've been waiting here," Jake said, indicating the corridor. There were a few blankets—rough sleeping places—and a small pile of emptied food packets. "We keep watch from the window, and we're close enough to the pipe where we came in to get there before anyone else."

"And push them into the Muffin Monster," Eben said.

Jake smiled and shrugged. "We only *nearly* diced you."

"Has anyone else been here?"

"No one," Denise said.

"We haven't searched the whole place," Lucy said.

Jake shook his head. "We haven't, but I'm pretty sure we're alone."

"Do you think we're all that's left?" Lucy asked, eyes wide. "Last defenders of the Alamo?"

Eben sighed. "I did think that until recently," he said. "But like I said, we found Gail Robbins. And Paul Jayko was alive in his house until . . ."

"Paul?" Jake said.

"*Was* alive," Eben said. "He isn't anymore. So yes, I'm pretty sure there are others still out there. And anyone who's survived this long . . . well, maybe they'll make it until sunrise."

"What then?" Jake asked. Nobody replied, because none of them could think of anything to say.

"Stella," Eben said again into the walkie-talkie. "I've reached where I was heading, are you okay?" Again, no response. He stared from the window.

DAY 29

"ANYONE?"

The voice ghosted from the mouth of the pipe leading outside. They'd left the maintenance hatch open so that they could hear any movement in there, and now the echo filtered out, alone and afraid.

"Who's that?" Jake whispered.

"Not sure," Eben said. "Sounded like Billy."

"It took him a day longer than you to get here?" Lucy asked suspiciously.

Eben shrugged. "I guess if it is him, he may have been followed." He had told the others about finding Billy's family dead, but he had not elaborated. Not because he felt a duty to the deputy, or believed that the Kitka family's death at Billy's hand should remain a secret. It was simply that the details sickened him so much.

Do I really wish they'd got him? Eben wondered. *I'm not sure. I can't say.* Deep, dark thoughts, and he could never share them with anyone.

"Let's go." Jake led the way, with Eben, Denise, and Lucy following.

The pipe soon grew dark and they felt their way

along, edging closer to the place where the floor opened up into the Muffin Monster. Eben kept his hand on Jake's shoulder, confident that his brother had scoped this place out and knew what he was doing.

"Hello?" the voice came again, and Eben knew for sure that it was Billy. He sounded tired and afraid, but Eben couldn't make out through the echoes whether or not he was being coerced.

How did he make it this far? He could barely walk.

They moved on, Eben wielding his ax.

He could hardly walk, and last thing I saw was that vampire going after him. Easy meal.

The tunnel started to vibrate from the shredder below, and the noise meant that they didn't have to be too cautious as they walked.

"Hello?" Billy called again, louder this time.

Jake switched on the flashlight he was carrying, flooding the tunnel with light.

Eben leaned forward and whispered into his brother's ear, "He may have been followed."

Billy was maybe thirty feet ahead of them, just on the other side of the shaft into the Muffin Monster. Another few seconds and he would have tumbled in. He brought his arms up to shield his eyes from the light, crouched down, obviously blinded to who was behind it.

"Who's there?" he asked. "Eben?"

"Were you followed, Billy?"

"Eben! No, I . . . I don't think so."

"Were you careful?"

"Of course. Kept to the snowbanks. Kept my eyes open."

"Your eyes," Eben said. He squeezed past Jake and shielded part of the light with his body. "Let me see your eyes."

"Eben, you really think—?"

"Easy to prove me wrong."

Billy stood and lowered his arms. His eyes were still squeezed closed against the light, but he was shivering from the cold and swaying with exhaustion.

"Look at me, Billy," Eben said.

"Eben, he's—"

"He could have been bitten."

"I *haven't* been bitten," Billy said. "We gonna do this every time we meet?" Billy opened his eyes. They were his own.

"How did you get away from the vampire?"

"I thought it went after you?" Billy said.

Eben shook his head. "Saw it following you."

Billy frowned. "Never saw it. Went into a crawl space and stayed there for a while. Heard gunshots, so I ran again. Circled round to the edge of town. Saw nothin'."

"Eben, what are you doing?" Lucy asked.

Eben stared across at Billy. "You see anything of Stella and Gail?"

"No, Eben."

Eben sighed. "Okay, jump over," he said, walking forward. "I'll catch you."

Billy stepped forward to the edge of the chute, squatted, and readied himself to jump.

A shadow moved behind him.

Eben tensed, hand going to the ax on his belt. *Something there?* he thought. *Or maybe just the light?* He glanced back at Jake where he stood holding the flashlight, but his brother obviously hadn't noticed anything amiss. Neither had Lucy and Denise; they watched Billy, eyes wide.

Billy jumped over the chute, landed, and stood up beaming. "Piece of cake," he said.

The shadow manifested then, growing a face and arms and legs that pounded at the pipe. It leapt the chute and knocked Billy to the floor, scrabbling at his face and neck, snapping its jaws at his waving hands.

"Billy!" Denise shouted.

The vampire looked up, dark eyes glittering in the flashlight beam. It wore jeans, T-shirt, and a black waistcoat, and its left ear was pierced.

Eben swung the ax at the monster. It knocked his hand aside.

Jake came, the light waving wildly as he ran, throwing struggling shadows against the walls and ceiling of the pipe.

The creature bit down into Billy's throat and shook its head, and then the roaring and growling was replaced with the sickening sound of swallowing.

Eben swung the ax again just as the creature raised its arm to strike him. The blade bit into its arm just above the elbow and it howled, flipping back from Billy and thumping into the tunnel wall.

"Billy, here!" Eben called, but already he knew it was

too late. The deputy held both hands to his throat and blood pulsed through his fingers. He tried to crawl but couldn't move.

"Back, Eben!" Jake shouted.

Eben edged back, locking gazes with Billy for a few dreadful seconds, but then he slipped on a patch of spilled blood.

The creature pried the ax from its arm, threw it back along the tunnel, and scrambled over Billy to get to Eben.

Eben raised one foot and kicked the vampire in the face. It smacked his leg aside and fell on him, and he was sure it was grinning past those ferocious teeth, mocking him even in those final seconds before it would tear out his throat and drink his blood.

He fought and kicked, poked at its eyes, kneed it between the legs, but it seemed to feel no pain.

"Eben!" Jake shouted.

"Back!" Eben shouted back. *Not Jake, too. Not him as well.*

As if reading his thoughts, the vampire paused in its attack, raised its head, and looked past him at his brother. It chuckled.

And then Billy was on it, grabbing it around the neck with one arm and pulling hard. Its claws snagged in Eben's jacket, and Eben quickly unzipped, wriggling his arms from the sleeves as Billy pulled the creature closer and closer to the chute. It thrashed and jumped, but Billy had a good hold . . . and Eben could see that he was strong once again.

Eben stood, swaying uncertainly. Jake appeared beside him and shined the beam straight into the creature's eyes. The light caught Billy's eyes, too . . . and they were already changing.

Billy spun around at the last moment, kicked out at the wall and pushed both himself and the monster into the mouth of the chute.

Eben leapt and grabbed hold of Billy's legs, hugging them to his chest and holding on.

The vampire growled and lashed out with its clawed hands, and Billy let it go. It fell howling, clanging against the sides of the chute, and there was a piercing squeal as it tried to slow its descent against the metal. To no avail. It gave a brief shriek, the Muffin Monster's tone changed for a few seconds, and the vampire was gone.

Eben let go of Billy's feet, and Billy glared back at him. *Now what?* Eben thought. *Has he turned so quickly?* He stood, moved quickly past Billy, jumped the chute and retrieved the ax. It was still black with the creature's blood, and Eben was careful not to get any on his hands.

Billy was still lying beside the hole, but now he was looking down at the whirring blades of the shredder.

Eben signaled to Jake and the others to move back. They did not need telling twice.

"I can't do it, Eben," Billy said. His voice was low—almost a growl—yet Eben was sure he saw tears falling from his darkening eyes.

"It's okay, Billy," he said.

"No, it isn't. I'm dead. I can feel it." The deputy looked up and caught Eben's gaze. "I can smell your blood."

Eben knew he had to act fast. He jumped the chute again, wary of Billy's hands and teeth. There were so many things he could say, but in the end they were all platitudes.

There was alive and dead, and anything in between could not be allowed.

Billy did not even look up as Eben swung the ax at his neck.

Jake, Denise, and Lucy moved back along the tunnel, not wanting to see. Billy's head had tumbled into the shredder, and Eben was about to shove the body in after it when he paused. *Why not leave it here?* he thought. *As a warning?* He shook his head. It didn't make sense, but he went with his gut instinct.

He left Billy's headless body where it lay and followed the others back into the storage tower.

"If one found us, the others will, too." Lucy was staring at the hatchway leading into the pipe.

"It followed Billy," Jake said. "Doesn't mean to say others will find us. Right, Eben?"

Eben paced back and forth, walkie-talkie in his hand. "If more than one had come, the others would be in by now." He frowned, staring from the window. "I saw them take Paul Jayko down, and there was a definite hierarchy. The leader took his fill and the other two held back. Maybe the one Billy threw into the shredder was out for a bit of solo meat."

"Solo meat," Lucy said. "That's nice. But I dunno if we can risk that, Eben."

"What else can we do?" Eben held his hands out, facing Jake and Lucy and inviting their replies. "Really, what can we do other than just sit here and wait? We've made it this far, this long." He trailed off and held the walkie-talkie up to his mouth, lowered it again.

"She may still be all right," Jake said.

"Yeah." Eben nodded, smiling at his brother. *She said the same thing to me about you. And she was right.*

"Try one more time?" Lucy said.

Eben sighed and pressed the send button on the walkie-talkie. "Stella?" he said, releasing the button and listening to nothing in response. He took the inhaler from his trouser pocket and puffed.

He was wearing a thick jacket he had found in Carter's office. It smelled of the cigars Carter used to smoke, and he couldn't shake the image from his mind of his friends' heads parting from their bodies.

If Stella gets bitten . . .

"Fuck it!" he shouted.

"Eben, please don't," Jake said.

Eben bit his lip to hold in another shout, turned back to the window and rested his forehead against the glass. The snow was dying out. "Snow's stopping again," he said quietly. *No more cover for Stella if she's still trying to make her way out of Barrow.*

"Good," Lucy said.

Eben turned around.

"Sun's due up soon," she continued. "Wouldn't want it so overcast we can't tell the difference."

Eben nodded and smiled, desperate for hope but unable to cling onto the chance that this could all be over soon. He looked at the others and realized just how close they all were to the end. Their eyes were bloodshot, lips split, skin pale and sickly, clothes hanging on their wasting frames. If anything they looked something like vampires themselves. But for the eyes . . . the life in their eyes and the tired, painful determination.

"Yeah," he said. "Sun's up soon. I'm so cold." He hugged Carter's old coat around himself and still shivered.

Denise appeared from along the corridor carrying a bottle of vodka, a box of chocolates, and a jar of vitamins. She held them out to the others and almost managed a smile.

"Found these behind the first-aid kit: three of the four basic food groups. So let's mark the occasion. One day till sunrise."

Jake glanced at the bottle then up at Eben. "I guess I'm too young for this?"

"Nobody's too young in this town," Denise said, twisting off the top. She took a glug, grimaced, coughed, and took another.

"But what if the storm starts again," Lucy asked, nibbling on a chocolate. "What if the sun can't come up?"

"We don't know the rules," Eben said. "Maybe it'll hurt them even if it's behind clouds. Maybe it's the absence of night that hurts, not the sunlight. Maybe . . . . anything. Let's just survive today and when tomorrow comes, we'll survive that, too."

Jake took the proffered bottle of vodka from Denise and glanced at Eben.

"Just a little," Eben said. "Don't need you drunk. Any of you."

They ate chocolates and passed around the bottle of vodka, but none of them took the vitamins. One day left until sunrise, and Eben really couldn't see what good a few tablets could do now.

They took turns keeping watch from the window, scanning the open ground between the Utilidor and the edge of town for any signs of movement. They wished for people they knew and dreaded seeing the stalking, hunting shadows of vampires coming their way. Eben said they should check out the rest of the facility, make plans, lay traps. But deep down he knew that they were now waiting for the end. Hoping against hope that the fighting and running was over, and all there was left to do was hide. Desperate to feel the kiss of the sun on their skins and find their town empty of vampires once more.

The others slept more than they should have as they were all utterly exhausted.

Eben, though, could not sleep. He held the walkie-talkie in his hand, keeping it warm, as though that would keep a spark of hope alive. He tried to imagine where its twin could be: tucked away in Stella's coat pocket, forgotten and switched off; lying on the ground next to a patch of frozen blood; crushed, destroyed by the vampires that had taken Stella and Gail.

He tried it now and then but static was the only response.

As the Dark came toward an end, so did hope.

And then the voice came from nowhere, and Eben knew that this final day would be a long one.

DAY 30

"Eben, are you there? Eben, come in." It was Stella, quiet and drained.

He almost dropped the walkie-talkie, then depressed the button and answered, "I'm here, Stella!"

"Whisper," Stella said. *"They've been looking around, haven't stopped searching. But I needed to hear your voice. Got Gail with me."*

Eben looked at the others, unable to keep a smile from his face. "Where the hell are you?"

"Under Paul Jayko's Chevy. So cold, Eben. Got snow packed around to keep in some heat, but . . . cold. Gail's not good."

"Eben," Jake said. "I've taken a look around this place. We go up three flights and there's an open balcony around the tops of the containers. We may be able to see the Jayko place from there, now that the storm's cleared again."

Eben nodded and signaled to the others to go. He spoke again to Stella as they hurried to the internal staircase. "The sun comes up later today, Stella. You and I, we'll see it together. You remember that ridge where we had our first date? We'll make it back there, baby, I promise."

"This way," Jake said. He opened a door and indicated an almost vertical stairway, without handles and heading up into darkness.

"Stella, I'm signing off for a few seconds, we're getting to a place where we can see you. Speak again in a minute."

"'kay."

"Stay quiet."

"'kay." Eben didn't like the sound of her voice.

They climbed two flights quickly, mounting landings in between, then headed up another stairway until they reached a larger landing. On one side, there was a door that led inside the storage container, but Jake went for the other door.

The gust of cold took their breath away.

"No cover out here," Jake said. "Just a balcony and low railings. We should crawl."

Eben looked at the frozen snow covering the balcony. "Great."

They moved slowly and cautiously, and a minute later all four of them were looking out between railings at the sprawl of Barrow before them. The area of open ground between the town and Utilidor seemed much narrower from this perspective; Eben guessed fear had made it seem larger.

"We're up," he said into the walkie-talkie. "We're gonna see if we can see you."

"Waving a red scarf . . . dancing on my head," Stella said.

Eben smiled and looked silently for a moment, trying to make out where the Jayko house would be. He'd never seen the town from this angle; had never seen this much of Barrow in one go, in fact. Much of it was still hidden from view by the darkness, but this end of town glowed from the moonlight peering through breaks in the cloud cover. Some houses had burned. All were dark and silent. It was an eerie feeling, wondering which homes still contained survivors, and which only the grisly dead.

"There," Jake said.

"Where?"

"Look straight along the main street ahead of us, four blocks, and left of the intersection you can just make out the Jaykos' big black Chevy."

Eben looked, saw it, shook his head. "You sure?"

"Certain," Jake said.

"He's right," Lucy said.

Denise gasped. "Oh fuck."

Eben swallowed and blinked a few times, but still saw what he saw. Half a block from the Chevy, six vampires were gathering in the street. They came in from different directions, all heading toward the tall, bald one that Eben took to be their leader. From this distance, they almost seemed human.

"No way we can get past them," Lucy said.

Eben felt a pang of annoyance, but he knew for sure she was right.

"Baby, we need to cut off, they're half a block from you. I'll call again when it's safe. I love you." He said it without thinking, three words as natural as breathing and just as vital for his survival.

Stella did not answer for a while and he wondered whether she'd heard.

"I'm sorry, baby," she said at last. *"I never should've left you."*

They clicked off and Eben stared down at the gathering vampires. There were even more arriving, and he made a silent promise to Stella, Jake, and to himself. *I won't let you down. Not now, not ever again.* He looked at the Jaykos' Chevy, trying to imagine how cold and uncomfortable it would be down there. *Stay safe just a little while longer.*

Eighteen had come in, and there were eleven remaining.

The cattle had exacted a large toll on his brethren. Impressive for mere humans.

But Marlow was full, and he could see from the others that this had been a feast like never before.

Now it was almost over, but for the final part of the plan.

"It took centuries for us to mesh with the living world," Marlow said. "To make them believe we were only bad dreams. We cannot put that at risk. We cannot leave clues that will allow us to become the hunted once again, as our fathers and brothers were years in the past. This night is almost over . . . but our lives are long, and there will be nights even darker. Any evidence of what happened here—any signs that *we* were here—must be destroyed. Before the sun comes back, this town must die. Rip it from the face of the earth."

The other vampires hissed and sighed, anticipating the destruction to come.

"And one more thing," Marlow said. "There are other survivors, and they will be driven out. When they are . . . bring two to me. Our pack has been denuded. We should build it back up to strength. And *no one* turns anyone but *me.*"

He watched his brethren fade away into the night. Then he opened his mouth and sniffed at the air, wondering who his new children would be.

A dozen times since scampering beneath the Chevy, Stella had questioned whether it had been the right thing to do. It had seemed sensible at the time. After shooting the female vampire through the eyes and fleeing the scene, she had made a snap judgment. Run, with a good chance of bumping into another one of those things? Or hide for a while? She'd thought then that hiding would fool the vampires—they'd *expect* their prey to run. And she guessed she'd been right, because she and Gail were still alive.

But hiding beneath a car had also trapped them. Because once down here, the cold had quickly begun to sap their strength. And there was no way to see whether or not it was safe to leave.

She'd managed to slowly compact snow between the wheels and the car's undercarriage, insulating them somewhat from the outside in an attempt to retain some of their body heat. But even that had started to feel unsafe. What if a vampire noticed and decided to investigate?

She would not know until one of those things had her.

She had even ignored Eben's increasingly desperate voice calling for her on the walkie-talkie. Afraid that she'd be heard if she replied. Terrified that the eyeless vampire was still out there, crawling through the snow and leaving bloody trails all across Barrow as it searched for her, ready to exact its terrible revenge.

Now, she felt more hope than she had in a while. Eben knew where they were, and soon the sun would rise.

"Cold," Gail said again, the only word she'd uttered for the past couple of hours.

"Me too, honey." Stella tried to hug the girl even tighter. Gail's teeth had started chattering and Stella made her bite on the sleeve of her jacket. Their skin was brittle and blue, and Stella had lost sensation in her toes. It was likely that she'd lose them to frostbite, even if they did make it out of here.

She'd give anything for some heat.

The walkie-talkie crackled into life and Eben's voice came in. *"Stella, click twice to let me know you're okay."*

She struggled to clench her hand, but eventually managed two clicks.

"Baby, they're up to something, can't tell what. Just get ready to run like hell if I tell you to."

Stella clicked twice. *Run like hell?* she thought. *Not sure if I could even crawl.* She started tensing and relaxing her legs, shifting her arms, turning her shoulders, and rolling her hips, warming the muscles and trying to prepare herself for Eben's call. She whispered to Gail to do the same. *They're up to something,* Eben had said. And she wondered just how much Eben was trying to keep her from the dreadful truth of what was really happening.

Denise volunteered to keep watch from the balcony while the others went back down to the corridor. Eben suggested that they take fifteen-minute shifts; any longer than that lying motionless in the cold could be dangerous. And even as he said that, it dawned on him how long Stella and Gail had been beneath the car.

"We wait until the sun comes up, those things leave, then we go and get them," Jake said.

Eben shook his head. "They could be dead by then. You heard her voice, Jake. I can't and won't leave her that long."

"So what?" Lucy asked. "Come on Eben, you have to be real here. We can't just—"

"Real?" he asked quietly. "Barrow's been taken over by vampires, most of its inhabitants slaughtered, drained of blood, and decapitated."

"Yeah, so face it," Lucy said. She put her hands on her hips and gave Eben a long, hard stare. "Go out there and you'll die, and maybe we will too. Don't give them the opportunity to have any more of us, not *one*."

"And Stella? Gail?"

Lucy shook her head. "If the cold gets them . . ."

"I won't even listen to that, Lucy. That's defeat. What, 'If the cold gets them, so be it'?"

She sighed. "Sorry, Eben. Just don't think Stella would appreciate you getting yourself killed for nothing."

"We have weapons," Jake said. "Eben, your ax. And there's bound to be other stuff lying around here, if we only look. Tools. Maybe Carter even kept a gun."

"I counted eleven of them out there," Eben said. He looked from the window. He could see along the main street, but the Jaykos' Chevy was out of sight from this angle. "And no one's even thought about where these things came from, or where they'll go when the sun comes up."

"What do you mean?" Jake said.

"Where will they hide from the sun?" Eben asked, the realization hitting him only now. "There's less than a day by my reckoning. They must have an escape plan."

"Or maybe they plan on staying here," Lucy suggested. "Down in the ground, basements, covered crawlways. And to do that, they'll have to make sure *everyone* in Barrow is dead."

"Hey!" Denise called from the stairway. She looked worried and excited at the same time. "Something's happening!" She disappeared back up the stairs.

"Looks like they've just called our hand," Eben muttered.

They followed Denise.

• • •

"They've ruptured the pipeline," Eben said.

"How could they do that?" Jake asked. "It's bombproof!"

"But not vampire proof." Eben watched the black tendrils spreading in from the south of the town, flowing through the streets and forming puddles in the lowest areas, pooling around houses, seeping into crawl spaces, and making islands of snowbanks. It was darker than the shadows and promised a danger much more familiar.

"They're going to burn the town," he said. Dread had him now, the certainty that the vampires were going to win one way or another. If they could not take Barrow for themselves and kill everyone in it, then they would leave nothing behind worth saving. "This must have been their plan all along. No survivors, no evidence, and they can melt back into the night."

"Everything we've built," Denise said. "Everything we've *been* through! Nobody'll know what happened. They'll think it was a stupid accident, and even if we make it out no one will believe. They'll *blame* us."

Lucy nodded. "And next time, they'll take out Point Hope or Wainwright."

"This building's strong," Jake said. "Can't we ride it out here?"

"Maybe," Eben said. But his eyes were fixed on the Chevy.

"Look," Denise said. She pointed as a small group of vampires walked a block to the south, pausing where a tendril of oil snaked along a frozen wheel rut. The tall creature was with them, and he took something from his pocket.

"Oh fuck, can't we do something?" Jake said.

"Just watch," Eben said. "That's all we can do. For now."

They didn't see the flame of the match from this distance, but they did see the tall vampire raise his hand and seem to take delight in dropping it. Fire leapt from the oil-drowned wheel rut, followed quickly by greasy black smoke that drifted like angry ghosts in the moonlight.

"That's it," Lucy remarked. "The end of Barrow."

The fire spread quickly across the oil already flowing through the town. Houses started to catch, cars exploded with pops and thuds, and the silvery moonlit scene was turned an angry, roaring yellow. A whole street of houses—a dozen in all—caught on fire from beneath, crawl spaces erupting. Their windows and doors began to glow, as though their lights had been switched on by returning inhabitants. But then the windows blew out, the rush of air turned the fires into infernos, and soon the roofs were bursting apart. Scalding ash from the houses' demise rose into the Arctic air. Oily smoke billowed with steam from melting snow. And the long, dark silence of Barrow's night of hell was silent and dark no more.

"Down there!" Lucy said. "Survivors!"

Two people burst from a burning house close to

the edge of town, dodging a stream of burning oil by leaping from one snowbank to the next. One of them carried fire with him in his hair and clothes, screaming, arms waving. Three shapes fell on them from the roofs of neighboring houses, dragging them to higher ground and then beginning to feed.

"Oh shit," Eben said. "Shit, shit, shit." *She runs, they get her. She stays put, she burns.*

"We should tell her what's happening," Jake said.

"Not yet." Eben's head was spinning with possibilities, but every thought now orbited the idea that had suddenly been seeded in his mind. A loathsome, grotesque idea, but one which would not go away. "I'm thinking," he said.

"Eben—"

"I'm thinking!" he snapped, and Jake flinched back. *My boy, my brother, you never deserved any of this.*

"It feels warmer," Gail whispered. "And what's that noise?"

"Don't worry, sweetie," Stella said, hugging Gail tight. "We're gonna make it. Not long to wait now."

Fire, she thought, *they're burning buildings, looking for survivors.* She heard the crackle of flames and the tinkle of shattering glass, and smelled the stench of burning things. *But that's okay. So long as they're burning houses and not cars we'll be safe.*

She continued flexing her muscles, waiting for Eben's signal to run.

• • •

Fire raged through Barrow. The south of the town was already an inferno, and slowly but surely the burning oil was spreading like lava.

Eben tried to trace the path of the flames, tried to figure out how long Stella had left, but it was impossible.

"Soon as she knows what's happening, she'll run," Lucy said.

"Shit," Eben whispered. "Fucking shit." The head vampire and his pack had gathered between the edge of town and the Utilidor, almost as if they knew where any survivors would flee to. They were strung out in a long, uneven line facing the town, shadows thrown behind them by the rising flames seeming to dance. Eben and the others had already seen two survivors taken down and slaughtered while attempting to flee the flames. If Stella broke cover and came that way . . .

Eben cursed and shook his head. Then he fell still and silent, and closed his eyes. "I've got an idea," he said.

"What?" Jake asked.

Eben looked at his brother, trying to stay strong. "Not a good one. But I'm not going to sit here and watch her die, Jake. I can't do that."

"What are you saying?"

"I don't know what else to do." He stood and headed for the stairs, already trying to plan ahead without actually dwelling on the results of his actions. *Saving Stella. And everyone else left alive. They're the results. Anything beyond that is unimportant.*

"Eben," Jake said, "please wait. At least tell me what you're up to so I can help."

Eben paused in the doorway, hunkered down so that he was out of sight of the vampires. "Not sure you would."

"You're scaring me," Lucy said.

Eben nodded. "Me, too. Come on, then."

Back down in the corridor Eben went for the first-aid kit Denise had left resting against the wall. Jumping shadows and drifting light came through the window, bathing them in the flames of Barrow's destruction. The glow helped him find exactly what he was looking for. The glass syringe glinted.

"Along the sewer pipe," he said. The others followed, Jake right at Eben's side.

Maybe he's already guessed, Eben thought. *He's quiet. Maybe—*

Jake shoved him into the side of the pipe, pinning him against the metal with an arm across his throat. He snatched the ax from Eben's belt and raised it over his head. "No, Eben!" he said. "I won't let you." He looked determined and petrified, tears and fear twisting his expression.

"Jake, listen to me—"

"No." Jake shook his head, never taking his eyes from his brother. "No, because you'll talk sense, and I'll hear the logical side of it, and then you'll go and do it, and *I've already seen too many people die.*"

"What's happening?" Denise asked.

Lucy was silent, and Eben thought she finally understood. She glanced at the syringe in his hand, then up at his face. She shook her head.

"No, Eben," Jake said again.

"What're you going to do with the ax?" Eben asked. He remembered the vampire girl in the store, and looking into Jake's eyes, he knew that his brother was remembering it as well.

Jake raised it higher, as though ready to swing it down. "Your arm," he said. "Or your leg. Something to stop you." He was really crying now, and all the strength suddenly seemed to flow from him.

Eben shoved Jake gently away from him, took the ax from his brother's hand and backed up a few paces toward the chute. "Everyone just *listen* to me! Jake . . . listen."

Jake sobbed and went to his knees.

"I can't let her die," Eben said. "That's all there is to it. And maybe when the sun comes up . . . I don't know . . ."

"Maybe nothing, Eben," Lucy said.

"I'm not thinking that far ahead anymore," Eben said. "I saw how Carter and Billy fought it, and I know I can fight it harder. I've got more reason." He looked at Jake. "I've got more to fight for."

He turned and went to Billy's corpse where he'd left it beside the chute. *Even back then I was planning this,* he thought. Deep down, maybe, but the idea was already there.

He slid the needle into Billy's arm and drew a

syringe full of blood. It looked black in Denise's flashlight beam. He wondered how it would look in daylight.

In daylight it'll burn, he thought, but then he shoved that image away.

"Eben . . ." Jake said, begging.

Eben closed his eyes and stuck the syringe in his arm.

They helped Eben back to the corridor and sat him against the wall. He was sweating and shivering and his limbs were weak. The arm into which he'd injected Billy's blood felt as though it was on fire. *Spreading through me like it's spreading through Barrow. One fire to save another.*

"I'm so cold," he said. *I never said good-bye to Stella. I can't talk to her now, not like this, knowing what I've done to our future . . .*

He shoved any thoughts of the future from his mind.

"You look hot," Jake said. "Sweating. Burning up." His brother was holding the ax. Eben pretended not to notice.

"How's it outside?" Eben said.

Lucy was at the window. "Fire's spreading. They just took down another survivor."

"From where?"

"North of the town. Don't know who it was. A woman."

Come on, Eben thought, *come on!* The fire spread up

his arm and into his shoulder. "I wonder, will it hurt?" he said, not meaning to speak out loud.

Jake moved back slightly, eyes welling up, ax scraping against the floor.

"Jake," Eben said. "Lot depends on you. While they're watching me—while I'm keeping them occupied—you get on the walkie-talkie and tell Stella and Gail to run for it." He started shivering more violently as the fire bled into his chest. His heart sped up, stuttering and jumping, and his lungs felt as though he could expel flames. "Tell her . . . tell her not to stop for anything."

"You sure this will work?" Jake asked through his tears.

"Carter and Billy changed—they were only bitten. They managed to hold on to who they were for a while. I'm stronger. And like I said . . . Jake . . . more reason."

"You think that'll be enough?" Lucy asked.

"Soon find out." Eben felt his senses weakening, and the voices starting to come from farther away. He sniffed, but his sense of smell had vanished. His vision blurred, and as he reached out he could not tell whether anyone was holding his hand. *Jake,* he tried to say, but he was not certain that he actually spoke at all.

"Eben," he heard from some distance, and for a wonderful moment he thought Stella had arrived and was emerging from the pipe. But then the voice spoke again and he recognized Jake, speaking close to him but now feeling so very far away.

The fire hit his heart and suddenly pumped quickly through his body, scorching into his pelvis and legs, stomach, and head, and delving into his brain. His heart shuddered and stopped, and Eben went away.

The walkie-talkie crackled and Stella snatched it up.

"Stella, it's Jake. Eben's doing something. When I say run, run."

"What's he doing?" she whispered. "Jake, what's going on? Are they burning every house looking for us?"

"They've ruptured the pipeline," Jake said. *"South of the town's burning, and the oil's moving north."* Stella gasped. Water was dripping on her and Gail from the Chevy's chassis, and the sounds and smells of burning had been growing closer and stronger. But she'd never thought of the pipeline. That would mean . . .

"The *whole* town?" she said.

"Yeah. Stella, listen for my signal," Jake said. *"And when you run, come for the Utilidor and don't stop for anything. Eben said to tell you that. Just* don't *stop!"*

"Jake?" Stella tried. "What is he doing, Jake?" But there was no response.

Stella hugged Gail and whispered into her ear. "We may have to run soon, honey. I'll help you, but you think your legs will be okay?"

"I'll try," Gail said.

"Good, honey." But Stella was worried. Jake had not sounded like himself. *Just what the hell are you up to now, Eben? Just what the hell?*

Eben Oleson, or at least the thing that had once been him, surfaced from a nightmare of nothing into the hell of a new existence.

He reached with everything he had, trying to grasp hold of something to haul himself from the void where he seemed to have been floating forever. Something grabbed on—his new senses, sharper and keener than ever before—and as his eyes snapped open, he drew in a huge, shuddery breath.

He smelled blood, and Jake sat before him.

"Eben!"

"Jake . . . stay away. Just for a second." He closed his eyes again and his breathing came harsher, hardening in his lungs like ice.

"Here." Jake placed something in his hand, and when Eben looked he saw the inhaler. He'd been using one for years, sometimes just once every few days, sometimes several times each day. Since Stella had gone, the latter . . .

"Stella?" he asked.

"She's okay," Jake said.

"I don't need this." Eben threw the inhaler to one side and stood, feeling an unaccustomed strength surging through his body. He stretched, and heard and felt his joints crackle as he loosened up. But the strength came with a price, and it was one which he was not prepared to pay.

"Eben?" Jake said uncertainly, backing away.

"I've changed," Eben said. The words hurt his throat, as though they were a language other than his own.

"Your eyes . . ." Jake began.

"Listen, Jake," Eben said. "My little brother, not so little anymore. Take care of Stella for me. Tell her . . .

no, she doesn't need to be told." He closed his eyes and things beckoned him from the shadows. He resisted them, as he knew he could, but their calling was strong. He didn't know how long he would be able to fight.

"He's one of them," Denise whispered.

Eben opened his eyes again and looked at her. She flinched back under his gaze. Lucy, too, backing away from the window and toward the stairs leading up to the balcony. He smiled, and he felt a pearl of blood dribble from his receding gums. He ran his tongue across his teeth, surprised at how long they suddenly felt, and then he realized what the movement would suggest.

Jake stood his ground. The ax still hung from his right hand.

"How do we know he won't attack us?" Lucy said, speaking as if Eben was no longer there. And in a way, he supposed he was not.

Denise whispered again. "Maybe we should stop him now."

Jake spun on them, brandishing the ax and backing up until he was standing directly in front of Eben. "Shut up! Shut up, now!" he shouted. "You touch him and you can kill me, too! Don't you see what he's doing? Don't you understand what he's *done*?"

Eben could sense the heat of Jake before him, the thrum of his blood, the smell of his flesh. He reached out and touched his brother's shoulder, and Jake didn't even flinch.

"You're a good boy," he said. He turned and entered the pipe that led outside. None of them followed.

On the way he shoved Billy's corpse into the shredder, realizing for the first time how brave and strong his deputy had actually been.

"Stella," Jake's voice said from the walkie-talkie. *"Get ready."*

"What's happening, Jake?" she asked. "What's Eben doing?"

But Jake fell silent again.

Eben kicked the hatch from the pipe and emerged into the moonlight. He glanced up at the sky, relishing the view, and looking across the ice plains to the east he thought perhaps it was a shade lighter.

Smoke billowed above Barrow in a huge column. It stank, and even from this far away he could feel the heat of his town's destruction. There was no comfort there, and no peace. This heat could not reach his bones. Even if he threw himself into the flames, he would be cold. Such was his doom, but his destiny was yet to be fulfilled.

Silhouetted against the flames, eleven vampires. And in their midst stood the tall leader.

Eben started walking. He felt stronger than he ever had before. And *starving* for something fresh, red, and bloody. *Such hunger,* he thought.

He fought the shadows that gathered at the periphery of his consciousness. They strove to crush in and squeeze the last of his humanity from him—open him to this raging hunger—but he was something they could not understand. He felt the full impact of the confusion within him and enjoyed it. It would not affect what he had come here to do.

As he crossed the open ground, smoke swirled around him, and steam, and then one of the vampires turned and saw him coming. It crouched down low and hissed. Eben stopped thirty paces away, pulling his coat tight around him and tucking the hood down over his changing eyes.

First test, he thought. He appraised the vampire with a quick glance. It was tall and long limbed, bearing a human head with far too many teeth. And Eben was not the slightest bit afraid.

Others had turned to watch him now, and already they seemed uncertain. Shocked by his foolish courage, perhaps? Or maybe just confused?

"The one who fights," the tall vampire said. There was hatred in his voice.

"Fuck you," Eben said.

"Defiant, too."

"Fuck you and all your stinking—"

The leader hissed something in a guttural, phlegmy language, and the crouching vampire seemed to flow across the snow at Eben.

He let it come, backing away a few steps to give the impression that he was afraid.

This is for Helen, he thought.

The vampire leapt when it was ten feet from him, arms outstretched, mouth wide open, and Eben stood to his full height and swung his fist. The vampire's jaw shattered under the impact. It howled and fell at his feet, scrabbling for purchase in the snow, astounded by Eben's actions and confused at the strength of his attack.

"Who were you?" Eben said, looking down at the inhuman face below him. "Someone's son? Someone's lover?"

The creature only hissed up at him, so Eben crushed his foot down onto its skull. He stamped again and again until he felt the bone rupture.

He looked up as fluids splashed against his leg, and somewhere deep in his mind a shadow screamed its last.

The lead vampire stared at him, amazed.

"You want someone to bite?" Eben asked. He stepped forward, and the vampires gathered before him moved back. He grinned. "Bite me."

"*Stella,* now!" Jake said.

"What's happening?" Stella asked, already pushing her way through the snow piled beneath the car. Jake's voice sounded strange; not terrified, but shocked. Shaken. "Jake, just what the hell—"

"Run, *Stella*!" he shouted, and she was certain that he was crying as well. *"Run here as fast as you can, and* don't stop for anything!"

Ironically, Eben had never felt so alive. Here they were, the monsters, scared of him. Here they were, the destroyers of Barrow, backing away before his emergence. And why? Did they sense something different in him, some purpose other than blood and death and destruction?

Perhaps. Or maybe it was the fury he exuded like heat from his burning town.

Two more vampires came at him, one from either side. He stepped back at the last moment and lashed out, grasping one creature around the neck and driving it down into the ice. Teeth broke. The other vampire came at him and he rolled across the first, kicking out and catching it beneath the jaw. He felt the power in his veins, driving through his body like electricity, and he opened his muscles and mind to let it in.

He straightened his fingers and plunged them into the prone creature's neck, ripping its head away from its body. The second creature backed away uncertainly, then retreated a few more steps at a hiss from the lead vampire.

Eben stood and kicked the head away.

The tall vampire came forward, all surprise now wiped from his face. "Back," it growled at its pack, "keep back."

It's afraid I'll destroy them all, Eben thought.

"Give us space," it said. It came to within six feet of Eben and looked him up and down.

Eben lowered his hood and the vampire saw his eyes.

"Interesting," it said. "My name is Marlow."

"You have no name," Eben said. "Not here."

Marlow shrugged. "Whatever you say, dead man."

Eben could feel the subtle sting of the brightening sky at his back, and the thrill of confidence surging through his veins. Empowered by both he leaped forward and reached for Marlow's throat.

The vampire backhanded him into the snow.

And the final fight for Barrow began.

Stella pulled Gail from beneath the car and they both stood, legs shaking, looking around in amazement at the destruction of Barrow. Stella checked the pistol again—not many shots left—and slung an arm around Gail's shoulders.

"Come on, honey," she said. "We need to get away from the fires." She was amazed at how close the burning pools of oil were to the Chevy. *Could have cut it a bit closer, Eben,* she thought, but then she remembered Jake's voice, the fear and grief that even the walkie-talkie could not disguise. And as she helped Gail run toward the Utilidor, she wondered where all the vampires had gone.

Eben was on his feet again in seconds, ducking beneath Marlow's taloned hands and going for his stomach. Marlow shifted aside seemingly without moving, grabbed Eben's head and drove a knee into his face.

Eben fell forward and rolled, spinning as soon as he found his feet again, swinging his fist in a roundhouse that would have taken off a polar bear's head.

Marlow grabbed Eben's fist in its own and squeezed.

That hurts, Eben thought. He kicked out at the vampire's shins, his heavy boots never making contact.

Marlow seemed to dance on the spot. He kicked higher and the vampire let go, backing away, circling him like a predator toying with its prey.

Eben went in again, low and fast, and Marlow stepped aside almost too quickly to see. Eben felt the vampire's hands close around his arm and leg and he was lifted, twisted, and slammed down onto the ice. Marlow fell on him, hands thrashing and claws ripping, battering him around the head, face, and neck, tearing his coat away and shredding his clothes.

Eben tried to slide away, but the vampire had him held fast against the ice. He felt his skin shredding, and his view of Marlow's snarling face became blurred with sprays of his own blood.

Groaning, feeling his newfound strength ebbing with every splash of blood, Eben heaved up and threw Marlow to one side, spilling the vampire into a drift of snow. He stood unsteadily, hands on knees for support. The ground around them was spattered with Eben's blood.

Marlow stood and came at him again.

Eben snarled and roared, but anger was not enough.

Emerging from the clouds of stinking smoke, Stella at last saw the shadow of the Utilidor in the distance, silhouetted against a slowly brightening sky. "At last," she said, a rush of emotion warming her insides. "Dawn."

A door smashed open to her left and she raised the gun, pointing it at a woman and young boy as they stepped down onto the pavement.

"No!" the woman said, and Stella saw how thin and exhausted they were.

"Utilidor," Stella said, too tired to say any more.

A few other survivors were emerging now, and Stella thought, *Is it all over? Did Eben's plan work?* Gail hurried along stronger at her side, encouraged by the brightening sky.

As they reached the edge of town and started out across the open ground before the Utilidor, Stella saw the vampires.

She dropped to her knees and took Gail with her. Brought up the gun. Saw that they were gathered in a circle, and in their midst two shapes were slashing, punching, and gnawing at each other. The watchers were uneasy, glancing east at the coloring horizon. *Now the sun rises,* she thought, *they start to fight amongst themselves.*

And then she realized that one of the combatants was Eben.

He was being pummeled and thrashed by a tall vampire, kicked across the ice, head beaten against the ground again and again, arm twisted until it snapped with an audible crack . . .

Eben screamed.

Stella screamed as well, running forward and raising her pistol.

Eben looked up at her and she saw the blackness in his eyes, and everything made some sort of crazy sense.

He looked at her through a mask of blood and broken flesh.

"Eben," she whispered.

The tall vampire stepped over Eben's prone body and came for her.

Eben watched Marlow walking toward Stella and raised himself into a kneeling position. *So much pain,* he thought, *so much blood. Just a little more of my own to spill and this will be over.*

He looked around at the vampires surrounding him, sensing their confusion and fear at what was coming from the east. *Soon,* he tried to say. He managed a broken grin instead.

Eben turned back to Marlow, stood, and ran, gathering all his strength for one last attack.

Marlow stumbled beneath his assault, then slipped out from beneath him and pressed Eben's face into the ice, then flipping Eben onto his back, and baring his monstrous teeth.

"They'll make fine vampires," it hissed.

Not all for nothing, Eben thought.

The vampire growled, twisting Eben's head to one side to expose his throat.

I can't fail them now.

He could see a dozen shapes milling beyond the vampires. Survivors, and among them were Jake and Stella, Denise and Lucy and Gail. They had to *remain* survivors. After everything they had been through, anything else was inconceivable.

Marlow's mouth opened wider, like a snake readying to swallow its prey.

No more, Eben thought.

As Marlow's head fell for his throat, Eben gathered every last shred of strength and punched upward. His fist smashed the vampire's teeth and plunged into its mouth up to the wrist.

Eben raised his broken hand and pressed it against Marlow's face.

Then he grabbed the vampire's jaw and pulled its head apart.

Stella fell to her knees as the top of the vampire's head tumbled into the snow. Its lower jaw was still attached to its torso, tongue twisting at the air like a dying snake. It landed beside Eben and spilled blood onto the ice, black as the burning oil.

The other vampires stepped back, silently edging away from the Sheriff as he stood. He dripped blood and exuded power over all those watching.

Eben took one step forward and the vampires broke, running away from Barrow and toward the stain of dawn now painting the horizon with its palette of oranges and yellows.

"Eben," Stella whispered. She ran to him and did not hesitate for a second—she hugged him, hating the coolness of his body, the smell of him, but loving him for the choice he had made.

"What have you *done* to yourself?" she asked.

"What I had to," he croaked, and she knew that every word pained him.

Eben held her and looked around, watching the fleeing shapes. "I should go after them," he said.

"They won't come back," Stella said, but then a terrible thought came to her. *Is that really what he meant?* She leaned back and looked at him, and cursed herself for ever doubting.

"I'm so cold," Eben said. "So cold, Stella."

Jake appeared beside them, still carrying the ax, and he did not hesitate to hug Eben. "You did it," he said. "I knew you would."

"Yeah," Eben said. "Guy was a wimp."

Gail wandered to Stella's side, and she and Eben swapped glances. When the girl fell into Stella's embrace she held her tight, making a silent vow to Gail that Eben still heard and understood: *I'll look after you, honey.*

"Almost dawn," Jake said, and they fell silent.

Stella looked at Eben, trying to hold back her tears. *Not yet,* she thought. *Not while he's still here.* "We can hide you, find blood for you—"

"No blood," Eben said.

"Eben . . ."

"The firehouse," Eben said.

"Right," Denise said. She and Lucy headed off, followed by the other survivors.

Eben looked past Stella at the flaming town. "Maybe they'll save some of it."

"So what now?" Jake asked.

Eben turned and looked past the Utilidor, squinting against the dawn colors. "Now I have to go," he said. And he started walking away.

Stella turned to Jake. "Look after Gail."

"Where are you going?" he asked, eyes wide and terrified. He kept glancing past her at his brother, walking away into the snow.

She smiled. "I'm going to look after Eben."

She came, and he was glad. He didn't want to be on his own at the end.

"The hunger . . . it's getting hard to fight it," Eben murmured. "I'm forgetting everything but the pain."

"I'm coming with you," she said. "I won't run again."

They walked hand in hand across the snow and ice. Eben's strength was leaking away, but this was one last journey he had to make. Neither of them spoke; being alone said enough. Behind them, the roar of fire and the shouts of survivors trying to save their town. Ahead, the snowfields, and the sun.

After a while they walked slowly, steadily up the incline to the ridge where they had hugged and kissed on their first date. Eben sank to his knees, strength leaving him, and turned back to look at Barrow.

A lot of the town was visible from here, and much of it had been destroyed. But the billowing black clouds were already diminishing as the few survivors set to work with the fire extinguishers, and he felt a brief, unexpected pang of hope.

"It'll be all right, won't it?" he said.

"Barrow? I don't know. Its heart's been ripped out." Stella knelt next to him and he leaned into her, resting his head on her shoulder.

"No," he said, smiling. "It's been hurt, but its heart's still beating."

"I hope you're right."

The sky to the east was a deep blue now, and a sliver of sun became visible on the horizon, blindingly bright where it reflected from the plains of snow and ice.

"Baby . . ." Eben whispered. His skin was stinging, blood turning hot, and already he felt his senses beginning to withdraw. He'd felt that once today already, and he knew what it meant.

"I'm here. I'm here with you."

"Listen . . . listen to me . . ." Stella faded from his sight, only a shadow now.

"I'm listening."

"I could live forever," he said, even his own voice distant now. "But I don't want to breathe another second . . . if I can't remember what it feels like to love you."

"Neither of us ever forgot," she said.

Eben asked her to hold him tight.

She felt his death approach. He winced, gasped in pain, but never cried out. Not even when his skin blistered and his flesh began to smoke.

By the time the sun broke from the horizon, Eben had gone to nothing, and Stella had started to remember him.

ABOUT THE AUTHOR

TIM LEBBON is the winner of two British Fantasy Awards, a Bram Stoker Award, and a Tombstone Award, and is a finalist for the International Horror Guild and World Fantasy Awards. His books include *Hellboy: Unnatural Selection, Dusk, Face, The Nature of Balance, Changing of Faces, Exorcising Angels* (with Simon Clark), *Dead Man's Hand, Pieces of Hate, Fears Unnamed, White and Other Tales of Ruin, Desolation,* and *Berserk.* His novella *White* is soon to be a feature film from Rogue Pictures. He lives in South Wales with his wife and two children. Find out more about the author at www.timlebbon.net and www.noreela.com.

Not sure what to read next?

Visit Pocket Books online at

www.simonsays.com

Reading suggestions for
you and your reading group

New release news

Author appearances

Online chats with your favorite writers

Special offers

Order books online

And much, much more!

13456